TRAPPED IN A MADMAN'S UNIVERSE!

As Jack Hamilton ascended higher into the strato-sphere, he could see the great blob of Earth spread be-neath him. *And it was standing still!* Around it, in an orbit, swung a tiny mass of glowing matter—the sun. It was the ancient geocentric universe come true—a uni-verse with Earth at dead center and all other celestial bodies subservient to it.

As he rose still higher, he found that he was peering into a gigantic lake, a lake roomy enough to hold all Earth without a ripple. And then, with a shocked gasp, Jack Hamilton realized that it wasn't a lake at all. He was peering into a colossal eye—an EYE IN THE SKY.

Eye in the Sky

by

PHILIP K. DICK

ace books
A Division of Charter Communications Inc.
1120 Avenue of the Americas
New York, N.Y. 10036

EYE IN THE SKY

Copyright ©, 1957, by A. A. Wyn, Inc.

All Rights Reserved

I

THE PROTON BEAM DEFLECTOR of the Belmont Bevatron
betrayed its inventors at four o'clock in the afternoon of
October 2, 1959. What happened next happened instantly. No longer adequately deflected—and therefore no
longer under control—the six billion volt beam radiated
upward toward the roof the chamber, incinerating,
along its way, an observation platform overlooking the
doughnut-shaped magnet.

There were eight people standing on the platform at
the time: a group of sight-seers and their guide. De-
prived of their platform, the eight persons fell to the
floor of the Bevatron chamber and lay in a state of injury and shock until the magnetic field had been drained
and the hard radiation partially neutralized.

Of the eight, four required hospitalization. Two, less
severely burned, remained for indefinite observation.
The remaining two were examined, treated, and then released. Local newspapers in San Francisco and Oakland
reported the event. Lawyers for the victims drew up the
beginnings of lawsuits. Several officials connected with
the Bevatron landed on the scrap heap, along with the

Wilcox-Jones Deflection System and its enthusiastic inventors. Workmen appeared and began repairing the physical damage.

The incident had taken only a few moments. At 4:00 the faulty deflection had begun, and at 4:02 eight people had plunged sixty feet through the fantastically charged proton beam as it radiated from the circular internal chamber of the magnet. The guide, a young Negro, fell first and was the first to strike the floor of the chamber. The last to fall was a young technician from the nearby guided missile plant. As the group had been led out onto the platform he had broken away from his companions, turned back toward the hallway and fumbled in his pocket for his cigarettes.

Probably if he hadn't leaped forward to grab for his wife, he wouldn't have gone with the rest. That was the last clear memory: dropping his cigarettes and groping futilely to catch hold of Marsha's fluttering, drifting coat sleeve. . . .

All morning Hamilton sat in the missile research labs, doing nothing but sharpening pencils and sweating worry. Around him his staff continued their work; the corporation went on. At noon Marsha showed up, radiant and lovely, as sleekly dressed as one of the tame ducks in Golden Gate Park. Momentarily, he was roused from his brooding lethargy by the sweet-smelling and very expensive little creature he had managed to snare, a possession even more appreciated than his hi-fi rig and his collection of good whiskey.

"What's the matter?" Marsha asked, perching briefly on the end of his gray metal desk, gloved fingers pressed together, slim legs restlessly twinkling. "Let's hurry and eat so we can get over there. This is the first day they have that deflector working, that part you wanted to see. Had you forgotten? Are you ready?"

"I'm ready for the gas chamber," Hamilton told her bluntly. "And it's about ready for me."

Marsha's brown eyes grew large; her animation took on a dramatic, serious tone. "What is it? More secret stuff you can't talk about? Darling, you didn't tell me something important was happening today. At breakfast you were kidding and frisking around like a puppy."

"I didn't know at breakfast." Examining his wrist watch, Hamilton got gloomily to his feet. "Let's make it a good meal; it may be my last." He added, "And this may be the last sightseeing trip I'll ever take."

But he didn't reach the exit ramp of the California Maintenance Labs, let alone the restaurant down the road beyond the patrolled area of buildings and installations. A uniformed messenger stopped him, a tab of white paper folded neatly and extended. "Mr. Hamilton, this is for you. Colonel T. E. Edwards asked me to give it to you."

Shakily, Hamilton unraveled it. "Well," he said mildly to his wife, "this is it. Go sit in the lounge. If I'm not out in an hour or so, go on home and open a can of pork and beans."

"But—" She gestured helplessly. "You sound so—so *dire*. Do you know what it is?"

He knew what it was. Leaning forward, he kissed her briefly on her red, moist, and rather frightened lips. Then, striding rapidly down the corridor after the messenger, he headed for Colonel Edwards' suite of offices, the high-level conference rooms where the big brass of the corporation were sitting in solemn session.

As he seated himself, the thick, opaque presence of middle-aged businessmen billowed up around him: a

compound of cigar smoke, deodorant, and black shoe
polish. A constant mutter drifted around the long steel
conference table. At one end sat old T. E. himself, fortified by a mighty heap of forms and reports. To some
degree, each official had his mound of protective papers,
opened briefcase, ashtray, glass of tepid water. Across
from Colonel Edwards sat the squat, uniformed figure
of Charley McFeyffe, captain of the security cops who
prowled around the missile plant, screening out Russian
agents.

"There you are," Colonel T. E. Edwards murmured,
glancing sternly over his glasses at Hamilton. "This won't
take long, Jack. There's just this one item on the conference agenda; you won't have to sit through anything
else."

Hamilton said nothing. Tautly, with a strained expression, he sat waiting.

"This is about your wife," Edwards began, licking his
fat thumb and leafing through a report. "Now, I understand that since Sutherland resigned, you've been in full
charge of our research labs. Right?"

Hamilton nodded. On the table, his hands had visibly
faded to a stark, bloodless white. As if he were already
dead, he thought wryly. As if he were already hanging
by the neck, squeezed out from all life and sunshine.
Hanging, like one of Hormel's hams, in the dark sanc-
tity of the abattoir.

"Your wife," Edwards rumbled ponderously on, his
liver-spotted wrists rising and falling as he flipped pages,
"has been classified as a plant security risk. I have the
report here." He nodded toward the silent captain of the
plant police. "McFeyffe brought it to me. I should add,
reluctantly."

"Reluctantly as hell," McFeyffe put in, directly to

Hamilton. His gray, hard eyes begged to apologize. Stonily, Hamilton ignored him.

"You, of course," Edwards rambled on, "are familiar with the security setup here. We're a private concern, but our customer is the government. Nobody buys missiles but Uncle Sam. So we have to watch ourselves. I'm bringing this to your attention so you can handle it in your own way. Primarily, it's your concern. It's only important to us in that you head our research labs. That makes it our business." He eyed Hamilton as if he had never set eyes on him before—in spite of the fact that he had originally hired him in 1949, ten solid years ago, when Hamilton was a young, bright, eager electronics engineer, just bursting out of MIT.

"Does this mean," Hamilton asked huskily, watching his two hands clench and unclench convulsively, "that Marsha is barred from the plant?"

"No," Edwards answered, "it means *you* will be denied access to classified material until the situation alters."

"But that means . . ." Hamilton heard his voice fade off into astonished silence. "That means all the material I work with."

Nobody answered. The roomful of company officials sat fortified by their briefcases and mounds of forms. Off in a corner, the air conditioner struggled tinnily.

"I'll be goddammed," Hamilton said suddenly, in a very loud, clear voice. A few forms rattled in surprise. Edwards regarded him sideways, with curiosity. Charley McFeyffe lit a cigar and nervously ran a heavy hand through his thinning hair. He looked, in his plain brown uniform, like a pot-bellied highway patrolman.

"Give him the charges," McFeyffe said. "Give him a chance to fight back, T. E. He's got *some* rights."

For an interval Colonel Edwards fought it out with the massed data of the security report. Then, his face darkening with exasperation, he shoved the whole affair across the table to McFeyffe. "Your department drew it up," he muttered, washing his hands of the matter. "You tell him."

"You mean you're going to read it here?" Hamilton protested. "In front of thirty people? In the presence of every official of the company?"

"They've all seen the report," Edwards said, not unkindly. "It was drawn up a month or so ago and it's been circulating since then. After all, my boy, you're an important man here. We wouldn't take up this matter lightly."

"First," McFeyffe said, obviously embarrassed, "we have this business from the FBI. It was forwarded to us."

"You requested it?" Hamilton inquired acidly. "Or did it just happen to be circulating back and forth across the country?"

McFeyffe colored. "Well, we sort of asked for it. As a routine inquiry. My God, Jack, there's a file on *me*— there's even a file on President Nixon."

"You don't have to read all that junk," Hamilton said, his voice shaking. "Marsha joined the Progressive Party back in '48 when she was a freshman in college. She contributed money to the Spanish Refugee Appeals Committee. She subscribed to *In Fact*. I've heard all that stuff before."

"Read the current material," Edwards instructed.

Picking his way carefully through the report, McFeyffe found the current material. "Mrs. Hamilton left the Progressive Party in 1950. *In Fact* is no longer published. In 1952 she attended meetings of the California Arts, Sciences, and Professions, a front organization with

pro-Communist leanings. She signed the Stockholm
Peace Proposal. She joined the Civil Liberties Union,
described by some as pro-left."

"What," Hamilton demanded, "does *pro-left* mean?"

"It means sympathetic to groups or persons sympathetic with Communism." Laboriously, McFeyffe continued. "On May 8, 1953, Mrs. Hamilton wrote a letter to
the San Francisco *Chronicle* protesting the barring of
Charlie Chaplin from the United States—a notorious
fellow-traveler. She signed the Save the Rosenbergs Appeal: convicted traitors. In 1954 she spoke at the Ala-
meda League of Women Voters in favor of admitting
Red China to the UN—a Communist country. In 1955
she joined the Oakland branch of the International Coexistence or Death Organization, with branches in Iron
Curtain Countries. And in 1956 she contributed money
to the Society for the Advancement of Colored People."
He translated the figure. "Forty-eight dollars and fifty-
five cents."

There was silence.

"That's it?" Hamilton demanded.

"That's the relevant material, yes."

"Does it also mention," Hamilton said, trying to keep
his voice steady, "that Marsha subscribed to the Chicago
Tribune? That she campaigned for Adlai Stevenson in
1952? That in 1953 she contributed money to the Hu-
mane Society for the advancement of dogs and cats?"

"I don't see what relevance these have," Edwards said
impatiently.

"They complete the picture! Sure, Marsha subscribed
to *In Fact*—she also subscribed to the *New Yorker*. She
left the Progressive Party when Wallace did—she joined
the Young Democrats. Does it mention that? Sure, she
was curious about Communism; does that make her a

Communist? All you're saying is that Marsha reads left-wing journals and listens to left-wing speakers—it doesn't prove she endorses Communism or is under Party discipline or advocates the overthrow of the government or—"

"We're not saying your wife is a Communist," McFeyffe said. "We're saying she's a security risk. The possibility that Marsha is a Communist *exists*."

"Good God," Hamilton said futilely, "then I'm supposed to prove she *isn't?* Is that it?"

"The possibility is there," Edwards repeated. "Jack, try to be rational; don't get upset and start bellowing. Maybe Marsha is a Red; maybe not. That isn't the issue. What we have here is material showing your wife is interested in politics—radical politics, at that. And that isn't a good thing."

"Marsha is interested in everything. She's an intelligent, educated person. She has all day to find out about things. Is she supposed to sit home and just"—Hamilton groped for words—"and dust off the mantel? Fix dinner and sew and cook?"

"We have a pattern, here," McFeyffe said. "Admittedly, none of these items in itself is indicative. But when you add them up, when you get the statistical average . . . it's simply too damn high, Jack. Your wife is mixed up in too many pro-left movements."

"Guilt by association. She's curious; she's interested. Does her being there prove she *agrees* with what they're saying?"

"We can't look into her mind—and neither can *you*. All we can judge is what she does: the groups she joins, the petitions she signs, the money she contributes. That's the only evidence we have—we've *got* to go on that. You say she goes to these meetings but she doesn't agree with the sentiments expressed. Well, let's suppose the police break up a lewd show and arrest the girls and the management. But the audience gets off by saying it didn't enjoy the show." McFeyffe spread his hands. "Would they be there if they didn't enjoy the show? One show, maybe. For curiosity. But not one after another, all down the line.

"Your wife has been mixed up in left-wing groups for ten years, since she was eighteen. She's had plenty of time to make up her mind about Communism. But she still goes to these things; she still turns up when some Commie group organizes to protest a lynching in the South or to squall about the latest armament budget. It seems to me the fact that Marsha also reads the Chicago *Trib* is no more relevant than the fact that the man watching the lewd show goes to church. It proves he has many facets, maybe even contradictory facets . . . but the fact remains that one of those facets includes enjoying smut. He isn't booked because he goes to church; he's booked because he likes smut and because he goes to see smut.

"Ninety-nine percent of your wife may be average red-blooded American—she may cook well, drive carefully, pay her income tax, give money to charity, bake cakes for church raffles. But the remaining one percent may be tied into the Communist Party. And that's it."

After a moment Hamilton admitted begrudgingly, "You put your case pretty well."

"I believe in my case. I've known you and Marsha as long as you've worked here. I like both of you—and so does Edwards. Everybody does. That's not the issue, though. Until we have telepathy and can get into people's minds, we're going to have to depend on this statistical stuff. No, we can't prove Marsha is an agent of a foreign power. And you can't prove she isn't. In abeyance, we'll have to resolve the doubt against her. We simply can't afford to do otherwise." Rubbing his heavy lower lip, McFeyffe asked, "Has it ever occurred to you to wonder if she *is* a Communist?"

It hadn't. Perspiring, Hamilton sat gazing mutely down at the gleaming surface of the table. He had always assumed Marsha was telling the truth, that she was merely curious about Communism. For the first time, a miserable, unhappy suspicion was beginning to grow. Statistically, it *was* possible.

"I'll ask her," he said out loud.

"You will?" McFeyffe said. "And what'll she say?"

"She'll say no, of course!"

Shaking his head, Edwards said, "That isn't worth anything, Jack. And if you think it over, you'll agree."

Hamilton was on his feet. "She's out in the lounge. You can all ask her—bring her in here, ask her yourselves."

"I'm not going to argue with you," Edwards said. "Your wife is classed as a security risk, and until further notice you're suspended from your job. Either bring conclusive evidence to show she isn't a Communist, or get rid of her." He shrugged. "You have a career, boy. This is your lifework."

Getting to his feet, McFeyffe came heavily around the side of the table. The meeting was breaking up; the conference on Hamilton's clearance was over. Taking hold of the technician's arm, McFeyffe led him insistently toward the door. "Let's get out of here, where we can breathe. How about a drink? The three of us, you and me and Marsha. Whiskey sours down at the Safe Harbor. I think we can use them."

II

"I don't want a drink," Marsha said emphatically, in clipped, brittle tones. Pale and determined, she faced McFeyffe, ignoring the company officials who filed through the lounge. "Right now Jack and I are going over to the Bevatron and watch them start up their new equipment. We've planned on it for weeks."

"My car's in the lot," McFeyffe said. "I'll drive you over." Ironically, he added, "I'm a cop—I can get you right in."

As the dusty Plymouth sedan ascended the long slope to the Bevatron buildings, Marsha said, "I don't know whether to laugh or cry or what. I can't believe it. Are you all really serious about this?"

"Colonel Edwards suggested that Jack shed you like an old coat," McFeyffe said.

Dazed, shaken, Marsha sat stiffly clutching her gloves and purse. "Would you do that?" she asked her husband.

"No," Hamilton answered. "Not even if you were a pervert, a Communist, and an alcoholic put together."

"You hear that?" Marsha said to McFeyffe.

"I hear."

"What do you think of that?"

"I think you're both swell people. I think Jack would

15

be a sonofabitch to do otherwise." McFeyffe finished;
"I told Colonel Edwards that."

"One of you two," Hamilton said, "shouldn't be here.
One of you should get kicked out the door. I ought to
flip a coin."

Stricken, Marsha gazed up at him, brown eyes swimming, fingers plucking aimlessly at her gloves. "Can't
you see?" she whispered. "This is a terrible thing. It's
a conspiracy against you and me. Against all of us."

"I feel sort of lousy, myself," McFeyffe acknowledged.
Turning the Plymouth off the state road, he guided it
past the check-station and into the Bevatron grounds.
The cop at the entrance saluted and waved; McFeyffe
waved back. "After all, you're friends of mine . . . my
duty comes along and pushes me into drawing up reports
on my friends. Listing derogatory material, investigat-
ing gossip—you think I enjoy it?"

"Take your dut—" Hamilton began, but Marsha cut
him off.

"He's right; it's not his fault. We're all in this together,
all three of us."

The car came to a halt before the main entrance. Mc-
Feyffe shut off the engine, and the three of them got out
and listlessly moved up the wide concrete steps.

A handful of technicians were visible, and Hamilton
looked back at them, at the group of them assembled on
the steps. Well-dressed young men with crew cuts, bow
ties, chatting affably together. With them was the usual
trickle of sightseers, who, having been cleared at the
gate, were on their way inside to enjoy the sight of the
Bevatron in action. But it was the technicians who interested Hamilton; he was thinking to himself, *There I
am.*

Or, he thought, *there I've been up until now.*

"I'll meet you in a minute," Marsha said faintly, dabbing at her tear-streaked eyes. "I'm going to the powder room and put myself back together."

"Okay," he murmured, still deep in thought.

She trotted off, and Hamilton and McFeyffe stood facing each other in the echoing corridor of the Bevatron building.

"Maybe it's a good thing," Hamilton said. Ten years was a long time, long enough in any kind of job. And where had he been going? It was a good question.

"You got a good right to be sore," McFeyffe said.

Hamilton said, "You mean well." He walked off by himself and stood with his hands in his pockets.

Of course he was sore. And he would be sore until he had settled the loyalty business one way or another. But it was not that; it was the jolt to his system, the jolt to his manner of life, to his whole range of habits. To the various things he believed in and took for granted. McFeyffe had cut all the way through to his deepest level of existence; to his marriage, and the woman who meant more to him than anyone else in the world.

More to him, he realized, than anyone or anything. More to him than his job. His own loyalty was to her, and that was a strange thing to realize. It was not really the loyalty business that bothered him; it was the idea that he and Marsha were cut off from each other, separated by what had happened.

"Yes," he said to McFeyffe. "I'm sore as hell."

"You can get another job. With your experience—"

"My wife," Hamilton said. "I'm talking about her. You think I'll have a chance to get back at you? I'd like one." But, he thought, it sounded childish when he said it. "You're sick," he said to McFeyffe, going on anyhow,

partly because he wanted to get it said and partly because he did not know what else to do. "You're destroying
innocent people. Paranoiac delusions—"

"Knock it off," McFeyffe said tightly. "You've had your
chance, Jack. Years of it. Too many years."

While Hamilton was framing his retort, Marsha reappeared. "They're letting in a group of regular sightseers. The big shots have already had their look." She
was a little more composed, now. "That thing—that new
deflector—is supposed to be in operation."

Reluctantly, Hamilton turned away from the heavy-
set security policeman. "Let's go, then."

McFeyffe followed along. "This should be interesting,"
he said to nobody in particular.

"That's right," Hamilton said distantly, aware that he
was trembling. Taking a deep breath he entered the
elevator after Marsha and turned automatically to face
the front. McFeyffe did the same; as the elevator ascended, Hamilton was treated to the sight of the man's fiery
red neck. McFeyffe, too, was upset.

On the second floor they found a young Negro, with
a broad arm band on his sleeve, assembling a group of
sightseers. They joined the group. Behind them, other
visitors waited patiently for their turn. It was three-
fifty; the Wilcox Jones Deflection System had already
been brought into focus and activated.

"Here we are, now," the young Negro guide was saying, in a thin, experienced voice, as he led them from
the hall toward the observation platform. "We want to
move quickly so others will have their chance. As you
know, the Belmont Bevatron was constructed by the
Atomic Energy Commission for the purpose of advanced
research into cosmic ray phenomena artificially generated within controlled conditions. The central element

of the Bevatron is the giant magnet whose field accelerates the beam of protons and provides them with increasing ionization. The positively charged protons are introduced into the linear chamber from the Cockroft-Walton acceleration tube."

According to their dispositions, the sightseers smiled vaguely or ignored him. One tall, slim, stern, elderly gentleman stood like a hardwood pole, arms folded, radiating detached contempt for science in general. A soldier, Hamilton observed: the man wore a tarnished wedge of metal on his cotton jacket. The hell with him, he thought bitterly. The hell with patriotism in general. In the specific and the abstract. Birds of a feather, soldiers and cops. Anti-intellectual and anti-Negro. Anti-everything except beer, dogs, cars and guns.

"Is there a pamphlet?" a plump, expensively dressed middle-aged mother was inquiring softly, but penetratingly. "We would like something we can read and take home, please. For school use."

"How many volts down there?" her boy shouted at the guide. "Is it over a billion volts?"

"Slightly over six billion," the Negro explained patiently, "is the electron volt push the protons will have received before they are deflected from their orbit and out of the circular chamber. Each time the beam makes a revolution, its charge and velocity are increased."

"How fast do they go?" a slender, competent woman in her early thirties asked. She wore severe glasses and a rough-woven, businesslike suit.

"At slightly under the velocity of light."

"How many times do they circle the chamber?"

"Four million times," the guide answered. "Their astronomical distance is three hundred thousand miles. That distance is covered in 1.85 seconds."

"Incredible," the expensively dressed mother gushed, in an awed, fatuous voice.

"When the protons leave the linear accelerator," the guide continued, "they have an energy of ten million volts, or, as we say, ten Mev. The next problem is to guide them into a circular orbit in exactly the right position and at exactly the right angle, so they can be picked up by the field of the big magnet."

"Can't the magnet do that?" the boy demanded.

"No, I'm afraid not. An inflector is utilized for this. Highly charged protons very easily leave a given path and wander in all directions. A complicated system of frequency modulation is required to keep them from entering a widening spiral. And, once the beam has attained its required charge, the fundamental problem of getting it out of the circular chamber remains."

Pointing down, below the railing of the platform, the guide indicated the magnet that lay beneath them. The magnet, vast and imposing, roughly resembled a doughnut. It hummed mightily.

"The accelerating chamber is inside the magnet. It is four hundred feet in length. You can't see it from here, I'm afraid."

"I wonder," the white-haired war veteran reflected, "whether the builders of this spectacular machine realize that one of God's ordinary hurricanes far exceeds the total of all man-made power, this and all other machines included?"

"I'm sure they realize it," the severe young woman told him archly. "They could probably tell you to a foot-pound what the power of a hurricane is."

The veteran surveyed her with aloof dignity. "Are you a scientist, madame?" he inquired mildly.

The guide had now induced most of his party out onto

the platform. "After you," McFeyffe said to Hamilton, stepping aside. Marsha moved blankly forward, and her husband followed. McFeyffe, drably pretending interest in the informational charts plastered on the wall overlooking the platform, brought up the rear.

Taking hold of his wife's hand, Hamilton squeezed hard and said in her ear, "You think I'd renounce you? We're not living in Nazi Germany."

"Not yet," Marsha said despondently. She was still pale and subdued; she had wiped off most of her make-up, and her lips were thin and bloodless. "Darling, when I think of those men getting you in there and confronting you with me and my activities, as if I was some sort of a—as if I was a prostitute or something, or maybe having secret relations with horses . . . I could just kill them. And Charley—I thought he was our friend. I though we could count on him. How many times has he been over to dinner?"

"We're not living in Arabia, either," Hamilton reminded her. "Just because we feed him doesn't mean he's a blood brother."

"That's the last time I ever bake a lemon meringue pie. And everything else he likes. Him and his orange garters. Promise me you'll never wear garters."

"Elastic socks and nothing else." Pulling her close to him, he told her: "Let's push the bastard into the magnet."

"You think it'd digest him?" Wanly, Marsha smiled a little. "Probably it would spit him back out. Too indigestible."

Behind them, the mother and her boy loitered. McFeyffe was trailing far behind, hands stuck in his pockets, beefy face sagging with dejection.

"He doesn't look very happy," Marsha observed. "In a way, I feel sorry for him. It's not his fault."

"Whose fault is it?" Lightly, as if he were making a joke, Hamilton asked, "The bloodsucking, capitalistic beasts of Wall Street?"

"That's a funny way of putting it," Marsha said, troubled. "I never heard you use words like that." Suddenly she clutched at him. "You don't really think there—" Breaking off, she jerked violently away from him. "You do. You think maybe it's true."

"Maybe what's true? That you used to belong to the Progressive Party? I used to drive you to meetings in my Chevvy coupé, remember? I've known that for ten years."

"Not that. Not what I did. What it *means*—what they say it means. You do think so, don't you?"

"Well," he said awkwardly, "you don't have a short-wave transmitter down in the basement. None that I've noticed, at least."

"Have you looked?" Her voice was cold and accusing. "Maybe I have; don't be so sure. Maybe I'm here to sabotage this Bevatron, or whatever the hell it is."

"Keep your voice down," Hamilton said warningly.

"Don't give me orders." Furious, wretched, she backed away from him directly into the thin, stern old soldier.

"Be careful, young lady," the soldier warned her, firmly guiding her from the railing. "You don't want to fall overboard."

"The greatest problem in construction," the guide was saying, "lay in the deflection unit used to bring the proton beam out of the circular chamber and into impact with its target. Several methods have been employed. Originally, the oscillator was turned off at a critical mo-

ment; this allowed the protons to spiral outward. But
such deflection was too imperfect."

"Isn't it true," Hamilton said harshly, "that up in the
old Berkeley cyclotron a beam got completely away, one
day?"

The guide eyed him with interest. "That's what they
say, yes."

"I heard it burned through an office. That you can
still see the scorch marks. And at night, when the lights
are off, the radiation is still visible."

"It's supposed to hang around in a blue cloud," the
guide agreed. "Are you a physicist, mister?"

"An electronics man," Hamilton informed him. "I'm
interested in the Deflector; I know Leo Wilcox very
slightly."

"This is Leo's big day," the guide observed. "They've
just put his unit to work down there."

"Which is it?" Hamilton asked.

Pointing down, the guide indicated a complicated apparatus at one side of the magnet. A series of shielded
slabs supported a thick pipe of dark gray, over which
an intricate series of liquid-filled tubes was mounted.
"That's your friend's work. He's around somewhere,
watching."

"How does it seem to be?"

"They can't tell yet."

Behind Hamilton, Marsha had retreated to the rear of
the platform. He followed after her. "Try to act like an
adult," he said in a low, angry whisper. "As long as we're
here, I want to see what's going on."

"You and your science. Wires and tubes—this stuff is
more important to you than my life."

"I came here to see this and I'm going to. Don't spoil
it for me; don't make a scene."

"You're the one who's making a scene."

"Haven't you done enough harm already?" Moodily turning his back to her, Hamilton pushed past the competent business woman, past McFeyffe, to the ramp that led from the observation platform back into the hallway. He was fumbling in his pockets for his pack of cigarettes when the first ominous wail of the emergency sirens shrieked up above the quiet hum of the magnet.

"Back!" the guide shouted, his lean, dark arms raised and flailing. "The radiation screen—"

A furious buzzing roar burst over the platform. Clouds of incandescent particles flamed up, exploded, and rained down on the terrified people. The ugly stench of burning stung their noses; wildly, they struggled and shoved toward the rear of the platform.

A crack appeared. A metal strut, burned through by the play of hard radiation, melted, sagged, and gave way. The middle-aged mother opened her mouth and screeched loudly and piercingly. In a frenzied scramble, McFeyffe struggled to get away from the corroded platform and the blinding display of hard radiation that sizzled everywhere. He collided with Hamilton; shoving the panic-stricken cop aside, Hamilton jumped past him and reached desperately for Marsha.

His own clothes were on fire. Around him, flaming people struggled and fought to clamber off, as slowly, ponderously, the platform spilled forward, hung for an instant, and then dissolved.

All over the Bevatron building, automatic warning bells squealed. Human and mechanical screams of terror mixed together in a cacophony of noise. The floor under Hamilton majestically collapsed. Ceasing to be solid, the steel and concrete and plastic and wiring became random particles. Instinctively, he threw up his hands; he was tumbling face-forward into the vague blur of machinery below. A sickening *whoosh* as the air rushed from his lungs; plaster rained down on him, scorched particles of ash that flickered and seared. Then, briefly, he was ripping through the tangled metal mesh that protected the magnet. The shriek of tearing material and the furious presence of hard radiation sweeping over him . . .

He struck violently. Pain became visible: a luminous ingot that grew soft and absorbing, like radioactive steel-wool. It undulated, expanded, and quietly absorbed him. He was, in his agony, a spot of moist organic matter, being soundlessly sopped up by the unlimited sheet of dense metallic fiber.

Then, even that ebbed out. Conscious of the grotesque brokenness of his body, he lay in an inert heap, trying aimlessly, reflexively, to get up. And realizing at the same time, that there would be no getting up for any of them. Not for a while.

III

IN THE DARKNESS, something stirred.

For a long time he lay listening. Eyes shut, body limp, he refrained from motion, and became, as much as possible, a single giant ear. The sound was a rhythmic *tap-*

tap, as if something had gotten into the darkness and was blindly feeling around. For an endless time he as giant ear examined it, and then he as giant brain realized foolishly that it was a venetian blind tapping against a window, and that he was in a hospital ward.

As ordinary eye, optic nerve, and human brain, he perceived the dim shape of his wife, wavering and receding, a few feet from the bed. Thankfulness enveloped him. Marsha hadn't been incinerated by the hard radiation; thank God for that. A mute prayer of thanks clouded his brain; he relaxed and enjoyed the sheer joy of it.

"He's coming around," a doctor's deep, authoritative voice observed.

"I guess so." Marsha was talking. Her voice seemed to come from a considerable distance. "When will we be sure?"

"I'm fine," Hamilton managed gruffly.

Instantly, the shape detached itself and fluttered over. "Darling," Marsha was gasping, tugging and pressing at him fondly. "Nobody was killed—everybody's all right. Even you." Like a great moon, she beamed ecstatically down at him. "McFeyffe sprained his ankle, but it'll mend. They think that boy has a brain concussion."

"What about you?" Hamilton asked weakly.

"I'm fine, too." She displayed herself, turning so he could see all of her. Instead of her chic little coat and dress, she had on a plain white hospital smock. "The radiation singed away most of my clothes—they gave me this." Embarrassed, she patted her brown hair. "And look —this is shorter. I clipped off the burned part. It'll grow back."

"Can I get up?" Hamilton demanded, trying to climb to a sitting position. His head swam dizzily; all at once he was prone again, and gasping for breath. Bits of darkness danced and swirled around him; closing his eyes he waited apprehensively for them to pass.

"You'll be weak for a time," the doctor informed him. "Shock, and loss of blood." He touched Hamilton's arm. "You were pretty badly cut. Torn metal, but we got the pieces out."

"Who's the worst off?" Hamilton asked, eyes shut.

"Arthur Silvester, the old soldier. He never lost consciousness, but I wish he had. Broken back, apparently. He's down in surgery."

"Brittle, I suppose," Hamilton said, exploring his arm. It was done up in a vast white-plastic bandage.

"I was the least hurt," Marsha said haltingly. "But I was knocked cold. I mean, the radiation did it. I fell right into the main beam; all I saw were sparks and lightning. They cut it right off, of course. It didn't really last over a fraction of a second." Plaintively, she added, "It seemed like a million years."

The doctor, a neat-appearing young man, pushed the covers back and took Hamilton's pulse. At the edge of the bed, a tall nurse hovered efficiently. Equipment was pulled up at Hamilton's elbow. Things seemed to be under control.

Seemed . . . but something was wrong. He could feel it. Deep inside him, there was a nagging sense that something basic was out of phase.

"Marsha," he said suddenly, "you feel it?"

Hesitantly, Marsha came over beside him. "Feel what, darling?"

"I don't know. But it's there."

After an anxious, undecided moment, Marsha turned to the doctor. "I told you something's the matter. Didn't I say that when I came back?"

"Everybody coming out of shock has a sense of unreality," the doctor informed her. "It's a common feeling. After a day or so it should fade. Remember, both of you have been given sedative injections. And you've had a terrible ordeal; that was highly charged stuff that hit you."

Neither Hamilton nor his wife spoke. They gazed at each other, each trying to read the expression on the other's face.

"I guess we were lucky," Hamilton said tentatively. His prayer of joy had faded to a doubtful uncertainty. *What was it?* The awareness was not rational; he couldn't pin it down. Glancing around the room he saw nothing odd, nothing out of place.

"Very lucky," the nurse put in. Proudly, as if she had been personally responsible.

"How long do I have to stay here?"

The doctor meditated. "You can go home tonight, I think. But you should be in bed a day or so. Both of you are going to need a lot of rest, the next week or so. I suggest a trained nurse."

Hamilton said thoughtfully, "We can't afford it."

"You'll be covered, of course." The doctor sounded offended. "The Federal Government manages this. If I were you, I'd spend my time worrying about getting back on my feet."

"Maybe I like it better this way," Hamilton said tartly. He didn't amplify; for a time he sank into somber reflections about his situation.

Accident or no accident, it hadn't changed. Unless, while he lay unconscious, Colonel T. E. Edwards had died of a heart attack. It didn't seem likely.

When the doctor and nurse had been persuaded to leave, Hamilton said to his wife, "Well, now we have an excuse. Something we can tell the neighbors, to explain why I'm not at work."

Forlornly, Marsha nodded. "I forgot about that."

"I'm going to have to find something that doesn't involve classified material. Something that doesn't bring in national defense." Somberly, he reflected, "Like Einstein said, back in '54. Maybe I'll be a plumber. Or a TV repairman; that's more along my line."

"Remember what you always wanted to do?" Perched on the edge of the bed, Marsha sat soberly examining her shortened, somewhat ragged hair. "You wanted to design new tape recorder circuits. And FM circuits. You wanted to be a big name in high fidelity, like Bogen and Thorens and Scott."

"That's right," he agreed, with as much conviction as possible. "The Hamilton Trinaural Sound System. Remember the night we dreamed that up? Three cartridges, needles, amplifiers, speakers. Mounted in three rooms. A man in each room, listening to each rig. Each rig is playing a different composition."

"One plays the Brahms double concerto," Marsha put in, with feeble enthusiasm. "I remember that."

"One plays the Stravinsky *Wedding*. And one plays Dowland music for the lute. Then the brains of the three men are removed and wired together by the core of the Hamilton Trinaural Sound System, the Hamilton Musiphonic Ortho-Circuit. The sensations of the three brains are mingled in a strict mathematical relationship, based on Planck's Constant." His arm had begun to throb; harshly, he finished: "The resultant combination is fed into a tape recorder and played back at 3:14 times the original speed."

"And listened to on a crystal set." Marsha bent quickly down and hugged him. "Darling, when I came around

I thought you were a corpse. So help me—you looked like a corpse, all white and silent and not moving. I thought my heart would break."

"I'm insured," he said gravely. "You'd be rich."

"I don't want to be rich." Rocking miserably back and forth, still hugging him, Marsha whispered: "Look what I've done to you. Because I'm bored and curious and fooling around with political freaks, you've lost your job and your future. I could kick myself. I should have known I couldn't sign the Stockholm Peace thing with you working on guided missiles. But whenever anybody hands me a petition, I *always* get carried away. The poor, downtrodden masses."

"Don't worry about it," he told her shortly. "If this were back in 1943, you'd be normal and McFeyffe would be out of a job. As a dangerous fascist."

"He is," Marsha said fervently. "He *is* a dangerous fascist."

Hamilton shoved the woman away from him. "McFeyffe is a rabid patriot and a reactionary. But that doesn't make him a fascist. Unless you believe that anybody who isn't—"

"Let's not talk about it," Marsha broke in. "You're not supposed to thrash around—right?" Intensely, feverishly, she kissed him on the mouth. "Wait until you're home."

As she moved away, he grabbed hold of her by the shoulder. *"What is it? What's gone wrong?"*

Numbly, she shook her head. "I can't tell. I can't figure it out. Since I came around, it always seems to be just behind me. I've felt it. As if—" She gestured. "I expect to turn around and see—I don't know what. Something hiding. Something awful." She shivered apprehensively. "It scares me."

"It scares me too."

"Maybe we'll find out," Marsha said faintly. "Maybe it isn't anything . . . just the shock and the sedatives, like the doctor said."

Hamilton didn't believe it. And neither did she.

They were driven home by a staff physician, along with the severe young businesswoman. She, too, wore a plain hospital smock. The three of them sat quietly in the back seat, as the Packard jitney made its way along the dark streets of Belmont.

"They think I've got a couple of cracked ribs," the woman told them dispassionately. Presently, she added, "My name's Joan Reiss. I've seen both of you before . . . you've been in my store."

"What store is that?" Hamilton asked, after he had sketchily introduced himself and his wife.

"The book and art supply shop on El Camino. Last August you bought a Skira folio of Chagall."

"That's so," Marsha admitted. "It was Jack's birthday . . . we put them up on the wall. Downstairs, in the audiophile room."

"The cellar," Hamilton explained.

"There was one thing," Marsha said suddenly, her fingers digging convulsively into her purse. "Did you notice the doctor?"

"Notice?" He was puzzled. "No, not particularly."

"That's what I mean. He was just sort of—well, a blob. Like doctors you see in toothpaste ads."

Joan Reiss was listening intently. "What's this?"

"Nothing," Hamilton told her shortly. "A private conversation."

"And the nurse. She was the same, a sort of composite. Like all the nurses you ever saw."

Pondering, Hamilton gazed out the car window at the

night. "It's the result of mass communication," he conjectured. "People model themselves after ads. Don't they, Miss Reiss?"

Miss Reiss said, "I wanted to ask you something. There was something I noticed that made me wonder."

"What's that?" Hamilton asked suspiciously; Miss Reiss couldn't possibly know what they were talking about.

"The policeman on the platform . . . just before it collapsed. Why was he there?"

"He came with us," Hamilton said, annoyed.

Miss Reiss eyed him intently. "Did he? I thought perhaps . . ." Her voice trailed off vaguely. "It seemed to me that he turned and started back just before it fell."

"He did," Hamilton agreed. "He felt it going. So did I, but I hurried the other way."

"You mean you deliberately came back? When you could have saved yourself?"

"My wife," Hamilton told her testily.

Miss Reiss nodded, apparently satisfied. "I'm sorry . . . all this shock and strain. We were fortunate. Some weren't. Isn't it odd: some of us got out with almost no injuries, and that poor soldier, Mr. Silvester, with a broken back. It makes you wonder."

"I meant to tell you," the physician driving the car spoke up. "Arthur Silvester doesn't have a broken spinal column. It seems to be a chipped vertebra and a damaged spleen."

"Great," Hamilton muttered. "What about the guide? Nobody's mentioned him."

"Some internal injuries," the physician answered. "They haven't released the diagnosis yet."

"Is he waiting out in the supply shack?" Marsha asked.

The doctor laughed. "You mean Bill Laws? He was

the first one they carted out; he's got friends on the staff."

"And another thing," Marsha said abruptly. "Considering how far we fell and all that radiation—none of us was really hurt. Here the three of us are running around again as if nothing had happened. It's unreal. It was too easy."

Exasperated, Hamilton said, "We probably fell into a bunch of safety gadgets. Goddam it—"

There was more he wanted to say, but he never got it out. At that moment, a stark, fierce pain lashed up his right leg. With a yell, he leaped up, banging his head on the roof of the car. Pawing frantically, he yanked up his trouser leg in time to see a small, winged creature scuttle off.

"What is it?" Marsha demand anxiously. And then she, too, saw it. "A bee!"

Furiously, Hamilton stepped on the bee, grinding it under his shoe. "It stung me. Right on the calf." Already, an ugly red swelling was taking shape. "Haven't I had enough trouble?"

The physician had pulled the car quickly to the side of the road. "You killed it? Those things get in while the car's parked. I'm sorry—will you be all right? I have some salve we can put on it."

"I'll live," Hamilton muttered, gingerly massaging the welt. "A bee. As if we hadn't had enough trouble for one day."

"We'll be home, soon," Marsha said soothingly, peering out the car window. "Miss Reiss, come on in and have a drink with us."

"Well," Miss Reiss equivocated, plucking at her lip with a thin, bony finger, "I could use a cup of coffee. If you can spare it."

"We certainly can," Marsha said quickly. "We ought to stick together, all eight of us. We've had such an awful experience."

"Let's hope it's over," Miss Reiss said uneasily.

"Amen to that," Hamilton added. A moment later, the car pulled up to the curb and halted: they were home.

"What a nice little place you have," Miss Reiss commented as they clambered from the car. In the evening twilight, the modern two-bedroom California ranch-style house sat quietly waiting for them to ascend the path to the front porch. And sitting on the porch, also waiting, was a large yellow tomcat, his paws tucked under his bosom.

"There's Jack's cat," Marsha said, fishing in her purse for her key. "He wants to be fed." To the cat she instructed, "Go on inside, Ninny Numbcat. You don't get fed out here."

"What a quaint name," Miss Reiss observed, with a touch of aversion. "Why do you call him that?"

"Because he's stupid," Hamilton answered briefly.

"Jack has names like that for all his cats," Marsha explained. "The last one was called Parnassus Nump."

The big, disreputable-looking tomcat had got to his feet and jumped down onto the walk. Sidling up to Hamilton, he rubbed loudly against his leg. Miss Reiss retreated with overt distaste. "I never could get used to cats," she revealed. "They're so sneaky and underhanded."

Normally, Hamilton would have delivered a short sermon on stereotypy. But at the moment, he didn't particularly care what Miss Reiss thought about cats. Sticking his key in the lock, he pushed open the front door and clicked on the living room lights. The bright little house flooded into being, and the ladies entered. After them came Ninny Numbcat, heading straight for the kitchen, his ragged tail stuck up like a yellow ramrod.

Still in her hospital smock, Marsha opened the refrigerator and got out a green plastic bowl of boiled beef hearts. As she cut up the meat and dropped the pieces to the cat, she commented: "Most electronics geniuses have mechanical pets—those phototropic moths and the like, things that go running and bumping around. Jack built one when we were first married, one that caught mice and flies. But that wasn't good enough; he had to build another that caught *it*."

"Cosmic justice," Hamilton said, taking off his hat and coat. "I didn't want them to populate the world."

While Ninny Numbcat greedily finished his dinner, Marsha went into the bedroom to change. Miss Reiss prowled around the living room, expertly inspecting the vases, prints, furnishings.

"Cats have no souls," Hamilton said morbidly, watching his tomcat avidly feed. "The most majestic cat in the universe would balance a carrot on his head for a bite of pork liver."

"They're animals," Miss Reiss acknowledged from the living room. "Did you get this Paul Klee print from us?"

"Probably."

"I've never been able to decide what Klee is trying to say."

"Maybe he's not trying to say anything. Maybe he's just having a good time." Hamilton's arm had begun to ache; he wondered how it looked under the bandage. "You say you want coffee?"

"Coffee—and strong," Miss Reiss corroborated. "Can I help you fix it?"

"Just make yourself comfortable." Mechanically, Hamilton reached around for the Silex. "The soft-cover edition of Toynbee's *History* is stuffed in the magazine rack, there by the couch."

"Darling," Marsha's voice came from the bedroom, sharp and urgent. "Could you come here?"

He did so, the Silex in his hand, sloshing water as he hurried. Marsha stood at the bedroom window, about to pull down the shade. She was gazing out at the night, a taut, worried frown wrinkling her forehead. "What's the matter?" Hamilton demanded.

"Look out there."

He looked, but all he saw was a vague blur of gloom, and the indistinct outline of houses. A few lights glowed weakly here and there. The sky was overcast, a low ceiling of fog that drifted silently around the roof tops. Nothing moved. There was no life, no activity. No presence of people.

"It's like the Middle Ages," Marsha said quietly.

Why did it look that way? He could see it, too; but objectively the scene was prosaic, the usual sight from his bedroom window at nine-thirty on a cold October night.

"And we've been talking that way," Marsha said, shivering. "You said something about Ninny's soul. You didn't talk like that before."

"Before what?"

"Before we came here." Turning from the window, she reached for her checkered shirt: it hung over the back of a chair. "And—this is silly, of course. But did you really see the doctor's car drive off? Did you say goodby? Did *anything* happen?"

"Well, he's gone," Hamilton pointed out noncommittally.

Eyes large and serious, Marsha buttoned her shirt and

stuffed the tails into her slacks. "I guess I'm delirious, like they said. The shock, the drugs . . . but it's all so quiet. As if we're the only people alive. Living in a gray bucket, no lights, no colors, just sort of a—primordial place. Remember the old religions? Before the cosmos came chaos. Before the land was separated from the water. Before the darkness was separated from the light. And things didn't have any names."

"Ninny has his name," Hamilton pointed out gently. "So do you; so does Miss Reiss. And so does Paul Klee."

Together, they returned to the kitchen. Marsha took over the job of fixing coffee; in a few moments the Silex bubbled furiously. Sitting stiffly upright at the kitchen table, Miss Reiss had a pinched, strained look; her severe, colorless face was set in rigid concentration, as if she were deep in turmoil. She was a plain determined-looking young woman, with a tight bun of mousy, sand-colored hair pulled against her skull. Her nose was thin and sharp; her lips were pressed into an uncompromising line. Miss Reiss looked like a woman with whom it was better not to trifle.

"What were you saying in there?" she asked as she stirred her cup of coffee.

Annoyed, Hamilton answered, "We were discussing a personal situation. Why?"

"Now, darling," Marsha reproved.

Bluntly facing Miss Reiss, Hamilton demanded, "Are you always this way? Snooping around, prying into things?"

There was no emotion visible on the woman's pinched face. "I have to be careful," she explained. "This accident today has made me especially conscious of the jeopardy I'm in." Correcting herself, she added, "So-called accident, I mean."

"Why you especially?" Hamilton wanted to know.

Miss Reiss didn't answer; she was watching Ninny Numbcat. The big battered tom had finished his meal; now he was looking for a lap. "What's the matter with him?" Miss Reiss asked, in a thin, frightened voice. "Why's he looking at me?"

"You're sitting down," Marsha said soothingly. "He wants to hop up and go to sleep."

Half-rising to her feet, Miss Reiss upbraided the cat, "Don't you come near me! Keep your dirty body away from me!" To Hamilton she confided, "If they didn't have fleas, it wouldn't be so offensive. And this one has a mean look. I suppose he kills his share of birds?"

"Six or seven a day," Hamilton answering, temper rising.

"Yes," Miss Reiss agreed, backing warily away from the puzzled tomcat. "I can see he's quite a killer. Certainly, in the city, there ought to be some kind of prohibitive ordinance. Destructive pets, vicious animals that are a menace, should at least have licenses. And the city really should—"

"Not only birds," Hamilton interrupted, a cold ruthless sadism sliding over him, "but snakes and gophers. And this morning he showed up with a dead rabbit."

"Darling," Marsha said sharply. Miss Reiss was shrinking away in genuine fear. "Some people don't like cats. You can't expect everybody to share your tastes."

"Little furry mice, too," Hamilton said brutally. "By the dozen. Part he eats, part he brings to us. And one morning he showed up with the head of an old woman."

A terrified squeak escaped from Miss Reiss' lips. In panic, she scrambled back, pathetic and defenseless. Instantly, Hamilton was sorry. Ashamed of himself, he

opened his mouth to apologize, to retract his misplaced
humor. . . .

From the air above his head a shower of locusts descended. Buried in a squirming mass of vermin, Hamilton
struggled frantically to escape. The two women and the
tomcat stood paralyzed with disbelief. For a time he
rolled and fought with the horde of crawling, biting,
stinging pests. Then, dragging himself away, he managed
to bat them off and retreat, panting and gasping, to a
corner.

"Merciful God," Marsha whispered, stricken, backing
away from the buzzing, flopping heap.

"What . . . happened?" Miss Reiss managed, eyes
fixed on the mound of quivering insects. "It's impossible!"

"Well," Hamilton said shakily, "it happened."

"But *how?*" Marsha echoed, as the four of them retreated from the kitchen, away from the spilling flood of
wings and chitinous bodies. "Things like this just can't
be."

"But it fits," Hamilton said, in a weak, soft voice. "The
bee—remember? We were right; something has happened. And it fits. It makes sense."

IV

MARSHA HAMILTON lay sleeping in bed. Warm yellow
morning sunlight splashed across her bare shoulders,
across the blankets and asphalt tile floor. In the bath-

room, Jack Hamilton stood relentlessly shaving, in spite of the throbbing pain in his injured arm. The mirror, fogged and dripping, reflected his lathered features, a distorted parody of his usual face.

By now, the house was calm and collected. Most of the locusts from the previous evening had dispersed; only an occasional dry scratching reminded him that some remained in the walls. Everything seemed normal. A milk truck rattled past the house. Marsha sighed drowsily and stirred in her sleep, raising one arm up over the covers. Outside, on the back porch, Ninny Numbcat was preparing to come indoors.

Very carefully, keeping a tight discipline on himself, Hamilton finished shaving, cleaned his razor, slapped talcum on his jowls and neck, and groped around for a clean white shirt. Lying sleepless the night before, he had decided on this moment to begin: the instant after shaving, when he was clean, combed, dressed, and fully awake.

Getting awkwardly down on one knee, he placed his hands together, closed his eyes, took a deep breath, and began.

"Dear Lord," he said grimly, in a half-whisper, "I'm sorry I did what I did to poor Miss Reiss. I'd appreciate being forgiven, if it's all right with You."

He remained kneeling for a minute, wondering if it had been enough. And if it had been correctly delivered. But gradually, a needling outrage displaced his humble contrition. It was unnatural, a grown man down on one knee. It was an undignified, unworthy posture for an adult . . . and one he wasn't accustomed to. Resentfully, he added a closing paragraph to his prayer.

"Let's face it—she deserved it." His harsh whisper drifted through the silent house; Marsha sighed again

and tumbled over in a fetal heap. Soon, she'd be awake.
Outside, Ninny Numbcat plucked fretfully at the screen
door and wondered why it was still locked.

"Consider what she said," Hamilton continued, choos-
ing his words with care. "It's attitudes like hers that lead
to extermination camps. She's rigid, a compulsive personality type. Anti-cat is one jump away from anti-Semi-
tism."

There was no response. Did he expect any? What,
exactly, *did* he expect? He wasn't sure. Something, at
least. Some sign.

Maybe he wasn't getting over. The last time he had
dipped into religion of any variety was in his eighth
year, in a vague Sunday School class. The labored reading of the night before had brought up nothing specific,
only the abstract realization that there was a great deal
on the subject. Proper forms, protocol . . . it was going
to be worse than arranging a discussion with Colonel
T. E. Edwards.

But somewhat the same thing.

He was still in a posture of supplication when a sound
came from behind him. Turning his head quickly, he
observed a shape walking gingerly through the living
room. A man, dressed in sweater and slacks; a young
Negro.

"Are you my sign?" Hamilton asked caustically.

The Negro's face was drawn with fatigue. "You remember who I am. I'm the guide who led you people
out on that platform. I've been thinking about it for fif-
teen hours straight."

"It wasn't your fault," Hamilton said. "You went down
with the rest of us." Getting stiffly to his feet, he came
out of the bathroom and into the hall. "Have you eaten
breakfast?"

"I'm not hungry." The Negro studied him intently. "What were you doing? *Praying?*"

"I was," Hamilton admitted.

"Is that customary with you?"

"No." He hesitated. "I haven't prayed since I was eight."

The Negro digested the information. "My name is Bill Laws." They shook hands. "You've figured it out, apparently. When did you figure it out?"

"Some time between last night and this morning."

"Anything special happen?"

Hamilton told him about the rain of locusts and the bee. "It wasn't hard to see the causal hookup. I lied—so I got punished. And before that, I blasphemed—and I got punished. Cause and effect."

"You're wasting your time praying," Laws told him curtly. "I tried that. No dice."

"What did you pray for?"

Ironically, Laws indicated the black surface of skin starting at his collar. "One guess. Things aren't quite that simple . . . they never were and they never will be."

"You sound pretty bitter," Hamilton said cautiously.

"This was quite a shock." Laws wandered around the living room. "Sorry to break right in. But the front door was unlocked, so I assumed you were up. You're an electronics research worker?"

"That's right."

Grimacing, Laws said, "Greetings, brother. I'm a graduate student in advanced physics. That's how I got the job as guide. A lot of competition in the field, these days." He added, "So they say."

"How did you find out?"

"This business?" Laws shrugged his shoulders. "It wasn't so tough." From his pocket he got a wad of cloth-

like material; unwrapping it, he produced a small sliver
of metal. "This is something my sister got me to carry,
years ago. Now it's a habit." He tossed the charm to
Hamilton. Inscribed on it were pious words of faith
and hope, worn smooth by years of handling.

"Go on," Laws said. "Use it."

"Use it?" Hamilton didn't understand. "Frankly, all
this is out of my line."

"Your arm." Laws gestured impatiently. "It works,
now. Put it on your gash. Better take off the bandage
first; works better if there's actual physical contact. *Con-
tiguity*, they call it. That's how I fixed up my various
aches and breaks."

Skeptically, and with great care, Hamilton peeled
away a section of the bandage; the livid, moist flesh
glowed bloodily in the morning sunlight. After a moment's hesitation, he laid the cold bit of metal against
it.

"There it goes," Laws said.

The ugly rawness of the wound faded. As Hamilton
watched, the meaty red waned to a dull pink. An orange
sheen crept over it; the gash shriveled, dried, and closed.
Only a narrow line, white and indistinct, remained. And
the throbbing pain was gone.

"That's it," Laws said, reaching for the charm.

"Did it work before?"

"Never. Just a lot of hot air." Laws pocketed it. "I'm
going to try leaving a few hairs in water overnight.
Worms in the morning, of course. Want to know how to
cure diabetes? Half a ground-up toad mixed with milk
of a virgin, wrapped around the neck in an old flannel
that's been dipped in pond water."

"You mean all that junk—"

"It's going to work. Like the rustics have been saying.

Up to now, they've been wrong. But now it's us who're wrong."

Marsha appeared at the bedroom doorway in her robe, hair tumbled about her face, eyes half-shut with sleep. "Oh," she said, startled, when she made out Laws. "It's you. How are you?"

"I'm all right, thanks," Laws answered.

Rubbing her eyes, Marsha turned quickly to her husband. "How did you sleep?"

"I slept." Something in her voice, a sharp urgency, made him ask: "Why?"

"Did you dream?"

Hamilton reflected. He had tossed, turned, experienced vague phantasmagoria. But nothing he could put his finger on. "No," he admitted.

A strange expression had appeared on Laws' sharp face. "You dreamed, Mrs. Hamilton? What did you dream?"

"The craziest thing. Not a dream, exactly. I mean, nothing happened. It just—was."

"A place?"

"Yes, a place. And us."

"All of us?" Laws asked intently. "All eight?"

"Yes." She nodded eagerly. "Lying down, where we fell. Down in the Bevatron. All of us, just stretched out there. Unconscious. And nothing happening. No time. No change."

"Off in the corner," Laws said, "is something moving? Some medical workers, maybe?"

"Yes," Marsha repeated. "But not moving. Just hanging on some kind of ladder. Frozen there."

"They're moving," Laws said. "I dreamed it, too. At first I thought they weren't moving. But they are. Very slowly."

There was an uneasy silence.

Searching his mind again, Hamilton said slowly, "Now that you talk about it . . ." He shrugged. "It's the traumatic memory. The moment of shock. It's cut right into our brains; we'll never be able to shake it."

"But," Marsha said tensely, "*it's still going on*. We're still there."

"There? Lying in the Bevatron?"

She nodded anxiously. "I feel it. I believe it."

Noting the alarm in her voice, Hamilton changed the subject. "Surprise," he told her, displaying his newly healed arm. "Bill just sat back and passed a miracle."

"Not me," Laws said emphatically, his dark eyes hard. "I wouldn't be caught dead passing a miracle."

Embarrassed, Hamilton stood rubbing his arm. "It was your charm that did it."

Laws reexamined his metal good luck charm. "Maybe we've sunk down to the real reality. Maybe this stuff has been there all the time, under the surface."

Marsha came slowly toward the two men. "We're dead, aren't we?" she said huskily.

"Apparently not," Hamilton answered. "We're still in Belmont, California. But not the same Belmont. There've been a few changes here and there. A few additions. There's Somebody hanging around."

"What now?" Laws inquired.

"Don't ask me," Hamilton said. "I didn't get us here. Obviously, the accident at the Bevatron produced it. Whatever *it* is."

"I can tell you what comes next," Marsha said calmly.

"What?"

"I'm going out and get a job."

Hamilton raised his eyebrows. "What kind of a job?"

"Any kind. Typing, working in a store, switchboard operator. So we can keep on eating . . . remember?"

"I remember," Hamilton said. "But you stay home and dust the mantel; I'll take care of the job-getting." He indicated his smooth-shaven chin and clean shirt. "I'm already two steps on my way."

"But," Marsha appealed, "it's my fault you're out of work."

"Maybe we won't have to work any more," Laws reflected, with ironic emphasis. "Maybe all we have to do now is open our mouths and wait for the manna to drift down."

"I thought you tried that," Hamilton said.

"I tried it, yes. And I got no results. But some people *do* get results. We're going to have to work out the dynamics of this thing. This world, or whatever it is, has its own laws. Different laws from the ones we were familiar with. We've had a few already. Charms function. That implies that the whole structure of blessing now works." Laws added, "And maybe damnation."

"Salvation," Marsha murmured, her brown eyes wide. "Good Lord, do you suppose there's really a Heaven?"

"Absolutely," Hamilton agreed. He returned to the bedroom; a moment later he emerged tying his necktie. "But that comes later. Right now I'm driving up the peninsula. We have exactly fifty dollars left in the bank, and I'm not going to starve to death trying to make this prayer-business function."

From the parking lot at the missile plant, Hamilton picked up his Ford business coupé. It was still parked in the slot reading: Reserved for John W. Hamilton.

Heading up El Camino Real, he left the town of Belmont. Half an hour later he was entering South San

Francisco. The clock in front of the South San Francisco branch of the Bank of America read eleven-thirty as he parked in the sedate gravel field beside the Cadillacs and Chryslers belonging to the staff of EDA.

The Electronics Development Agency buildings lay to his right; white blocks of cement set against the hills of the sprawling industrial city. Once, years ago, when he had done his first published paper in advanced electronics, EDA had tried to hire him away from California Maintenance. Guy Tillingford, one of the leading statisticians of the country, headed the corporation; a brilliant and original man, he had been in addition, a close friend of Hamilton's father.

This was the place to find a job—if he found one at all. And, most important, EDA was not currently engaged in military research. Doctor Tillingford, part of the group that had made up the Institute of Advanced Studies at Princeton (before that group had been officially disbanded), was more concerned with general scientific knowledge. From EDA came some of the most radical computers, the great electronic brains used in industries and universities all over the Western world.

"Yes, Mr. Hamilton," the efficient little secretary said, crisply examining his sheaf of papers. "I'll tell the doctor you're here . . . I'm sure he'll be glad to see you."

Tautly, Hamilton paced the lounge, rubbing his hands together and breathing a silent prayer. The prayer came easily; at this particular moment he didn't have to force it. Fifty dollars in the bank wasn't going to last the Hamilton family very long . . . even in this world of miracles and falling locusts.

"Jack, my boy," a deep voice boomed. Doctor Guy Tillingford appeared at the doorway of his office, aged face beaming, hand extended. "By golly, I'm glad to see you. How long has it been? Ten years?"

"Darn near," Hamilton admitted, as they heartily grasped hands. "You're looking well, Doctor."

Around the office stood consultant engineers and technicians; bright young men with crew cuts, bow ties, alert expressions on their smooth faces. Ignoring them, Doctor Tillingford led Hamilton through a series of wood-paneled doors into a private chamber.

"We can talk here," he confided, throwing himself down in a black leather easy chair. "I have this fixed up —a sort of personal retreat, where I can take time off to meditate and get my second wind." Sadly, he added, "I can't seem to stand the steady grind, the way I used to. I crawl in here a couple times a day . . . to get back my strength."

"I've left California Maintenance," Hamilton said.

"Oh?" Tillingford nodded. "Good for you. That's a bad place. Too much emphasis on guns. They're not scientists; they're government employees."

"I didn't quit. I was fired." In a few words, Hamilton explained the situation.

For a little while Tillingford said nothing. Thoughtfully, he picked at a front tooth, wrinkled brow pulled together in a frown of concentration. "I remember Marsha. Sweet girl. I always liked her. There's so darn much of this security-risk stuff these days. But we don't have to worry about that here. No government contracts at present. Ivory tower." He chuckled drily. "Last remnant of pure research."

"You suppose you could use me?" Hamilton asked, as dispassionately as possible.

"I don't see why not." Idly, Tillingford got out a small religious prayer wheel and began spinning it. "I'm familiar with your work . . . I wish we could have got hold of you sooner, as a matter of fact."

Fascinated, hypnotized with disbelief, Hamilton stared fixedly at Tillingford's prayer wheel.

"Of course, there're the regular questions," Tillingford observed, spinning. "The routine . . . but you won't have to fill out the written forms. I'll ask you orally. You don't drink, do you?"

Hamilton floundered. *"Drink?"*

"This business about Marsha poses a certain problem. We're not concerned with the security aspect, of course . . . but I will have to ask you this. Jack, tell me truthfully." Reaching into his pocket, Tillingford got out a black-bound volume, gold-stamped *Bayan of the Second Bab,* and handed it to Hamilton. "In college, when you two were mixed up in radical groups, you didn't practice—shall I say, 'free love'?"

Hamilton had no answer. Mute, dazed, he stood holding the *Bayan of the Second Bab;* it was still warm from Tillingford's coat pocket. A pair of EDA's bright young men had come quietly into the room; they now stood respectfully watching. Dressed in long white lab smocks, they seemed curiously solemn and obedient. Their smooth-cropped skulls reminded him of the polls of young monks . . . odd that he had never noticed how much the popular crewcut resembled the ancient ascetic practice of religious orders. These two men were certainly typical of bright young physicists; where was their usual brashness?

"And while we're at it," Doctor Tillingford said, "I might as well ask you this. Jack, my boy, hold onto that Bayan and tell me truthfully. Have you found the One True Gate to blessed salvation?"

All eyes were on him. He swallowed, flushed beet-red,

stood helplessly struggling. "Doctor," he managed finally, "I think I'll come back some other time."

Concerned, Tillingford removed his glasses and carefully eyed the younger man. "Jack, don't you feel well?"

"I've been under a lot of strain. Losing my job . . ." Hastily, Hamilton added: "And other difficulties. Marsha and I were in an accident, yesterday. A new deflector went wrong and bathed us with hard radiation, over at the Bevatron."

"Oh, yes," Tillingford agreed. "I heard about that. Nobody killed, fortunately."

"Those eight people," one of his ascetic young technicians put in, "must have walked with the Prophet. That was a long drop."

"Doctor," Hamilton said hoarsely, "could you recommend a good psychiatrist?"

A slow, incredulous glaze settled over the elderly scientist's face. "A—*what*? Are you out of your head, boy?"

"Yes," Hamilton answered. "Apparently."

"We'll discuss this later," Tillingford said shortly, in a choked voice. Impatiently, he waved his two technicians out of the room. "Go down to the mosque," he told them. "Meditate until I call for you."

They departed, with an intent, thoughtful scrutiny of Hamilton.

"You can talk to me," Tillingford said heavily. "I'm your friend. I knew your father, Jack. He was a great physicist. They don't come any better. I always had high hopes for you. Naturally, I was disappointed when you went to work for California Maintenance. But, of course, we have to bow to the Cosmic Will."

"Can I ask you a few questions?" Cold perspiration poured down Hamilton's neck, into his starched white collar. "This place is still a scientific organization, isn't it? Or is it?"

"Still?" Puzzled, Tillingford took back his Bayan from Hamilton's lifeless fingers. "I don't get the drift of your questions, boy. Be more specific."

"Let's put it this way. I've been—cut off. Deep in my own work, I've lost contact with what the rest of the field is doing. And," he finished desperately, "I don't have any idea what other fields are up to. Maybe—could you briefly acquaint me with the current overall picture?"

"Picture," Tillingford echoed, nodding. "Very commonly lost sight of. That's the trouble with overspecialization. I can't tell you too much, myself. Our work at EDA is fairly well delineated; one might even say *prescribed*. Over at Cal Main you were developing weapons for use against the infidels; that's simple and obvious. Strictly applied science, correct?"

"Correct," Hamilton agreed.

"Here, we're working with an eternal and basic problem, that of communication. It's our job—and it's quite a job—to insure the fundamental electronic structure of communication. We have electronics men—like yourself. We have top-notch consulting semanticists. We have very good research psychologists. All of us form a team to tackle this basic problem of man's existence: keeping a well-functioning wire open between Earth and Heaven."

Doctor Tillingford continued: "Although of course you're already familiar with this, I'll say it again. In the old days, before communication was subjected to rigid scientific analysis, a variety of haphazard systems existed. Burnt sacrifices; attempts to attract God's attention by tickling His nose and palate. Very crude, very unscientific. Loud prayer and hymn singing, still practiced by the uneducated classes. Well, let them sing their hymns and chant their prayers." Pressing a button, he caused one wall of the room to become transparent. Hamilton found himself gazing down at the elaborate research labs that lay spread out in a ring around Tillingford's office: layer after layer of men and equipment, the most advanced machines and technicians available.

"Norbert Wiener," Tillingford said. "You recall his work in cybernetics. And, even more important, Enrico Destini's work in the field of theophonics."

"What's that?"

Tillingford raised an eyebrow. "You *are* a specialist, my boy. Communication between man and God, of course. Using Wiener's work, and using the invaluable material of Shannon and Weaver, Destini was able to set up the first really adequate system of communication between Earth and Heaven in 1946. Of course, he had the use of all that equipment from the War Against the Pagan Hordes, those damned Wotan-Worshiping, Oak-Tree-Praising Huns."

"You mean the—Nazis?"

"I'm familiar with that term. That's sociologist jargon, isn't it? And that Denier of the Prophet, that Anti-Bab. They say he's still alive down in Argentina. Found the elixir of eternal youth or something. He made that pact with the devil in 1939, you remember. Or was that before your time? But you know about it—it's history."

"I know," Hamilton said thickly.

"And yet, there were still people who didn't see the handwriting on the wall. Sometimes I think the Faithful deserve to be humbled. A few hydrogen bombs set off here and there, and the strong current of atheism that just can't be stamped out—"

"Other fields," Hamilton interrupted. "What are they doing? Physics. What about the physicists?"

"Physics is a closed subject," Tillingford informed him. "Virtually everything about the material universe is known—was known centuries ago. Physics has become an abstract side of engineering."

"And the engineers?"

In answer, Tillingford tossed him the November '59 issue of the *Journal of Applied Sciences*. "The lead article gives you a good idea, I think. Brilliant man, that Hirschbein."

The lead article was entitled *Theoretical Aspects of the Problem of Reservoir Construction.* Underneath was a subtitle. *The necessity of maintaining a constant supply of untainted grace for all major population centers.*

"Grace?" Hamilton said feebly.

"The engineers," Tillingford explained, "are mainly preoccupied with the job of piping grace for every Babi-ite community the world over. In a sense, it's an analogue to our problem of keeping the lines of communication open."

"And that's all they do?"

"Well," Tillingford acknowledge, "there's the constant task of building mosques, temples, altars. The Lord is a strict taskmaster, you realize; His specifications are quite exact. Frankly, just between you and me, I don't envy those fellows. One slip and"—he snapped his fingers—*"poof."*

"Poof?"

"Lightning."

"Oh," Hamilton said. "Of course."

"So very few of the brighter boys go into engineering. Too high a mortality rate." Tillingford scrutinized him with fatherly care. "My boy, you see, don't you, that you're really in a good field?"

"I never doubted that," Hamilton said hoarsely. "I was just curious to find out what that field is."

"I'm satisfied as to your moral status," Tillingford told him. "I know you're from a good, clean, God-fearing family. Your father was the soul of honesty and humility. I hear from him occasionally, still."

"Hear?" Hamilton said weakly.

"He's getting along quite well. He misses you, naturally." Tillingford indicated the intercom system on his desk. "If you'd like—"

"No," Hamilton said, backing away. "I'm still under the weather from my accident. I couldn't stand it."

"Suit yourself." Tillingford clapped a friendly hand on the younger man's shoulder. "Want to have a look at the labs? We've got some darn good equipment, let me tell you." In a confidential whisper, he revealed, "Took a mighty lot of praying, though. Over at your old bailiwick, Cal Main, they were sending up quite a noise themselves."

"But you got it."

"Oh, yes. After all, we set up the communication lines." Grinning and winking slyly, Tillingford led him toward the door. "I'll turn you over to our Personnel Director . . . he'll do the actual hiring."

The Personnel Director was a florid, smooth-jowled man who beamed happily at Hamilton as he fumbled in his desk for his forms and papers. "We'll be happy to accept your application, Mr. Hamilton. EDA needs men of your experience. And if the Doctor knows you personally—"

"Put him right through," Tillingford instructed. "Waive

the bureaucratic stuff; get right to the qualifications test."

"Right," the Director agreed, getting out his own copy of the *Bayan of the Second Bab*. Laying it on the desk, closed, he shut his eyes, ran his thumb down the pages, and opened the book at random. Tillingford leaned intently over his shoulder; conferring and murmuring, the two men examined the passage.

"Fine," Tillingford said, withdrawing in satisfaction. "It's a go."

"It certainly is," the Director agreed. To Hamilton he said, "You might be interested; it's one of the clearest okays I've seen this year." In a rapid, efficient voice he read: "Vision 1931: Chapter 6, verse 14, line 1. 'Yes, the True Faith melts the courage in the unbeliever; for he knows the measure of God's wrath; he knows the measure to fill the clay vessel.'" With a snap, he closed the Bayan and put it back on his desk. Both men beamed fondly at Hamilton, radiating good will and professional satisfaction.

Dazed, not sure how it felt, Hamilton reverted to the thin, clear thread that had brought him here. "Can I ask about the salary? Or is that too—" He tried to make a joke out of it. "Too crass and commercial?"

Both men were puzzled. "Salary?"

"Yes, salary," Hamilton repeated, in rising hysteria. "You remember, that stuff the bookkeeping department hands out every two weeks. To keep the hired help from getting restive."

"As is customary," Tillingford said, with quiet dignity, "you will be credited with the IBM people every ten days." Turning to the Personnel Director, he inquired, "What is the exact number? I don't remember those things."

"I'll check with the bookkeeper." The Personnel Director left his office; a moment later he returned with the information. "You'll go on as a Four-A rating. In six months you'll be Five-A. How's that? Not bad for a young man of thirty-two."

"What," Hamilton demanded, "does Four-A mean?"

After a surprised pause, the Personnel Director glanced at Tillingford, wet his lips, and answered, "IBM maintains the Book of Debits and Credits. The Cosmic Record." He gesticulated. "You know, the Great Unalterable Scroll of Sins and Virtues. EDA is doing the Lord's work; ergo, you're a servant of the Lord. Your pay will be four credits every ten days, four linear units toward your salvation. IBM will handle all the details; after all, that's why they exist."

It fitted. Taking a deep breath, Hamilton said: "That's fine. I forgot—excuse my confusion. But"—frantically, he appealed to Tillingford—"how'll Marsha and I live? We have to pay our bills; we have to *eat*."

"As a servant of the Lord," Tillingford said sternly, "your needs will be provided for. You have your Bayan?"

"Y-yes," Hamilton said.

"Just make certain you don't run short on faith. I should say a man of your moral caliber, engaged in this work, should be able to pray for and get at least—" He computed. "Oh, say, four hundred a week. What do you say, Ernie?"

The Personnel Director nodded in agreement. "At least."

"One thing more," Hamilton said, as Doctor Tillingford started briskly off, the matter—to his satisfaction—settled. "A little earlier I was asking about a psychiatrist . . ."

"My boy," Tillingford said, halting. "I have one thing

and one thing only to say to you. It's your life and you can conduct it as you please. I'm not trying to tell you what to do and what to think. Your spiritual existence is strictly a matter between yourself and the One True God. But if you wish to consult quacks and—"

"Quacks!" Hamilton echoed feebly.

"Borderline crackpots. It's all right for the layman. Uneducated persons, I realize, flock to psychiatrists in vast numbers. I've read the statistics; it's a sorry commentary on the state of public misinformation. I'll do this for you." From his coat he got a note pad, pencil, and quickly scribbled a note. "This is the only correct road. I suppose if you haven't got onto it by now, this won't make any difference. But we're instructed to keep trying. After all, eternity is a long time."

The note read *The Prophet Horace Clamp. Sepulcher of the Second Bab. Cheyenne, Wyoming.*

"Exactly," Tillingford said. "Right up to the top. Does that surprise you? It shows how concerned I am, my boy."

"Thanks," Hamilton said, mindlessly pocketing the note. "If you say so."

"I do say so," Tillingford repeated, in tones of absolute authority. "Second Babiism is the only True Faith, my boy; it's the sole guarantee of obtaining Paradise. God speaks through Horace Clamp and no one else. Take tomorrow and go out there; you can report for work some other time, it doesn't matter. If anybody can save your immortal soul from the fires of Eternal Damnation, the Prophet Horace Clamp can."

V

As HAMILTON uncertainly made his way from the EDA buildings, a small group of men followed quietly along behind, hands in their pockets, faces blank and benign. While he was fumbling for his car keys, the men moved purposefully forward, across the gravel parking lot, and up to him.

"Hi," one of them said.

All were young. All were blond. All had crew cuts and wore ascetic white lab smocks. Tillingford's bright young technicians, super-educated employees of EDA.

"What do you want?" Hamilton asked.

"You're leaving?" the leader inquired.

"That's right."

The group considered the information. After a time the leader observed, "But you're coming back."

"Look," Hamilton began, but the young man cut him off.

"Tillingford hired you," he stated. "You're showing up for work next week. You passed your entrance tests and now you've been poking and nosing around the labs."

"I may have passed my tests," Hamilton acknowledged, "but that doesn't mean I'm showing up for work. As a matter of fact—"

"My name's Brady," the leader of the group broke in. "Bob Brady. Maybe you saw me in there. I was with Tillingford when you showed up." Eying Hamilton, Brady finished: "Personnel may be satisfied, but we're not. Personnel is run by laymen. They have a few routine bureaucratic qualification tests and that's all."

"We're not laymen," one of Brady's group put in.

"Look," Hamilton said, with partially regained hope. "Maybe we can get together. I wondered how you qualified people could agree to that random book-opening test. That's no adequate measure of an applicant's training and ability. In advanced research of this type—"

"So as far as we're concerned," Brady continued inexorably, "you're a heathen until proved otherwise. And no heathens go to work at EDA. We have our professional standards."

"And you're not qualified," one of the group added. "Let's see your N-rating."

"Your N-rating." Extending his hand, Brady stood waiting. "You've had a nimbusgram taken recently, haven't you?"

"Not that I can recall," Hamilton answered uncertainly.

"That's what I thought. No N-rating." From his coat pocket Brady got out a small punched card. "There isn't anybody in this group with less than a 4.6 N-rating. Offhand, I'd guess you don't reach 2.0 class. How about that?"

"You're a heathen," one of the young technicians said severely. "Some nerve, trying to worm your way in here."

"Maybe you better get going," Brady said to Hamilton. "Maybe you better drive the hell out of here and not come back."

"I have as much right here as any of you," Hamilton said, exasperated.

"The ordeal approach," Brady said thoughtfully. "Let's settle this once and for all."

"Fine," Hamilton said with satisfaction. Pulling off his coat, and tossing it in the car, he said, "I'll wrestle any of you."

Nobody paid attention to him; the technicians were clustered around in a circle, conferring. Overhead, the late afternoon sun was beginning to set. Cars moved along the highway. The EDA buildings sparkled hygienically in the fading light.

"Here we go," Brady decided. Brandishing an ornate cigarette lighter, he solemnly approached Hamilton. "Stick out your thumb."

"My—thumb?"

"Ordeal by fire," Brady explained, igniting the lighter. A flash of yellow flame glowed. "Show your spirit. Show you're a man."

"I'm a man," Hamilton said angrily, "but I'll be damned if I'm going to stick my thumb into that flame just so you lunatics can have your frat-boy ritualistic initiation. I thought I got out of this when I left college."

Each technician extended his thumb. Methodically, Brady held the lighter under one thumb after another. No thumb was even slightly singed.

"You next," Brady said sanctimoniously. "Be a man, Hamilton. Remember you're not a wallowing beast."

"Go to hell," Hamilton retorted hotly. "And keep that lighter away from me."

"You refuse to subject yourself to ordeal by fire?" Brady inquired significantly.

With reluctance, Hamilton extended his thumb. Perhaps, in this world, cigarette lighters did not burn. Perhaps, without realizing it, he was immune to fire. Perhaps—

"Ouch!" Hamilton shouted, jerking his hand violently away.

The technicians shook their heads gravely. "Well," Brady said, putting away his lighter with a flourish of triumph. "That's that."

Hamilton stood impotently rubbing his injured thumb. "You sadists," he accused. "You God-mongering zealots. All of you belong back in the Middle Ages. You—Moslems!"

"Watch it," Brady warned. "You're talking to a Champion of the One True God."

"And don't forget it," one of his assistants chimed in.

"You may be a Champion of the One True God," Hamilton said, "but I happen to be a top-flight electronics man. Think that over."

"I'm thinking," Brady said, undisturbed.

"You can stick your thumb into the arc of a welding torch. You can dive into a blast furnace."

"That's so," Brady agreed. "I can."

"But what's that got to do with electronics?" Glaring at the young man, Hamilton said, "Okay, wise guy. I challenge you to a contest. Let's find out how much you know."

"You challenge a Champion of the One True God?" Brady demanded, incredulous.

"That's right."

"But—" Brady gestured. "That's illogical. Better go home, Hamilton. You're letting your thalamus get hold of you."

"Chicken, eh?" Hamilton taunted.

"But you can't win. Axiomatically, you lose. Consider the premises of the situation. By definition, a Champion of the One True God triumphs; anything else would be a denial of His power."

"Stop stalling," Hamilton said. "You can put the first

question to me. Three questions for each of us. Pertaining to applied and theoretical electronics. Agreed?"

"Agreed," Brady responded reluctantly. The other technicians crowded around wide-eyed, fascinated by the turn of events. "I'm sorry for you, Hamilton. Evidently you don't comprehend what's going on. I'd expect a layman to behave in this irrational fashion, but a man at least partly disciplined in scientific—"

"Ask," Hamilton told him.

"State Ohm's Law," Brady said.

Hamilton blinked. It was like asking him to count from one to ten; how could he miss? "That's your first question?"

"State Ohm's Law," Brady repeated. Silently, his lips began to move.

"What's happening?" Hamilton demanded suspiciously. "Why are your lips moving?"

"I'm praying," Brady revealed. "For Divine help."

"Ohm's Law," Hamilton said. "The resistance of a body to the passage of electrical current—" He broke off.

"What's wrong?" Brady inquired.

"You're distracting me. Couldn't you pray later?"

"Now," Brady said emphatically. "Later would be of no use."

Trying to ignore the man's twitching lips, Hamilton went on. "The resistance of a body to the passage of electrical current can be stated by the following equation: R equals . . ."

"Go on," Brady encouraged.

An odd, dead weight lay over Hamilton's mind. A series of symbols fluttered, figures and equations. Like butterflies, words and phrases leaped and danced, and refused to be pinned down. "An absolute unit of resistance," he said hoarsely, "can be defined as the resistance of a conductor in which—"

"That doesn't sound like Ohm's Law to me," Brady said. Turning to his group, he asked, "Does that sound like Ohm's Law to you?"

They shook their heads piously.

"I'm licked," Hamilton said, incredulous. "I can't even state Ohm's Law."

"Praise be to God," Brady answered.

"The heathen has been struck down," a technician noted scientifically. "The contest is over."

"This is unfair," Hamilton protested. "I know Ohm's Law as well as I know my own name."

"Face facts," Brady told him. "Admit you're a heathen and outside the Lord's grace."

"Don't I get to ask you something?"

Brady considered. "Sure. Go ahead. Anything you want."

"An electron beam is deflected," Hamilton said, "if it passes between two plates through which a voltage is applied. The electrons are subjected to a force at right angles to their motion. Call the length of the plates L_1. Call the distance from the center of the plates to the . . ."

He broke off. Slightly above Brady, close to his right ear, had appeared a mouth and hand. The mouth was quietly whispering into Brady's ear; directed by the hand, the words vanished before Hamilton could hear them.

"Who's that?" he demanded, outraged.

"I beg your pardon?" Brady said innocently, waving away the mouth and hand.

"Who's kibitzing? Who's giving you information?"

"An angel of the Lord," Brady said. "Naturally."

Hamilton gave up. "I quit. You win."

"Go on," Brady encouraged. "You were going to ask me to plot the deflection of the beam by this formula." In a few succinct phrases, he outlined the figures Hamilton had concocted in the privacy of his mind. "Correct?"

"It's not fair," Hamilton began. "Of all the flagrant, blatant cheating—"

The angelic mouth grinned coarsely and then said something crude in Brady's ear. Brady permitted himself a momentary smile. "Very funny," he acknowledged. "Very apt, too."

As the great vulgar mouth began to fade away, Hamilton said, "Wait a minute. Stick around. I want to talk to you."

The mouth lingered. "What's on your mind?" it said, in a loud, rumbling, thunder-like mutter.

"You seem to know already," Hamilton answered. "Didn't you just look?"

The mouth twisted contemptuously.

"If you can look into men's minds," Hamilton said, "you can also look into men's hearts."

"What's this all about?" Brady demanded uncomfortably. "Go bother your own angel."

"There's a line somewhere," Hamilton continued. "Something about the desire to commit a sin being as bad as actually committing it."

"What are you babbling about?" Brady demanded irritably.

"As I construe that ancient verse," Hamilton said, "it's a statement concerning the psychological problem of motivation. It classes motive as the cardinal moral point, an actually committed sin being merely the overt outgrowth of the evil desire. Right and wrong depend not on what a man does but on what a man feels."

The angelic mouth made an agreeing motion. "What you say is true."

"These men," Hamilton said, indicating the technicians, "are *acting* as Champions of the One True God. They are rooting out heathenism. But in their hearts lie evil motives. Back of their zealous actions lies a hard core of sinful desire."

Brady gulped. "What do you mean?"

"Your motive for screening me out of EDA is venal. You're jealous of me. And jealousy, as a motive, is unacceptable. I call attention to this as a coreligionist." Mildly, Hamilton added, "It's my duty."

"Jealousy," the angel repeated. "Yes, jealousy falls into the category of sin. Except in the sense of the Lord being a jealous God. In that usage, the term expresses the concept that only One True God can exist. Worship of any other quasi-God is a denial of His Nature, and a return to pre-Islamism."

"But," Brady protested, "a Babiist can jealously pursue the Lord's work."

"Jealously in the sense that he excludes all other work and loyalties," the angel said. "There is that one use of the term which does not involve negative moral characteristics. One can speak of jealously defending one's heritage. Meaning, in that case, a zealous determination to guard that which belongs to one. This heathen, however, asserts that you are jealous of him in the sense that you wish to gainsay him his rightful position. You are motivated by an envious, grudging, and malign greed—in essence, by a refusal to submit to the Cosmic Apportionment."

"But—" Brady said, flapping his arms foolishly.

"The heathen is right to point out that apparent good works which are motivated by evil intentions are only

pseudo-good works. Your zealous acts are negated by
your wicked covetousness. Although your actions are
directed toward sustaining the cause of the One True
God, your souls are impure and stained."

"How do you define the term impure," Brady began,
but it was too late. Judgment had been pronounced. Silently, the overhead sun dwindled to a gloomy, sickly
yellow and then faded out altogether. A dry, harsh wind
billowed around the group of frightened technicians.
Underfoot, the ground shriveled and became arid.

"You can make your appeals later," the angel said,
from the gloomy darkness. He prepared to depart. "You'll
have plenty of time to make use of the regular channels."

What had been a fertile section of the landscape sur-
rounding the EDA buildings was now a blighted square
of drought and barrenness. No plants grew. The trees,
the grass, had withered into dry husks. The technicians
dwindled until they became squat, hunched figures, dark-
skinned, hairy, with open sores on their filth-stained arms
and faces. Their eyes, red-rimmed, filled with tears as
they gazed about them in despair.

"Damned," Brady croaked brokenly. "We're damned."

The technicians were overtly and visibly no longer
saved. Now dwarfish, bent-over figures, they crept miserably around, aimless and wretched. Night darkness
filtered down on them through the layers of drifting dust
particles. Across the parched earth at their feet slithered a snake. Soon after it came the first rasping click-
click of a scorpion. . . .

"Sorry," Hamilton said idly. "But truth will out."

Brady glared up at him, red eyes gleaming balefully
in his whisker-stubbled face. Strands of filthy hair hung
over his ears and neck. "You heathen," he muttered, turning his back.

"Virtue is its own reward," Hamilton reminded him. "The Lord moves in mysterious ways. Nothing succeeds like success."

Going to his car, he climbed in and pushed the key into the ignition lock. Clouds of dust settled over the windshield as he began cranking the starter motor. Nothing happened; the engine refused to catch. For a time he continued pumping the accelerator and wondering what was wrong. Then, with dismay, he noticed the faded seat covers. The once brilliant and splendid fabrics had become drab and indistinct. The car, unfortunately, had been parked within the damned area.

Opening the glove compartment, Hamilton got out his well-thumbed auto repair manual. But the thick booklet no longer contained schemata of automotive construction; it now listed common household prayers.

In this milieu, prayer substituted for mechanical know-how. Folding the book open in front of him, he put the car into low gear, pressed down on the gas, and released the clutch.

"There is but one God," he began, "and the Second Bab is—"

The engine caught, and the car moved noisily forward. Backfiring and groaning, it crept from the parking lot toward the street. Behind Hamilton the damned technicians wandered around in their confined, blighted area. Already, they had begun arguing the proper course of appeal, citing dates and authorities. They'd have their status back, Hamilton reflected. They'd manage.

It took four different common household prayers to carry the car down the highway to Belmont. Once, as he passed a garage, he considered stopping for repairs. But the sign made him hurry on.

Nicholton and Sons
Auto Healing

And under it, a small window display of inspirational literature, with the leading slogan, *Every day in every way my car is getting newer and newer.*

After the fifth prayer, the engine seemed to be performing properly. And the seat covers had regained their usual luster. Some confidence returned to him; he had gotten out of a nasty situation. Every world had its laws. It was simply a question of discovering them.

Now evening had arrived everywhere. Cars raced along El Camino, their headlights blazing. Behind him, the lights of San Mateo winked in the darkness. Overhead, ominous clouds covered the night sky. Driving with utmost caution, he maneuvered his car from the lanes of commuter traffic over to the curb.

To his left lay California Maintenance. But there was no use approaching the missile plant; even in his own world he hadn't been acceptable. God knew what it would be like now. Somehow, he intuited that it could only be worse. Far worse. A man of Colonel T. E. Edwards' type in this world would surpass belief.

To his right lay a small, familiar, luminous oasis. He had loafed away many afternoons in the Safe Harbor . . . directly across from the missile plant, the bar was the favorite spot of the beer-drinking technicians on hot, mid-summer days.

Parking his car, Hamilton clambered out and strode down the dark sidewalk. A light rain beat quietly down on him as he headed gratefully for the flickering red *Golden Glow* neon sign.

The bar was full of people and friendly noise. Hamilton stood for a moment in the entrance, taking in the presence of sullied humanity. This, at least, hadn't changed. The same black-jacketed truck drivers hunched over their beers at the far end of the counter. The same noisy young blond sat perched on her stool: inevitable barfly drinking down her whiskey-colored water. The gaudy jukebox roared furiously in the corner next to the stove. To one side, two balding workmen were intently playing shuffleboard.

Shouldering his way among the people, Hamilton approached the line of stools. Seated directly in the center, before the great plate-glass mirror, waving his beer mug, shouting and yelling at a group of momentary pals, was a familiar figure.

A perverse gladness filled Hamilton's confused and weary mind. "I thought you were dead," he said, punching McFeyffe on the arm. "You miserable bastard."

Surprised, McFeyffe spun around on his stool, sloshing beer down his arm. "I'll be damned. The Red." Happily, he signaled the bartender. "Pour my pal a beer, goddam it."

Apprehensively, Hamilton said: "Pipe down. Haven't you heard?"

"Heard? About what?"

"About what's happened." Hamilton sank down on a vacant stool beside him. "Haven't you noticed? Can't you see any difference between things as they were and things as they are?"

"I've noticed," McFeyffe said. He did not appear disturbed. Lifting aside his coat, he showed Hamilton what he was wearing. Every conceivable good luck charm hung from him; an array of devices for each situation. "I'm twenty-four hours ahead of you, buddy," he said. "I don't know who this Bab is, or where they dug up this corny Arab religion, but I'm not worried." Stroking one of the charms, a gold medalion with cryptic symbols carved in interwoven circles, he said, "Don't trifle with me or I'll get a plague of rats in here to gnaw you apart."

Hamilton's beer arrived and he accepted it avidly. Noise, people, human activity blared around him; temporarily content, he relaxed and allowed himself to slide passively into the general uproar. When it came down to it, he didn't really have much choice.

"Who's your friend?" the sharp-faced little blond demanded, squirming over beside McFeyffe and draping herself around his shoulder. "He's cute."

"Take off," McFeyffe told her good-naturedly. "Or I'll turn you into a worm."

"Wise guy," the girl sniffed. Pulling up her skirt, she indicated a small white object slipped under her garter. "Try and beat that," she told McFeyffe.

Fascinated, McFeyffe gazed at the object. "What is it?"

"The metatarsal bone of Mohammed."

"Saints preserve us," McFeyffe said piously, sipping his beer.

Pushing down her skirt, the girl addressed Hamilton. "Haven't I seen you in here before? You work across the street at that big bomb factory, don't you?"

"I used to," Hamilton answered.

"This joker's a Red," McFeyffe volunteered. "And an atheist."

Horrified, the girl drew back. "No kidding?"

"Sure," Hamilton told her. At this point, it was all the same to him. "I'm Leon Trotsky's maiden aunt. I gave birth to Joe Stalin."

Instantly, a shattering pain snapped through his abdomen; doubled up, he fell from the stool onto the floor and sat clutching himself, teeth chattering with agony.

"That's what you get," McFeyffe said without pity.

"Help," Hamilton appealed.

Solicitous, the girl crouched down beside him. "Aren't you ashamed of yourself? Where's your Bayan?"

"Home," he whispered, ashen with pain. Renewed cramps lashed up and down inside him. "I'm dying. Burst appendix."

"Where's your prayer wheel? In your coat pocket?" Lithely she began searching his coat; her nimble fingers plucked and flew.

"Get—me to a—doctor," he managed.

The bartender leaned over. "Throw him out or fix him up," he told the girl brusquely. "He can't die here."

"Does somebody have a little holy water?" the girl called, in a penetrating soprano.

The crowd stirred; presently a small flat flask was passed forward. "Don't use it all," a voice cautioned peevishly. "That was filled at the font at Cheyenne."

Unscrewing the top, the girl dribbled the tepid water on her red-nailed fingers and quickly sprinkled drops over Hamilton. As they touched him, the fierce pain ebbed. Relief spread over his tortured body. After a time, with some help from the girl, he was able to sit up.

"The curse is gone," the girl remarked matter-of-factly, returning the holy water to its owner. "Thanks, mister."

"Buy that man a beer," McFeyffe said, without turning around. "He's a true follower of the Bab."

As the foaming mug of beer was passed back into the crowd, Hamilton crawled miserably back onto his stool. Nobody noticed him; the girl had now gone off to fondle the owner of the holy water.

"This world," Hamilton grated, between clenched teeth, "is crazy."

"Crazy, hell," McFeyffe answered. "What's crazy about

it? I haven't paid for a beer all day." He wagged his mighty array of charms. "All I have to do is appeal to these."

"Explain it," Hamilton muttered. "This place—this bar. Why doesn't God erase it? If this world operates by moral laws—"

"This bar is necessary to the moral order. This is a sinkpit of corruption and vice, a fleshpot of iniquity. You think salvation can function without damnation? You think virtue can exist without sin? That's the trouble with you atheists; you don't grasp the mechanics of evil. Get on the inside and enjoy life, man. If you're one of the Faithful, you've got nothing to worry about."

"Opportunist."

"Bet your sweet soul."

"So God lets you sit here lapping up booze and diddling these floozies. Swearing and lying, doing anything you want."

"I know my rights," McFeyffe said sleekly. "I know what's on top, here. Look around you and learn. Pay attention to what's going on."

Nailed to the wall of the bar beside the mirror was the motto, *What Would The Prophet Say If He Found You In A Place Like This?*

"I'll tell you what he'd say," McFeyffe informed Hamilton. "He'd say, 'Pour one for me, boys.' He's a regular fellow. Not like you egghead professors."

Hamilton waited hopefully, but no rain of stinging snakes descended. Confidently, complacently, McFeyffe guzzled his beer.

"Apparently, I'm not on the inside," Hamilton said. "If I said that, I'd be struck dead."

"*Get* on the inside."

"How?" Hamilton demanded. He was weighed down

by the sense of unfairness, the basic wrongness of it all. The world that to McFeyffe made perfect sense seemed to him a travesty on an equitably run universe. To him, only the mere glimmer of pattern beat intermittently through the haze, through the confusion that had surrounded him since the accident at the Bevatron. The values that made up his world, the moral verities that had underlined existence as long as he could remember, had passed away; in their place was a crude, tribal vengeance against the outsider, an archaic system that had come from—*where?*

Reaching unsteadily into his coat, he brought out the note which Doctor Tillingford had given him. Here was the name, the Prophet. The center, the Sepulcher of the Second Bab, the source-point of this non-Western cult that had somehow slipped in and absorbed the familiar world. Had there always been a Horace Clamp? A week ago, a few days ago, there had been no Second Bab, no Prophet of the One True God at Cheyenne, Wyoming. Or—

Beside him, McFeyffe peered to examine the writing on the bit of paper. On his face was a dark expression; the blustering humor had faded, and in its place was a somberness, hard and oppressive. "What's that?" he demanded.

"I'm supposed to look him up," Hamilton said.

"No," McFeyffe said. Suddenly his hand shot out; he snatched for the note. Get rid of it." His voice was shaking. "Don't pay any attention to that."

Struggling, Hamilton managed to retrieve the note. McFeyffe caught hold of his shoulder; his thick fingers dug into Hamilton's flesh. The stool under Hamilton tottered, and all at once he was falling. McFeyffe's massive weight descended on him, and then the two of them

were fighting on the floor, panting and perspiring, trying
to get possession of the note.

"No jihad in this bar," the bartender said, hopping
around the bar to put an end to the fight. "If you want
to mangle each other, go outside."

Muttering, McFeyffe crept unsteadily to his feet. "Get
rid of it," he said to Hamilton as he smoothed his clothes.
His face was still rigid, still distorted by some deep-
lying uneasiness.

"What's the matter?" Hamilton demanded, reseating
himself. He located his beer and began to lift it. Something was happening in McFeyffe's brutish mind, and he
did not know what it was.

At that moment, the little blond barfly made her way
over. With her was a doleful, gaunt figure. Bill Laws,
gripping a shot glass, bowed lugubriously to McFeyffe
and Hamilton. " 'Afternoon," he intoned. "Let's have no
more conflicts. We're all friends, around here."

Staring down at the bar, McFeyffe said, "All things
considered, we pretty well have to be." He did not
amplify.

VI

"THIS individual says he's acquainted with you," the
small blond barfly explained to Hamilton.

"That's right," Hamilton answered. "Pull up a stool

and sit down." He eyed Laws levelly. "Have you investigated the situation with advanced physics in the last day or so?"

"The hell with physics," Laws said, scowling. "I'm past that. I've outgrown that."

"Go construct a reservoir," Hamilton told him. "Stop reading so many books. Get out in the fresh air."

Laws placed his lean hand on the blond's shoulder. "Meet Grace. Full of reservoir. Full to the gills."

"Glad to meet you," Hamilton said.

The girl smiled uncertainly. "My name isn't Grace. My name—"

Pushing the girl aside, Laws leaned close to Hamilton. "I'm glad you mentioned the term reservoir."

"Why?"

"Because," Laws informed him, "in this world there is no such thing."

"But there has to be."

"Come along." Holding onto Hamilton's necktie, Laws pulled him away from the bar. "I'm going to let you in on something. Greatest discovery since the poll tax."

Threading his way among the patrons, Laws led Hamilton to the cigarette dispenser in the corner. Thumping the machine with the flat of his hand, Laws said triumphantly, "Well? What do you think of it?"

Hamilton cautiously examined the machine. The usual sight: a tall, metallic box with blue-tinted mirror, coin slot at the upper right, rows of little glass windows behind which rested various brands of cigarettes, the line of levers, and then the drop slot. "Looks all right," he commented.

"Notice anything about it?"

"No, nothing in particular."

Laws peered around to make certain no one was

listening. Then he dragged Hamilton close to him. "I've been watching that machine work," he whispered harshly. "I've figured out something. Try to grasp this. Try not to get thrown. *There are no cigarettes in that machine.*"

Hamilton considered. "None at all?"

Squatting down, Laws indicated the row of display packages visible behind their glass covering. "That's all there is. One of each. There is no reservoir. But watch." He dropped a quarter into the coin slot, selected the Camels lever, and pushed it firmly in. A package of Camels slid out, and Laws grabbed it. "See?"

"I don't get it," Hamilton admitted.

"The candy bar machine is the same." Laws led him over to the candy dispensing machine. "Candy comes out but there's no candy in it. Only the display packages. Get it? Comprehend?"

"No."

"Didn't you ever read about miracles? In the desert it was getting food and water; that's what came first."

"Oh," Hamilton said. "That's right."

"These machines work on the original principle. Division by miracle." From his pocket Laws got a screwdriver; kneeling, he began disassembling the candy bar machine. "I tell you, Jack, this is the greatest discovery known to man. This'll revolutionize modern industry. The whole concept of machine tool production, the whole assembly-line technique—" Laws waved his hand. "Out. Kaput. No more using up raw materials. No more depressed labor force. No more dirty, pounding factories. In this metal box lies a vast secret."

"Hey," Hamilton said, interested. "Maybe you've got something."

"This stuff can be utilized." Feverishly, Laws tore at

the back of the machine. "Give me a hand, man. Help me get the lock off."

The lock came off. Between them, the two men slid the back of the candy dispenser away and leaned it against the wall. As Laws had predicted, the upright columns that were the reservoirs of the machine were totally empty.

"Get a dime out," Laws instructed. Skillfully, he unbolted the inner mechanism until the display bars were visible from behind. To the right was the output chute; at its beginning was an elaborate series of stages, levers and wheels. Laws began tracing the physical circuit back to its point of origin.

"Looks like the candy bar starts here," Hamilton suggested. Leaning over Laws' shoulder, he touched a flat shelf. "The coin trips a switch and tilts that plunger over. It gives the candy bar a shove and starts it moving toward the slot. Gravity does the rest."

"Put the coin in," Laws said urgently. "I want to see where the damn candy bar *comes* from."

Hamilton inserted the dime and pulled a plunger at random. The wheels and levers spun. From the center of the grinding works emerged a U-no bar. The U-no bar slithered down the chute and came to rest in the slot outside the machine.

"It just grew out of nothing," Laws said, awed.

"But in a specific area. It appeared tangent to the model bar. That suggests it's a kind of binary fission process. The model bar splits into two whole bars."

"Drop another dime in. I tell you, Jack, this is *it*."

Again, a candy bar materialized and was expelled by the efficient machinery. Both men watched with admiration.

"A neat piece of equipment," Laws admitted. "A lovely job of designing and construction. Fine utilization of the miracle principle."

"But utilization on a small scale," Hamilton pointed out. "For candy, soft drinks and cigarettes. Nothing important."

"That's where we come in." Gingerly, Laws pushed a bit of tin foil into the empty stage beside a model Hershey bar. The tin foil met no resistance. "Nothing there, all right. If I take out the model bar and put something else in its place . . ."

Hamilton removed the model Hershey bar and placed a bottle cap in the display rack. When the lever was pulled, a duplicate bottle cap rustled down the chute and out the exit slot.

"That proves it," Laws agreed. "It duplicates anything tangent to it. We could duplicate anything." He got out some silver coins. "Let's get down to business."

"How does this sound?" Hamilton said. "An old electronic principle: *regeneration*. We feed part of the output back to the original model stage. So the supply continues to build—the more it turns out the more is fed back and duplicated."

"A liquid would be best," Laws reflected. "Where can we get some glass tubing to pipe it back?"

Hamilton tore down a neon display from the wall, while Laws trotted to the bar to order a drink. As Hamilton was installing the tubing, Laws reappeared, carrying a tiny glass of amber liquid.

"Brandy," Laws explained. "Genuine French cognac —the best they have."

Hamilton pushed the glass onto the model stage where the Hershey bar had been. The tubing, emptied of its neon gas, led from the tangent duplication area and divided. One nozzle led back to the original glass; the other led to the output slot.

"The ratio is four to one," Hamilton commented. "Four parts go out the slot as product. One part is fed back to the original source. Theoretically, we should get an ever-accelerating output. With infinite volume as a limit."

With a deft motion, Laws wedged open the lever that tripped the mechanism into action. After a pause, cognac began dripping from the slot, onto the floor in front of the machine. Getting to his feet, Laws grabbed up the detached back of the machine; the two men fitted it into place and turned the lock. Quietly, continuously, the candy dispenser drizzled a growing torrent of top-quality brandy.

"That's it," Hamilton said, pleased. "Free drinks—everybody line up."

A few bar patrons shambled over, interested. Very shortly there was a crowd.

"We've utilized the machinery," Laws said slowly, as the two of them stood watching the growing line that had formed in front of the ex-candy dispenser. "But we haven't worked out the basic principle. We know what it does and mechanistically how. But not *why*."

"Maybe," Hamilton conjectured, "there isn't any principle. Isn't that what 'miracle' means? No operating law —just a capricious event, without regularity or cause. It simply happens; you can't predict or trace back a source."

"But there's regularity here," Laws insisted, indicating the candy machine. "When the dime is put in a candy bar comes out, not a baseball or a toad. And that's all natural law is, simply a description of what happens. An account of regularity. There's no causality involved—

we merely say that if A and B are added we get C, and not D."

"Will we always get C?" Hamilton asked.

"Maybe and maybe not. So far we've got C; we've got candy bars. And now it's turning out brandy, not insect spray. We have our regularity, our pattern. All we have to do is find out what elements are necessary to make up the pattern."

Excitedly, Hamilton said, "If we can find out what has to be present to cause duplication of the model object—"

"Right. *Something* sets the process into motion. We don't care how it does it—all we have to do is know *what* does it. We don't need to know how sulphur, potassium nitrate and charcoal produce gunpowder, or even why. All we have to know is that when mixed together in a certain proportion, *they do.*"

The two of them moved back toward the bar, past the throng of patrons collecting the free brandy. "Then this world does have laws," Hamilton said. "Like our own. I mean, not like our own. But laws, anyhow."

A dark shadow passed over Bill Laws' face. "That's so." Suddenly his enthusiasm was gone. "I forgot."

"What's wrong?"

"It won't work back in our world. It'll only work here."

"Oh," Hamilton said, mollified. "True."

"We're wasting our time."

"Unless we don't want to go back."

At the bar, Laws seated himself on a stool and gathered up his shot glass. Hunched over, brooding, he murmured, "Maybe that's what we ought to do. Stay here."

"Sure," McFeyffe said genially, overhearing him. "Stay here. Be smart . . . quit while you're ahead."

Laws glanced briefly at Hamilton. "You want to stay here? You like it here?"

"No," Hamilton said.

"Neither do I. But maybe we don't have a choice. As yet, we don't even know *where* we are. And as far as getting out—"

"This is a nice place," the little blond barfly said indignantly. "I'm here all the time and I think it's fine."

"We're not talking about the bar," Hamilton said.

His hands gripped harshly around his shot glass, Laws said, "We're going to have to get back. Somehow, we're going to have to find our way out of here."

"I realize that," Hamilton said.

"You know what you can buy at the supermarket?" Laws inquired acidly. "I'll tell you. Canned burnt offerings."

"You know what you can buy at the hardware store?" Hamilton answered. "Scales to weigh your soul on."

"That's silly," the blond said petulantly. "A soul doesn't have any weight."

"Then," Hamilton reflected, "you could put one through the U. S. mail for nothing."

"How many souls," Laws conjectured ironically, "can be fitted into one stamped envelope? New religious question. Split mankind in half. Warring factions. Blood running in the gutters."

"Ten," Hamilton guessed.

"Fourteen," Laws contradicted.

"Heretic. Baby-murdering monster."

"Bestial drinker of unpurified blood."

"Accursed spawn of filth-devouring evil."

Laws considered. "You know what you can get on your TV set Sunday morning? I won't tell you; you can find out for yourself." Carefully holding his empty shot glass, he slid abruptly from his stool and disappeared into the crowd.

"Hey," Hamilton said, astonished. "Where'd he go?"

"He's crazy," the blond said, matter-of-factly.

For a moment the figure of Bill Laws reappeared. His dark face was gray with anguish. Addressing Hamilton across the murmuring, laughing crowd of patrons, he shouted, "Jack, you know what?"

"What?" Hamilton answered, perturbed.

The Negro's face twitched in a spasm of acute, helpless misery. "In this world—" Sorrow blurred his eyes. "In this damn place, I've started to shuffle."

He was gone, leaving Hamilton to ponder.

"What'd he mean?" the blond asked curiously. "Shuffle cards?"

"Shuffle *him*," Hamilton murmured moodily.

"They all do," McFeyffe commented.

Taking Bill Laws' vacated stool, the blond began systematically oozing up to Hamilton. "Buy me a drink, baby," she asked hopefully.

"I can't."

"Why not? Under age?"

Hamilton searched his empty pockets. "I haven't got any money. I spent it on that candy machine."

"Pray," McFeyffe told him. "Pray like hell."

"Dear Lord," Hamilton said bitterly. "Send Your unworthy electronics expert a glass of colored water for this tarnished young baggage." Dutifully, he concluded, "Amen."

The glass of colored water appeared on the surface of the bar beside his elbow. Smiling, the girl accepted it. "You're sweet. What's your name?"

"Jack."

"What's your *full* name?"

He sighed. "Jack Hamilton."

"My name's Silky." Playfully, she toyed with his collar. Is that your Ford coupé out there?"

"Sure," he answered dully.

"Let's go someplace. I hate this place, here. I—"

"Why?" Hamilton lashed out suddenly and loudly. "Why the hell did God answer that prayer? Why not some of the others? Why not Bill Laws'?"

"God approved of your prayer," Silky said. "After all, it's up to Him; He has to decide how He feels about it."

"That's terrible."

Silky shrugged. "Maybe so."

"How can you live with that? You never know what's going to happen—there's no order, no logic." It infuriated him that she did not object, that it seemed natural to her. "We're helpless; we have to depend on whim. It keeps us from being people—we're like animals waiting to be fed. Rewarded or punished."

Silky studied him. "You're a funny boy."

"I'm thirty-two years old; I'm not a boy. And I'm married."

Fondly, the girl tugged at his arm, half-pulling him from his precarious stool. "Come on, baby. Let's go where we can worship in private. I have a few rituals you might like to try."

"Will I go to Hell for it?"

"Not if you know the right people."

"My new boss has an intercom to Heaven. Will that do?"

Silky continued to urge him from his stool. "We'll talk about it later. Let's go, before that ape of an Irishman notices."

Raising his head, McFeyffe eyed Hamilton. In a strained, hesitant voice he said, "Are—are you leaving?"

"Sure," Hamilton said, getting unsteadily from his stool.

"Wait." McFeyffe followed after him. "Don't leave."

"Take care of your own soul," Hamilton said. But he caught in McFeyffe's face the element of basic uncertainty. "What's the matter?" he asked, sobered.

McFeyffe said, "I want to show you something."

"Show me what?"

Striding past Hamilton and Silky, McFeyffe picked up an immense black umbrella; he turned back to them, waiting. Hamilton followed, and Silky tagged along. Pushing the doors open, McFeyffe carefully raised the vast, tent-like umbrella over their heads. The light sprinkle had become a shower; cold autumn rain beat down on the shiny sidewalks, on the silent stores and streets.

Silky shivered. "It's dismal. Where're we going?"

Locating Hamilton's coupé in the gloom, McFeyffe was saying to himself, in a monotone. "It must still exist."

"Why do you suppose he shuffles?" Hamilton asked morbidly, as the car raced along the endless wet highway. "He never shuffled before."

Behind the wheel, McFeyffe drove reflexively, his body hunched, sunk down so that he seemed almost asleep. "Like I said," he muttered, rousing himself. "They're that way."

"It means something," Hamilton persisted. The swish-swish of the windshield wipers lulled him; he lay sleepily against Silky and closed his eyes. The girl smelled faintly of cigarette smoke and perfume. A good smell . . . he enjoyed it. Against his cheek her hair was dry, light, scratchy. Like certain weed spores.

McFeyffe said, "You know this Second Bab stuff?" His voice lifted, desperate and harsh. "It's a lot of hot air.

A nut cult; a bunch of crackpots. It's nothing but a bunch of Arabs coming over here with their ideas. Isn't that right?"

Neither Hamilton nor Silky answered.

"It won't last," McFeyffe said.

Peevishly, Silky said, "I want to know where we're going." Squeezing closer to Hamilton, she said, "Are you really married?"

Ignoring her, Hamilton said to McFeyffe, "I know what you're afraid of."

"I'm not afraid of anything," McFeyffe said.

"You sure are," Hamilton said. And he, too, in spite of himself, was uneasy.

Ahead of them San Francisco grew larger and closer, until the car was passing between houses and along streets which showed no sign of life, no motion or sound or light. McFeyffe seemed to know exactly where he wished to go; he made turn after turn, until the car was moving along narrow side streets. Suddenly he slowed the car. Raising himself, up, he peered through the windshield. His face was stiff with apprehension.

"This is awful," Silky complained, burying her head in Hamilton's coat. "What is this slum? I don't get it."

Stopping the car, McFeyffe pushed the door open and stepped out onto the empty street. Hamilton followed him, and the two of them stood together. Silky stayed behind, listening to insipid dinner music on the car radio. The tinny sound drifted out into the darkness, mixing with the fog that drifted among the closed-up stores and hulking, shabby buildings.

"Is that it?" Hamilton asked, at last.

"Yeah." McFeyffe nodded. Now, faced with the reality of it, he showed no emotion.

The two men faced a dingy, run-down store, a decrepit

board structure whose yellow paint had peeled away,
exposing the rain-soaked wood beneath. Heaps of trash
and newspapers littered the entrance. By the light of the
street lamp, Hamilton made out the notices pasted on the
windows. Tracts, yellow and fly-specked, were smeared
and arranged haphazardly. Beyond was a dingy curtain
and, past that, rows of ugly metal chairs. Behind the
chairs, the interior of the store was in darkness. Erected
above the entrance of the store was a hand-lettered sign,
aged and tattered. It read:

Non-Babiist Church
All Welcome

With a ragged groan, McFeyffe pulled himself together
and started toward the sidewalk.

"Better let it go," Hamilton said, following.

"No." McFeyffe shook his head. "I'm going in." Raising his black umbrella, he stepped up to the entrance
of the store; in a moment he was hammering methodically on the door with the umbrella handle. The sound
echoed up and down the empty street, a hollow, vacant
noise. Somewhere in an alley, an animal stirred among
the ash cans, startled.

The man who eventually opened the door a crack was
a tiny, bent figure. Timidly, he peeped out through a pair
of steel-rimmed glasses. His cuffs were threadbare and
unclean; his yellow, watery eyes darted warily. Trembling, he gazed without recognition at McFeyffe.

"What do you want?" he quavered in a thin, whining
voice.

"Don't you know me?" McFeyffe said. "What's happened, Father? Where's the church?"

Fumbling, muttering, the dried-up old man began to
tug the door shut. "Get away from here. A couple of

good-for-nothing drunks. Get away or I'll call the police."

As the door swung shut, McFeyffe stuck his umbrella into the opening, jamming it. "Father," he implored, "this is terrible. I can't understand it. They stole your church. And you're—small. It isn't possible." His voice ebbed, broken with disbelief. "You used to be . . ." He turned helplessly to Hamilton. "He used to be big. Bigger than me."

"Get away," the little creature buzzed warningly.

"Can't we come in?" McFeyffe asked, making no move to take away his umbrella. "Please let us in. Where else can we go? I have a heretic here . . . he wants to be converted."

The little man hesitated. Grimacing anxiously, he peered out at Hamilton. "You? What's the matter? Can't you come back tomorrow? It's after midnight; I was sound asleep." Releasing the door, he stepped reluctantly aside.

"This is all there is," McFeyffe said to Hamilton, as the two of them entered. "Did you ever see it *before?* It was made of stone, big as—" He gestured futilely. "The biggest of them all."

"It'll cost you ten dollars," the little man said, ahead of them. Bending down, he lugged a clay urn from under the counter. On the counter were heaps of tracts and pamphlets; several slid to the floor, but he didn't notice. "In advance," he added.

Fumbling in his pockets, McFeyffe gazed about him. "Where's the organ? And the candles? Don't you even have candles?"

"Can't afford that sort of business," the little man said, scurrying toward the rear. "Now, just what is it you want? You want me to convert this heretic?" He caught hold of Hamilton's arm and scrutinized him. "I'm Father O'Farrel. You'll have to kneel down, young man. And bow your head."

Hamilton said, "Has it always been like this?"

Momentarily pausing, Father O'Farrel said, "Like what? What do you mean?"

A wave of compassion touched Hamilton. "Let it go," he said.

"Our organization is very old," Father O'Farrel told him hesitantly. "Is that what you mean? It goes back centuries." His tone wavered. "Back before even the First Bab. I'm not positive of the exact date of origin. They say it's—" He faltered. "We don't have much authority. The First Bab, of course, that was 1844. But even before that—"

"I want to talk to God," Hamilton said.

"Yes, yes," Father O'Farrel agreed. "So do I, young man." He patted Hamilton's arm; the pressure was light, almost unfelt. "So does everybody."

"Can't you help me?" Hamilton said.

"It's very difficult," Father O'Farrel said. He disappeared into a back closet, a chaotic storeroom. Wheezing and groping, he reappeared carrying a wicker basket of assorted bones, fragments, bits of dried hair and skin. "This is everything we've got," he gasped, setting the basket down. "Maybe you can get some use out of these. You're welcome to help yourself."

As Hamilton gingerly lifted a few pieces out, McFeyfe said in a shattered voice, "Look at them. Phonies. Junk curios."

"We do what we can," Father O'Farrel said, pressing his hands together.

Hamilton said, "Is there any way we can get up there?"

For the first time, Father O'Farrel smiled. "You'd have to be dead, young man."

Gathering up his umbrella, McFeyffe moved toward the door. "Let's go," he said heavily to Hamilton. "Let's get out of here; I've had enough."

"Wait," Hamilton said.

Halting, McFeyffe asked, "Why do you want to talk to God? What good will it do? You can see the situation. Look around."

Hamilton said, "He's the only one who can tell us what's happened."

After a pause, McFeyffe said, "I don't care what's happened. I'm leaving."

Working rapidly, Hamilton laid out a circle of bones and teeth, a ring of relics. "Give me a hand," he said to McFeyffe. "You're in this, too."

"What you're after," McFeyffe said, "is a miracle."

"I know," Hamilton said.

McFeyffe walked back. "It won't do any good. It's hopeless." He stood gripping his great black umbrella. Father O'Farrel paced about restlessly, bewildered by what was happening.

"I want to know how this business got started," Hamilton said. "This Second Bab, this whole mess. If I can't find out there—" Reaching, he seized the great black umbrella from McFeyffe, and, taking a deep breath, raised it. Like the spread of a leathery vulture, the struts and fabric of the umbrella opened above him; a few drops of stagnant moisture dripped down.

"What's this?" McFeyffe demanded, stepping past the circle of relics to grope for his umbrella.

"Grab on." Holding tightly to the handle of the umbrella, Hamilton said to Father O'Farrel, "Is there water in that jug?"

"Y-yes," Father O'Farrel said, peering into an earthen-ware urn. "Some, at the bottom."

"As you toss the water," Hamilton said, "recite that up-going part."

"Up-going?" Perplexed, Father O'Farrel retreated. "I—"

"*Et resurrexit.* You remember."

"Oh," Father O'Farrel said. "Yes, I believe so." Nodding, he dubiously dipped his hand into the urn of holy water and began sprinkling it onto the umbrella. "I sincerely doubt if this will work."

"Recite," Hamilton ordered.

Uncertainly, Father O'Farrel murmured, "'*Et resurrexit tertia die secundum scripturas, et ascendit in coelum, sedet ad dexteram partis, et iterum venurus est cum gloria judicare vivos et mortuos, cujas regni non erit finis . . .*'"

In Hamilton's hands the umbrella quivered. Gradually, laboriously, it began to ascend. McFeyffe gave a terrified bleat and hung on for his life. In a moment the tip of the umbrella was bumping against the low ceiling of the store; Hamilton and McFeyffe dangled absurdly, their feet waving in the dusty shadows.

"The skylight," Hamilton gasped. "Open it."

Rushing to get the pole, Father O'Farrel scurried about like a disturbed mouse. The skylight was pushed aside; wet night air billowed in, displacing the staleness of years. Released, the umbrella shot upward; the tumble-down wooden building disappeared below. Cold fog plucked at Hamilton and McFeyffe as they rose higher and higher. Now they were level with Twin Peaks. Now they were above the great city of San Francisco, suspended by the handle of the umbrella over a dish of winking yellow lights.

"What—" McFeyffe shouted, "what if we let go?"

"Pray for strength!" Hamilton shouted back, closing his eyes and clutching frantically at the shaft of the umbrella. Up and up the umbrella shot, gaining velocity each instant. For a brief interval, Hamilton dared to open his eyes and peer upward.

Above lay a limitless expanse of ominous black clouds. What existed beyond? Was He waiting?

Up and up rose the umbrella, into the dark night. It was too late to back out, now.

VII

As THEY ascended, the chaotic darkness began to fade. The layer of clouds dribbled moistly past them; with a wet slither the umbrella burst through. Instead of the chill black of night, they were rising in a dull medium of indiscriminate gray, an unformed expanse of colorless, shapeless nothing.

Below lay the Earth.

It was the best view Hamilton had ever had of the Earth. In many ways it met his expectations. It was round and quite clearly a globe. Suspended in its medium, the globe hung quietly, a somber but impressive object.

Especially impressive because it was unique. Shocked, Hamilton realized that no other planets were heaving into view. He peered up apprehensively, gazed around him, gradually and reluctantly absorbing what his eyes made out.

The Earth was alone in the firmament. Around it wheeled a blazing orb, much smaller, a gnat buzzing and flickering around a giant, inert bulb of matter. That, he realized with a thrill of dismay, was the sun. It was *tiny*. And—it moved!

Si muove. But not Terra. *Si muove*—the sun!

Fortunately, the glowing, burning bit of phosphorescence was on the far side of the mighty Terra. It moved slowly; its total revolution was a twenty-four hour period. On this side came a smaller, almost unnoticed speck. A corroded wad of waste material that dully plodded along, trivial and dispensable.

The moon.

It wasn't far off; the umbrella was going to carry him almost within touching distance. Incredulous, he gazed at it, until it fell away into the gray medium. Was science, then, in error? Was the whole scheme of the universe mistaken? The vast and overwhelming structure of the Copernican heliocentric system all wrong?

He was seeing the ancient, outmoded, geocentric universe, with a giant, unmoving Earth the only planet. Now he could make out Mars and Venus, bits of material so tiny as to be virtually nonexistent. And the stars. They, too, were incredibly tiny . . . a canopy of insignificance. In an instant, the entire fabric of his cosmology had come tottering down into ludicrous ruin.

But it was only here. *This* was the ancient Ptolemaic universe. Not his world. Tiny sun, tiny stars, the great obese blob of an Earth, swollen and bloated, occupying dead center. That was true here—that was the way this universe was run.

But that meant nothing concerning his own universe . . . thank God.

Having accepted this, he was not particularly surprised to observe a deep underlayer far below the grayness, a reddish film beneath the Earth. It looked as if down at the very bottom of this universe, a primitive mining operation was going on. Forges, blast furnaces and, further into the distance, a kind of crude volcanic simmering sent vague flashes of sinister red to color the nondescript medium of gray.

It was Hell.

And above him . . . he craned his neck. Now it was clearly visible. Heaven. This was the other end of the phone system: this was the station to which the electronics men, the semanticists, the experts on communication, the psychologists, had linked Earth. This was point A on the great cosmic wire.

Above the umbrella, the drifting grayness faded out. For an interval there was nothing, not even the chill night wind that had frozen his bones. McFeyffe, clutching the umbrella, watched in growing awe as the abode of God grew closer. Not much of it was visible. An infinite wall of dense substance stretched out, a protective layer that blocked off any real view.

Above the wall drifted a few luminous specks. The specks darted and leaped like charged ions. As if they were alive.

Probably, they were angels. It was too soon to see.

The umbrella rose, and so did Hamilton's curiosity. Amazingly, he was quite calm. Under the circumstances it was impossible to feel emotion; either he was totally self-controlled or he was overwhelmed. It was one or

the other; there was no in-between. Soon, in another five
minutes, he would be carried above the wall. He and
McFeyffe would be looking into Heaven.

A long way, he thought. A long way from the moment
when they had stood in the hall of the Bevatron building, facing each other. Arguing over some petty trifle
. . .

Gradually, almost imperceptibly, the ascent of the
umbrella diminished. Now it was barely rising. This was
the limit. Above this, there was no *up*. Idly, Hamilton
wondered what would happen. Would the umbrella begin to descend, as patiently as it had climbed? Or would
it collapse and deposit them in the middle of Heaven?

Something was coming into view. They were parallel
with the expanse of protective material. An inane thought
crept into his mind: the material was there—not to keep
passersby from seeing in—but to keep inhabitants from
tumbling out. To keep them from tumbling back down
to the world from which over the centuries, they had
come.

"We're—" McFeyffe wheezed. "We're almost there."

"Yeah," Hamilton said.

"This—has—quite an effect on a—man's outlook."

"It really does," he admitted. Almost, he could see.
Another second . . . half-second . . . a vague glimpse
of landscape was already coming into view. A confusing vision; some kind of circular continuum, a sort of
vaguely misty place. Was it a pond, an ocean? A vast
lake; swirling waters. Mountains at the far end; an endless range of forest shrubbery.

Abruptly, the cosmic lake disappeared, a curtain had
swept down over it. But then the curtain, after an interval, swept back up. There was the lake again, the unlimited expanse of moist substance.

It was the biggest lake he had ever seen. It was big enough to contain the whole world. As long as he lived, he didn't expect to see a bigger lake. He wondered, idly, what the cubic capacity of it was. In the center was a denser, more opaque substance. A kind of lake within a lake. Was all Heaven just this titanic lake? As far as he could see, there was nothing but lake.

It wasn't a lake. It was an *eye*. And the eye was looking at him and McFeyffe!

He didn't have to be told Whose eye it was.

McFeyffe screeched. His face turned black; his wind rattled in his throat. A breath of utter fright swept over him; for an instant he danced helplessly at the end of the umbrella, trying to force his own fingers apart, trying futilely to pry himself loose from the field of vision. Trying, frantically and unsuccessfully, to scramble away from the eye.

The eye focused on the umbrella. With an acrid *pop* the umbrella burst into flame. Instantly, the burning fragments, the handle, and the two shrieking men dropped like stones.

They did not descend as they had come up. They descended at meteoric velocity. Neither of them was conscious. Once, Hamilton was dimly aware that the world was not far below. Then came a stunning impact; he was tossed high in the air again, almost all the way back up. Almost, on this vast first bounce, back to Heaven.

But not quite. Again he was descending. Again he struck. After a time of indescribable bouncing, his physical self lay inert and gasping, clutching at the surface of the Earth. Holding on desperately to a bunch of withered grass growing in a soil of dry, red clay. Cautiously, painfully, he opened his eyes and looked around.

He was spread out on a long plain of dusty, parched

country. It was very early morning of another day, and it was quite cold. Meager buildings rose in the distance. Not far off lay the unmoving body of Charley McFeyffe.

Cheyenne, Wyoming.

"I guess," Hamilton managed, after a long interval, "this is where I should have come first."

There was no answer from McFeyffe. He was totally unconscious. The only sound was the shrill twittering of birds perched in a scraggly tree a few hundred yards off.

Painfully pulling himself to his feet, Hamilton tottered over and examined his companion. McFeyffe was alive and with no apparent injuries, but his breathing was shallow and harsh. A thin ooze of saliva had made a path down his chin from his half-open mouth. His face still wore an expression of terror and wonder, and overpowering dismay.

Why dismay? Wasn't McFeyffe glad of the sight of his God?

More peculiar facts to file away. More odd-ball data in this odd-ball world. Here he was at the spiritual center of the Babiist universe, Cheyenne, Wyoming. God had corrected the errant bent in his direction. McFeyffe had put him on the wrong track, but he was surely and absolutely back. Tillingford had spoken the truth: it was to the Prophet Horace Clamp that Providence intended him to come.

With curiosity, he surveyed the chill, gray outline of the nearby town. In the center, among the otherwise nondescript structures, rose one single colossal spire. The spire glowed furiously in the early-morning sunlight. A skyscraper? A monument?

Not at all. This was the temple of the One True Faith. From this distance, several miles away, he was seeing the

Sepulcher of the Second Bab. The Babiist power, as experienced up to now, would seem a mere trifle compared with what lay ahead.

"Get up," he said to McFeyffe, noticing him stir.

"Not me," McFeyffe answered. "You go on. I'm staying here." He rested his head on his arm and closed his eyes.

"I'll wait." While he waited, Hamilton considered his situation. Here he was, set down in the middle of Wyoming, in the chill morning of an autumn day, with only thirty cents in his pockets. But what had Tillingford said? He shuddered. It was worth a try, though. And he didn't have much choice.

"Lord," he began, getting down in the customary posture; one knee to the ground, hands pressed together, eyes turned piously toward Heaven. "Reward Thy humble servant according to the usual pay scale for Class Four-A electronic workers. Tillingford mentioned four hundred dollars."

For a time nothing happened. A cold, barren wind whipped over the plain of red clay, rustling the dry weeds and rusty beer cans. Then, presently, the air above him stirred.

"Cover your head," Hamilton yelled at McFeyffe.

A shower of coins rained down, a glittering swirl of dimes, nickels, quarters, and half dollars. With a sound like coal pouring through a tin chute, the coins rattled down, deafening and blinding him. When the torrent had tapered off, he began collecting. Sullen disappointment was his next reaction, once the excitement had worn off. There was no four hundred dollars here; he was getting pocket change tossed to a beggar.

It was what he deserved, though.

The amount, when he tallied it, came to forty dollars

and seventy-five cents. It would help; at least he'd be able to keep himself eating. And when that was gone—

"Don't forget," McFeyffe muttered sickly, as he struggled to his feet. "You owe me ten bucks."

McFeyffe was not a well man. His large face was mottled and unwholesome; his thick flesh hung in ugly, doughlike folds around his collar. Nervously, his fingers plucked at a twitch in his cheek. The transformation was amazing; McFeyffe had been shattered by the sight of his God. The face to face encounter had completely demoralized him.

"Wasn't He what you expected?" Hamilton asked, as the two of them plodded dully toward the highway.

Grunting, McFeyffe spat red clay dust into a clump of weeds. Hands thrust deep in his pockets, he dragged himself along, eyes blank, slouched over like a broken man.

"Of course," Hamilton conceded, "it's none of my business."

"I can use a drink," was all McFeyffe had to contribute. As they stepped up onto the shoulder of the highway, he consulted his wallet. "I'll see you in Belmont. Hand over the ten bucks; I'll need it for plane fare."

Hamilton reluctantly counted out ten dollars in small change, which McFeyffe accepted without comment.

They were entering the suburbs of Cheyenne when Hamilton noticed something foreboding and ominous. On the back of McFeyffe's neck, a series of ugly, swollen red sores were forming. Fiery welts that grew and expanded even as he watched.

"Boils," Hamilton observed, astonished.

McFeyffe glanced at him in mute suffering. Presently he touched his left jaw. "And an abscessed wisdom tooth," he added, in a totally defeated tone. "Boils and an abscess. My punishment."

"For what?"

Again, there was no answer. McFeyffe was sunk into private gloom, battling with invisible comprehensions. He would be lucky, Hamilton realized, if he survived his encounter with his God. Of course, there was an elaborate mechanism of sin-expiation available; McFeyffe could shed his abscessed tooth and plague of boils with the proper absolutions. And McFeyffe, the innate opportunist, would find the way.

At the first bus stop they halted and threw themselves wearily down on the damp bench. Passers-by, on their journey into town for Saturday shopping, glanced at them curiously.

"Pilgrims," Hamilton said icily, in answer to an interested stare. "Crawled on our knees from Battle Creek, Michigan."

This time, there was no punishment from above. Sighing, Hamilton almost wished there had been; the capricious personality element infuriated him. There was just too little relationship between deed and punishment; the lightning was probably cutting down some totally innocent Cheyennite, on the far side of town.

"Here's the bus," McFeyffe said gratefully, struggling to his feet. "Get out your dimes."

When the bus reached the airfield, McFeyffe tottered off and wretchedly made his way toward the office building. Hamilton rode on, toward the towering, radiant, imposing structure that was the Only True Sepulcher.

The Prophet Horace Clamp met him in the glorious entrance-way. Awesome marble columns rose on all sides; the Sepulcher was an overt copy of the traditional tombs of antiquity. A kind of seedy, middle-class vulgarity hung about it, vast and impressive as it was. Massive, threatening, the mosque was an esthetic atrocity. Like a government building in the Soviet Union, it had been designed by men lacking artistic sensibility. Unlike the Soviet office buildings, it was larded and smeared with fretwork, embossed with rococo railings and flutings, infinite bric-a-brac, lavishly polished brass knobs and pipings. Recessed indirect lights played over the terra cotta surfaces. Stupendous bas-reliefs stood out in pompous stateliness: greater-than-life representations of Middle Eastern pastoral scenes. The characters portrayed were moral and fatuous. And elaborately clothed.

"Greetings," the Prophet announced, holding up one plump, pale hand in benediction. Horace Clamp might have stepped from some vividly colored Sunday school poster. Fat, waddling, with an absent, benign expression, robed and hooded, he gathered Hamilton up and prodded him into the mosque proper. Clamp was the living manifestation of the Islamic spiritual leader. As the two of them entered a richly furnished study, Hamilton wondered dismally why he was here. Was this what God had in mind?

"I was expecting you," Clamp said, in a businesslike manner. "I was informed of your coming."

"Informed?" Hamilton was puzzled. "By whom?"

"Why, by (Tetragrammaton), of course."

Hamilton was baffled. "You mean you're the Prophet of a god named—"

"The Name cannot be spoken," Clamp interrupted with sly agility. "Much too sacred. He prefers to be referred to by the term (Tetragrammaton). I'm rather surprised that you don't know this. It's common public knowledge."

"I'm somewhat ignorant," Hamilton said.

"You have, I understand, recently experienced a vision."

"If you mean did I just see (Tetragrammaton), the answer is yes." Already, he had developed an aversion to the pudgy Prophet.

"How is He?"

"He seemed in good health." Hamilton couldn't refrain from adding, "For Someone His age."

Clamp roamed busily around the study. Almost bald, his head shone like a polished stone. He was the epitome of theological dignity and pomp. And he was, Hamilton reflected, virtually a caricature. All the timeless, stuffy elements were there . . . Clamp was just too majestic to be true.

Caricature—or somebody's idea of what the spiritual head of the One True Faith ought to be like.

"Prophet," Hamilton said bluntly, "I might as well lay it on the line. I've been in this world approximately forty hours, no longer. Frankly, all this baffles me. As far as I'm concerned, this is an absolutely crackpot universe. A moon the size of a pea—it's absurd. Geocentric—the sun revolving around the Earth. It's primitive! And this whole archaic, non-Western concept of God; this old man showering down coins and snakes, loosing plagues of boils . . ."

Clamp eyed him acutely. "But my dear sir, this is the way things are. This is His creation."

"*This* creation, maybe. But not mine. Where I come from—"

"Perhaps," Clamp interrupted, "you had better tell me where you come from. (Tetragrammaton) didn't acquaint me with this aspect of the situation. He merely informed me that a lost soul was on its way here."

Without much enthusiasm, Hamilton outlined what had happened.

"Ah," Clamp said, when he had finished. Distressed and skeptical, he flounced about the study, arms behind his back. "No," he declared, "I really can't accept this. But it could be so; it really could. You assert, you actually stand there and claim, that up until Thursday you lived in a world untouched by His presence?"

"I didn't say that. Untouched by a crude, bombastic presence. None of this—tribal deity stuff. This bluster and thunder. But He could very well be there. I always took it for granted that He was. In a subtle way. Behind the scenes, not kicking them over with His hoof every time somebody steps out of line."

The Prophet was clearly moved by Hamilton's revelation. "This is a sensational affair . . . I hadn't realized there were whole worlds still infidel."

At that, Hamilton lost his temper. "Can't you grasp what I'm saying? This second-rate universe, this Bab or whatever—"

"The Second Bab," Clamp interrupted.

"What is a Bab? And where's the First Bab? Where did all this nonsense come from?"

After a haughty moment, Clamp said, "On July 9, 1850, the First Bab was executed at Tabriz. Twenty thousand of his followers, the Babiis, were horribly murdered. The First Bab was a True Prophet of the Lord; he died transcendentally, causing even his jailers to weep. In 1909, his remains were carried to Mount Carmel." Clamp paused dramatically, his eyes full of emotion. "In 1915, sixty-five years after his death, *the Bab reappeared on Earth.* In Chicago, at eight o'clock on the morning of

August 4, he was witnessed by a group of persons eating in a restaurant. This, despite the proven fact that the remains at Mount Carmel are still intact!"

"I see," Hamilton said.

Raising his hands, Clamp said, "What further proof could be asked? What greater miracle has the world seen? The First Bab was a mere Prophet of the One True God." His voice trembling, Clamp finished, "And the Second Bab—is He!"

"Why Cheyenne, Wyoming?" Hamilton inquired.

"The Second Bab ended His days on Earth at this exact spot. On May 21, 1939, He ascended to Paradise, carried by five angels, in plain sight of the Faithful. It was a thrilling moment. I, myself—" Clamp was unable to speak. "I, personally, received from the Second Bab during His last hour on Earth, His—" He pointed to a niche in the wall of the study. "In that mihrab is the Second Bab's watch, His fountain pen, His wallet, and one false tooth—the rest were genuine and went with Him bodily to Paradise. I, during the lifetime of the Second Bab, was His recorder. I wrote down many sections of the Bayan with this typewriter you see here." He touched a glass case in which was an old Underwood Model Five office machine, battered and obsolete.

"And now," the Prophet Clamp continued, "let us consider this world you describe. Obviously, you've been sent here to acquaint me with this extraordinary situation. An entire world, billions of people, living their lives cut off from the sight of the One True God." In his eyes a fervent glow appeared; the glow burgeoned as the Prophet's mouth formed the word, "Jihad."

"Look," Hamilton began apprehensively. But Clamp cut him brusquely off.

"A jihad," Clamp said excitedly. "We'll get hold of

Colonel T. E. Edwards at Califorania Maintenance . . .
immediate conversion to long-range rockets. First, we'll
bombard this blighted region with informational literature of a scriptural nature. Then, when we've sparked
some kind of spiritual light in the wilderness, we'll follow
through with instructional teams. And after that, a general concentration of peripatetic messengers, presenting
the True Faith through various mass-media. Television,
movies, books, recorded testimonials. I would think
(Tetragrammaton) could be persuaded to do a fifteen-
minute kinescope. And some long-playing messages for
the benefit of the unbelievers."

And was this, Hamilton wondered, why he had been
summarily dropped at Cheyenne, Wyoming? Surrounded
by the certitude of the Prophet Clamp, he was beginning to falter. Maybe he was a sign, sent to fulfill the
Realization of Submission; maybe this was the real world
after all, clutched to (Tetragrammaton)'s bosom.

"Can I look around the sepulcher?" he hedged. "I'd
like to see what the spiritual hub of Second Babiism is
like."

Preoccupied, Clamp glanced up. "What? Certainly."
Already, he was punching buttons on his intercom. "I'm
getting in touch with (Tetragrammaton) immediately."
He halted long enough to lean toward Hamilton, raise
his hand, and ask, "Why do you suppose He didn't in-
form us of this darkened world?" On his face, on the lush,
complacent face of the Prophet of the Second Bab, a
floating measure of uncertainty appeared. "I would have
thought . . ." Shaking his head, he murmured, "But the
Path of God is sometimes strange."

"Damn strange," Hamilton said. Leaving the study,
he made his way out into the echoing marble corridor.
Even at this early hour, devout worshipers roamed

here and there, fingering holy exhibits and gawking. The sight of them depressed Hamilton. In one large chamber, a group of well-dressed men and women, most of them middle-aged, were singing hymns. Hamilton started to pass by, and then thought better of it.

Over the group of the Faithful hung a faintly luminous—and faintly jealous—Presence. Perhaps, he decided, it would be a good idea to follow along.

Halting, he joined the group and reluctantly sang along with them. The hymns were unfamiliar to him, but he quickly picked up the general beat. The hymns had a redundant simplicity; the same phrases and tones appeared and reappeared. The same monotonous ideas, repeated indefinitely. The appetite of (Tetragrammaton) was insatiable, he concluded. A childish, nebulous personality that required constant praise—and in the most obvious terms. Quick to anger, (Tetragrammaton) was equally quick to sink into euphoria, was eager and ready to lap up these blatant flatteries.

A balance. A method of lulling the Deity. But what a delicate mechanism. Danger for everyone . . . the easily-aroused Presence that was always nearby. Always listening.

Having discharged his religious duty, he wandered grimly on. Both the building and the people were infested with the stern nearness of (Tetragrammaton). He could feel Him everywhere; like a thick, oppressive fog, the Islamic God lay over everything. Uneasily, Hamilton examined an immense illuminated wall plaque.

Roll Call Of The Faithful. Is Your Name Here?

The list was alphabetical; he scanned it and discovered that his name was lacking. So, he observed caustically, was McFeyffe's Poor McFeyffe. But he would manage. Marsha's name, too, was absent. The list, in toto, was

astonishingly short; of all mankind, was this meager
portion the only group fit to be taken into Paradise?

Dull resentment boiled inside him. At random, he
sought some of the great names he had lived by: Ein-
stein, Albert Schweitzer, Gandhi, Lincoln, John Donne.
None was there. His rage increased. What did it signify?
Were they condemned to Hell because they hadn't been
Followers of the Second Bab of Cheyenne, Wyoming?

Naturally. Only the Believers were saved. Everybody
else, countless billions, were destined to sink into the
corroding fires of Hell. The rows of smug names were
the rustic provincials who made up the One True Faith.
Trivial personalities, tiny blots of mediocrity nonentities
. . .

One name was familiar. For a long time he stood staring at it, wondering in a troubled fashion what it meant;
wondering, with growing concern, why it was there
and what its presence meant.

                    Silvester, Arthur

The old war veteran! The severe old soldier lying in
the hospital at Belmont. He was a charter member of
the One True Faith.

It made sense. It made so much sense that, for a time,
he could only stand gazing sightlessly up at the graven
name.

Feebly, in a dim manner, he was beginning to see
how the parts and pieces fitted together. The dynamics
were swimming up into plain view. He had finally, at
long last, found the structure.

The next step was getting back to Belmont. And finding Arthur Silvester.

At the Cheyenne airfield, Hamilton pushed all his
money across the counter and said, "One-way ticket to

San Francisco. The baggage compartment, if necessary."

It lacked. But a quick telegram to Marsha brought the balance . . . and closed out his savings account. With the money came a cryptic, plaintive message: *Maybe you shouldn't come back. Something awful is happening to me.*

He wasn't particularly surprised . . . in fact, he had a good idea what it was.

The plane deposited him at the San Francisco airport just before noon. From there he took a Greyhound bus to Belmont. The front door of the house was locked; sitting despondently in the picture window was the yellow shape of Ninny Numbcat, watching him as he searched his pockets for his doorkey. Marsha was not in sight—but he knew she was there.

"I'm home," he announced, when he had got the door open.

From the darkened bedroom came a faint, sniffling sob. "Darling, I'm going to die." In the gloom, Marsha thrashed helplessly around. "I can't come out. Don't look at me. *Please* don't look at me."

Hamilton removed his coat and then picked up the telephone. "Get over here," he said, when Bill Laws finally answered. "And round up all of the group you can. Joan Reiss, that woman and her son, McFeyffe if you can find him."

"Edith Pritchet and her son are still at the hospital," Laws told him. "God knows where some of the others are. Does it have to be now?" He explained, "I have a sort of hangover."

"This evening, then."

"Make it tomorrow," Laws said. "Sunday's soon enough. What's up?"

"I think I've got this business figured out."

"Just when I was beginning to enjoy it." Ironically, Laws continued: "And tomorrow's the big day in this hear place. Lordy, Lordy. We'uns am sho' gwan to hab' ourselfs a ball."

"What's wrong with you?"

"Nuthin', suh." Laws chuckled humorlessly. "Nuthin' at all."

"I'll see you Sunday, then." Hamilton hung up and turned toward the bedroom. "Come on out," he called sharply to his wife.

"I won't," Marsha said with stubborn determination. "You can't look at me. I've made up my mind."

Standing in the entrance of the bedroom, Hamilton fumbled for his cigarettes. They were gone; he had left them with Silky. He wondered if she were still sitting in his Ford coupé, parked across the street from Father O'Farrel's Non-Babiist Church. Perhaps she had seen him and McFeyffe rise to Paradise. But she was a sophisticated girl; she wouldn't be surprised. So no harm was done—except that it might be a while before he got his car back.

"Come on, baby," he said to his wife. "I'm hungry for some breakfast. And if it's what I think it is—"

"It's awful." Loathing and pain shuddered through Marsha's voice. "I was going to kill myself. *Why?* What have I done? What's it punishment for?"

"It's not punishment," he told her gently. "And it'll go away."

"Really?" Slim hope touched her. "Are you positive?"

"If we handle this situation right. I'll go sit in the living room with Ninny; we'll be waiting."

"He's seen, already," Marsha said, in a strained, choked voice. "He's disgusted."

"Cats disgust easily." Returning to the living room,

Hamilton threw himself down on the couch and waited patiently. For a time nothing stirred. Then, from the dark bedroom, came the first sounds of ponderous movement. A shape, awkward and clumsy, was making its way forward. A pang of compassion rose in Hamilton's breast. The poor darn creature . . . and not to understand it.

At the doorway, a figure emerged. Gross, squat, it stood facing him. Forewarned as he was, the shock overwhelmed him. The resemblance to Marsha was only slight. Was this tubby, bloated monstrosity his wife?

Tears leaked down her coarse cheeks. "What—" she whispered. "What'll I do?"

Getting up, he came rapidly toward her. "It won't last long. And you're not the only one. Laws shuffles. And talks in dialect."

"I don't care about Laws. I care about *me*."

The change had touched every part of her. What had once been soft brown hair was now dirty, stringy fibers hanging over her neck and shoulders, an unclean tangle of twisted strands. Her skin was gray and pebbled, broken out with acne. Her body was a lumpy pudding, shapeless, grotesque. Her hands were immense, the nails chipped and blackened. Her legs were two white, furry columns that ended in massive flat feet. Instead of her usual chic dress she wore a coarse wool sweater, stained tweed skirt, tennis shoes—and wrinkled bobby socks.

Hamilton walked critically around her. "It makes sense."

"Is this God's—"

"This has nothing to do with God. This has to do with an old war veteran named Arthur Silvester. A crackpot old soldier who believes in his religious cult and his stereotyped ideas. To him, people like you are dangerous radicals. And he has a very clear idea what a rad-ical—a young radical woman—looks like."

Marsha's coarse features twisted painfully. "I look like—like a *cartoon*."

"You're what Silvester imagines a young radical col-lege woman would look like. And he thinks all Negroes shuffle. This is going to be tough on all of us . . . unless we get out of Silvester's world pretty damn soon, it's going to be our finish."

VIII

ON SUNDAY morning, Hamilton was awakened at the crack of dawn by a frenzied yammering that filled the house. As he crept stiffly from bed, he recalled that Bill Laws had predicted some dire event in the early hours of the Lord's Day.

The blaring, screeching racket came from the living room. Entering, Hamilton found that the television set had miraculously turned itself on; the screen was alive with animation. Turgid blurs drifted and pulsed; the entire picture was an angry swirl of dangerous reds and purples. From the hi-fi speaker system came deafening thunder, relentless and impassioned, a genuine hellfire-and-damnation roar.

This, he realized, was a Sunday morning sermon. And the sermon was being delivered by (Tetragrammaton) Himself.

Turning the set down, he padded back to the bedroom to dress. In the bed, Marsha lay huddled in an unhappy heap, trying to evade the bright glare of sunlight filtering through the window. "Time to get up," he informed her. "Don't you hear the Almighty bellowing in the living room?"

"What's He saying?" Marsha murmured crossly.

"Nothing in particular. Repent or suffer eternal damnation. The usual tribal tub-thumping."

"Don't watch me," Marsha begged. "Turn your back while I dress. Good God, I'm a *monster*."

In the living room, the television set had turned itself up full-blast again; nobody was going to interfere with the weekly harangue. Trying his best not to hear, Hamilton padded into the bathroom and went through the timeless routine of washing and shaving. He was back in the bedroom, getting on his clothes, when the door chimes rang.

"They're here," he said to Marsha.

Marsha, now dressed and struggling with her hair, gave an agonized wail. "I can't face them. Make them go away."

"Darling," he told her firmly, lacing up his shoes, "if you hope to get your old self back—"

"You-all home?" Bill Laws' voice came. "Ah jes' push open de' do' an' wahk raht in."

Hamilton hurried into the living room. There was Laws, graduate student in advanced physics. Arms dangling at his sides, white eyeballs popping, knees bent, body lank and shambling, he grotesquely swiveled his way over to Hamilton.

"You-all looka yhar," he told Hamilton. "Look, man, how Ah bin done in. This yhar goddam wuhl' done kick me square in de ass."

"Are you doing this on purpose?" Hamilton demanded, not sure whether to be amused or outraged.

"Puhpus?" The Negro gazed vacantly at him. "What you-all mean, Massah Hamilton?"

"You're either completely in Silvester's hands, or you're the most cynical man I've ever met."

Suddenly Laws' eyes flickered. "Silvester's hands? What do you mean?" His dialect was gone; instantly he was alert, tense. "I thought it was His Everlasting Majesty."

"The dialect was an act, then?"

Laws' eyes gleamed. "I'm beating it, Hamilton. The *pull* is there—I can feel it slipping in. But I'm going it one better." At that moment he caught sight of Marsha. "Who's that?"

Lamely, Hamilton explained, "My wife. This thing has hold of her."

"Jesus," Laws said softly. "What are we going to do?"

The door chimes sounded again. With a wail, Marsha disappeared back into the bedroom. This time it was Miss Reiss. Brisk and severe, she strode into the living room, dressed in a strict gray business suit, low heels, horn-rimmed glasses. "Good morning," she said, in a clipped staccato. "Mr. Laws told me there is—" She broke off, surprised. "That racket." She indicated the yammer and din of the television set. "It's on yours, too?"

"Of course. He's giving everybody the works."

Noticeably, Miss Reiss relaxed. "I thought it was just me He had singled out."

Through the half-open front door came the pain-wracked shape of Charley McFeyffe. "Greetings," he muttered. His now violently swollen jaw was bandaged. A white cloth was wrapped around his neck, pushed down inside his collar. Picking his way with care, he crossed the living room toward Hamilton.

"Can't you beat it?" Hamilton asked sympathetically.

McFeyffe glumly shook his head. "Can't."

"What's this all about?" Miss Reiss wanted to know. "Mr. Laws said you have something to tell us. Something about this peculiar conspiracy going on."

"Conspiracy?" Hamilton eyed her uneasily. "That's hardly the term for it."

"I agree," Miss Reiss said fervently, misunderstanding him. "It goes far beyond any mere conspiracy."

Hamilton gave up. Going to the closed bedroom door he knocked urgently. "Come on out, sweetheart. Time to head for the hospital."

After a tormented interval, Marsha emerged. She had put on a heavy overcoat and jeans, and in an attempt to conceal her ratty hair, she had tied it up in a red kerchief. She wore no make-up; it would have been a waste of time. "All right," she said wanly. "I'm ready."

Hamilton parked McFeyffe's Plymouth in the hospital lot. As the five of them trooped across the gravel toward the hospital buildings, Bill Laws said, "Silvester is the key to all this?"

"Silvester *is* all this," Hamilton said. "The dream you and Marsha had is the key. And various other facts— such as your shuffling, and her altered appearance. The status of the Second Babiists. This whole geocentric universe. I get the feeling that I know Arthur Silvester inside and out. Mostly inside."

"Are you positive?" Laws said doubtfully.

"All eight of us dropped into the proton beam of the

Bevatron. During the interval there was only one consciousness, one frame of reference, for the eight of us. Silvester never lost consciousness."

"Then," Laws said practically, "we're not actually here."

"Physically, we're stretched out on the floor of the Bevatron. But mentally, we're here. The free energy of the beam turned Silvester's personal world into a public universe. We're subject to the logic of a religious crank, an old man who picked up a screwball cult in Chicago in the 'thirties. We're in his universe, where all his ignorant and pious superstitions function. We're in the man's *head*." He gestured. "This landscape. This terrain. The convolutions of a brain; the hills and valleys of Silvester's mind."

"Oh, dear," Miss Reiss whispered. "We're in his power. He's trying to destroy us."

"I doubt if he's aware of what's happened. That's the irony of it. Silvester probably sees nothing odd about this world. Why should he? It's the private fantasy-world he's lived in all his life."

They entered the hospital building. Nobody was in sight; from all rooms boomed the aggressive roar of (Tetragrammaton)'s Sunday morning sermon.

"That's right," Hamilton admitted. "I forgot about that. We'll have to be careful."

The information desk was untended. Probably the whole staff was off watching the sermon. Examining the mechanical directory, Hamilton found Silvester's room number. A moment later they were ascending in the silent hydraulic elevator.

The door to Arthur Silvester's room was wide open. Inside sat the thin, upright old man, intently facing his television set. With him were Mrs. Edith Pritchet and her son David. Mrs. Pritchet and David fidgeted uneasily; with a sigh of weak relief they greeted the group as it filed into the room. Silvester, however, did not stir. Relentlessly, with fanatic sternness, he sat facing his God, absorbed in the angry swirl of bellicose, chest-beating sentiments that poured out into the room.

Clearly, Arthur Silvester was not surprised to find himself addressed by his Maker. It was obviously a part of his Sunday routine. On Sunday morning he ingested his week's supply of spiritual nourishment.

David Pritchet strolled peevishly over to Hamilton. "Who the heck is that?" he demanded, pointing at the screen. "I can't get with it."

His mother, plump, middle-aged, sat daintily gnawing on a cored apple, her bland face devoid of comprehension. Except for a nebulous aversion to the dinning blare, she was indifferent to the phenomenon on the screen.

"It's hard to explain," Hamilton told the boy. "You probably never ran into Him before."

The aged, bony skull of Arthur Silvester turned slightly; two harsh and uncompromising gray eyes fixed themselves on Hamilton. "No talking," he said, in a voice that chilled Hamilton. Without another word, he turned back to the screen.

This was the man whose world they had got themselves into. For the first time since the accident, Hamilton felt authentic and unmistakable fear.

"Ah guess," Laws muttered, out of the side of his mouth, "we-all am gwan tuh heb' tuh listen tuh this yhar speechifyin'."

What Laws said appeared to be so. How long, once He had got the stage, did He customarily hold forth?

Ten minutes later Mrs. Pritchet had had all she could stand. With an exasperated moan, she climbed to her feet and made her way to the back of the room where the others stood.

"Good heavens," she complained, "I never could abide those ranting evangelists. It doesn't seem to me I've heard one so noisy in all my life."

"He'll give up," Hamilton said, amused. "He's getting winded."

"Everybody in this whole hospital is watching," Mrs. Pritchet revealed, her face clouding into a displeased pout. "It's not good for David . . . I've tried to bring him up to see the world rationally. This isn't a good place for him."

"No," Hamilton agreed, "it certainly isn't."

"I want my son to be well educated," she confided gushily, her ornate hat dancing and swaying. "I want him to know the great classics, to experience the beauties of life. His father was Alfred B. Pritchet; he did that wonderful rhymed translation of the *Iliad.* I think great art should play a part in the ordinary man's life, don't you? It can make his existence so much richer and more meaningful."

Mrs. Pritchet was almost as much a bore as (Tetragrammaton).

Miss Joan Reiss, her back to the screen, said, "I just don't think I can stand another minute of it. That awful old man sitting there lapping that rubbish up." Her intense face twitched spasmodically. "I'd like to pick up something—anything—and smash it over his head."

"Ma'am," Laws told her, "dat dare ol' man, he fix you-all up like you nevuh been fix' up, iffen you-all do dat."

Mrs. Pritchet listened to Laws' dialect with vapid pleasure. "Regional accents ring so sweetly on the ear," she told him fatuously. "Where are you from, Mr. Laws?"

"Clinton, Ohio," Laws said, losing his accent. He shot

her a look of wrath; this was one reaction he hadn't an-
ticipated.

"Clinton, Ohio," Mrs. Pritchet repeated, retaining her
bland delight. "I've passed through there. Doesn't Clinton have a very lovely opera company?"

As Hamilton turned back to his wife, Mrs. Pritchet
was listing her favorite operas. "There's a woman who
wouldn't notice if *no* world existed," he said to Marsha.

He had spoken softly. But, at that moment, the roar
ing sermon came to an end. The muddled swirl of temper faded from the screen; in an instant the room
dropped into silence. Hamilton was chagrined to hear his
last words blare out noisily in the abrupt quiet.

Slowly, inexorably, Silvester's aged head swiveled on
the broomstick neck. "I beg your pardon?" he said, in
a quiet, frigid voice. "Did you have something to say?"

"That's right," Hamilton said; he couldn't back out
now. "I want to talk to you, Silvester. The seven of us
have a bone to pick. And you're on the other end."

In the corner, the television set showed a group of
angels happily singing close-harmony versions of popular hymns. Faces vacant and empty, the angels swayed
languidly back and forth, generating a mildly jazzy
touch to the lugubrious cadences.

"We have a problem," Hamilton said, his eyes on the
old man. Probably, Silvester had the power to hurl the
seven of them down into Hell. After all, this was his
world; if anybody had pull with (Tetragrammaton), it
was certainly Arthur Silvester.

"What problem is that?" Silvester asked. "Why aren't
the lot of you at prayer?"

Ignoring him, Hamilton continued, "We've made a

discovery about our accident. How are your injuries mending, by the way?"

A smirk of calm satisfaction covered the withered face. "My injuries," Silvester informed him, "are gone. Faith is responsible, not these meddling doctors. Faith and prayer will carry a man through any trial." He added, "What you refer to as an 'accident' was the method by which Providence tested us. God's way of discovering what kind of fiber we're made out of."

"Oh, dear," Mrs. Pritchet protested, smiling confidently. "I'm sure Providence wouldn't subject people to such an ordeal."

The old man studied her relentlessly. "The One True God," he stated categorically, "is a stern God. He deals out punishment and reward as He sees fit. It is our fate to submit. Mankind was put here on this Earth to fulfill the Will of the Cosmic Authority."

"Of the eight of us," Hamilton said, "seven were knocked unconscious by the impact of the fall. One of us remained conscious. That was you."

Silvester nodded in complacent agreement. "As I fell," he explained, "I prayed to the One True God to protect me."

"From what?" Miss Reiss broke in. "His own ordeal?"

Waving her away, Hamilton continued: "There was a lot of free energy running around the Bevatron. Normally, each individual has a unique frame of reference. But because we all lost consciousness while we were in the energy beam, and you didn't—"

Silvester was not listening. He was gazing intently past Hamilton, toward Bill Laws. A righteous indignation glowed in his sunken cheeks. "Is that," he said thinly, "a person of color standing there?"

"That's our guide," Hamilton said.

"Before we continue," Silvester said evenly, "I'll have to ask the colored person to step outside. This is the private quarters of a white man."

What Hamilton said came from a level beyond careful reasoning. He had no excuse for saying it; the words rose too naturally and spontaneously to be defended. "The hell with you," he said, and saw Silvester's face turn bleak as stone. Well, it had happened. So he might as well do it right. "A white man? If that Second Bab or whatever it's called, that (Tetragrammaton) rubbish you've invented, can sit back and listen to you say that, He's more of a worthless, broken-down travesty of a god than you are of a man. Which is saying a lot."

Mrs. Pritchet gasped. David Pritchet giggled. Stricken, Miss Reiss and Marsha involuntarily backed away. Laws stood rigid, his face pained and sardonic. Off in the corner, McFeyffe dully nursed his distended jaw and seemed barely to have heard.

Gradually, Arthur Silvester rose to his feet. He was no longer a man; he was an avenging force that transcended humanity. An agent of purification, he was defending his cultish deity, his country, the white race, and his personal honor all at once. For an interval he stood gathering his powers. A vibration shook through his gaunt frame; and from deep inside his body came a slow, gummy, poisonous hate. "I believe," he said, "that you are a nigger lover."

"That's so," Hamilton agreed. "And an atheist and a Red. Have you met my wife? A Russian spy. Have you met my friend Bill Laws? Graduate student in advanced physics; good enough to sit down at the dinner table with any man alive. Good enough to—"

On the television screen, the chorus of mixed angels had ceased singing. The image wavered; dark waves of light radiated menacingly, a growing anger of fluid motion. The speaker no longer carried lachrymose music; now a dull rumble rattled the tubes and condensers. The rumble grew to an ear-splitting thunder.

From the television screen emerged four vast figures. They were angels. Big, brutish, masculine angels, with mean looks in their eyes. Each must have weighed two hundred pounds. Wings flapping, the four angels directed themselves toward Hamilton. His wrinkled face smirking, Silvester stepped back to enjoy the spectacle of heavenly vengeance striking down the blasphemer.

As the first angel descended to deliver the Cosmic Judgment, Hamilton knocked it cold. Behind him, Bill Laws swept up a table lamp. Leaping forward, he smashed the second angel over the head; stunned, the angel struggled to get hold of the Negro.

"Oh, dear," Mrs. Pritchet wailed. "Somebody call the police."

It was hopeless. Off in the corner, McFeyffe awoke from his stupor and made a futile pass at one of the angels. A blast of clear energy lapped over him; very quietly, McFeyffe collapsed against the wall and lay still. David Pritchet, yelling excitedly, grabbed up bottles of medicine from the bedside table and lobbed them haphazardly at the angels. Marsha and Miss Reiss fought wildly, both of them hanging onto one hulking, dull-witted angel, dragging him down, kicking and scratching at him, pulling his feathers out in handfuls.

More angels soared from the television screen. Arthur Silvester watched with smug satisfaction as Bill Laws disappeared under a mound of vengeful wings. Only Hamilton remained, and there was little left of him. Coat torn, nose streaming blood, he was putting up a determined, last-ditch fight. Another angel went down, kicked squarely in the groin. But for every one put out of commission, a whole flock sailed from the twenty-seven-inch television screen and rapidly gained full stature.

Retreating, Hamilton backed toward Silvester. "If there was any justice in this stinky, run-down world of yours—" he gasped. Two angels leaped on him; blinded, choking, he felt his legs slide out from under him. With a cry, Marsha struggled to make her way over. Wielding a gleaming hatpin, she stabbed one of the angels in the kidney; the angel bellowed and let go of Hamilton. Snatching up a bottle of mineral water from the table, Hamilton swung it despairingly. The bottle exploded against the wall; shards of glass and foaming water spouted everywhere.

Sputtering, Arthur Silvester backed away. Miss Reiss collided with him; wary as a cat, she spun, gave him a violent shove, and scrambled away. Silvester, an astonished expression on his face, stumbled and fell. A corner of the bed rose to meet his brittle skull; there was a sharp *crack* as the two hit. Groaning, Arthur Silvester sagged into unconsciousness . . .

And the angels vanished.

The hubbub died. The television set became silent. Nothing remained but eight damaged human beings, strewn in various postures of injury and defense. McFeyffe was totally unconscious, and partly singed. Arthur Silvester lay inert, eyes glazed, tongue extended, one arm twitching reflexively. Bill Laws, sitting up, groped to pull himself to his feet. Terror-stricken, Mrs. Pritchet peeped into the room from the doorway, her soft face bubbling with dismay. David Pritchet stood winded, his arms still full of the apples and oranges he had been hurling.

Laughing hysterically, Miss Reiss cried, "We got him. We won. We *won!*"

Dazed, Hamilton gathered together the trembling form of his wife. Slim, panting, Marsha huddled against him. "Darling," she whispered, eyes bright with tears, "it's all right, isn't it? It's over."

Against his face her soft brown hair billowed. Her skin, smooth and warm, pressed against his lips; her body was frail, slender, the light, lithe body he remembered. And the sacklike garments were gone. In a trim little cotton blouse and skirt, Marsha hugged him in grateful, joyous relief.

"Sure," Laws muttered, standing upright with effort. One closed eye was swelling ominously; his clothes were in tatters. "The old bastard is out. We knocked him cold—that did it. Now he's no better than the rest of us. Now he's unconscious, too."

"We won," Miss Reiss was repeating, with compulsive emphasis. "We escaped from his conspiracy."

Doctors came racing from every part of the hospital. Most of the medical attention was directed toward Arthur Silvester. Grimacing weakly, the old man managed to clamber back into his chair before the television set.

"Thank you," he muttered. "I'm fine, thanks. I must have had a dizzy spell."

McFeyffe, who was starting to revive, pawed happily at his jaw and neck; his multiple curses were gone. With a glad shout he ripped away the bandage and wadded cloth. "Gone!" he yelled. "Thank God!"

"Don't thank God," Hamilton reminded him drily. "Quit while you're ahead."

"What was going on up here?" a doctor demanded.

"A little scuffle." Ironically, Laws indicated the box

of strewn chocolates that had spilled from the bedside table. "Over who got the last buttercream."

"There's only one thing wrong," Hamilton murmured, deep in preoccupied thought. "It's probably just a technical matter."

"What's that?" Marsha asked, pressed tight against him.

"Your dream. Aren't we all lying in the Bevatron, more or less unconscious? Aren't we physically suspended in time?"

"Gosh," Marsha said, sobered. "That's so. But we're back—we're safe!"

"Apparently." Hamilton could feel her heart beating, and, more slowly, the rise and fall of her breathing. "And that's what counts." She was warm, soft, and wonderfully slim. "As long as I have you put together the way you were . . ."

His voice died away. In his arms, his wife was slim, all right. *Too* slim.

"Marsha," he said quietly, "something *has* gone wrong."

Instantly, her lithe body stiffened. "Wrong? What do you mean?"

"Take off your clothes." Urgently, he caught hold of the zipper of her skirt. "Come on—hurry!"

Blinking, Marsha edged away from him. "Here? But darling, with all these people—"

"Come on!" he ordered sharply.

Bewildered, Marsha began unfastening her blouse. Slipping out of it, she tossed it on the bed and then bent to remove her skirt. Shocked and horrified, the group of people watched as she stepped from her underclothing and stood naked in the center of the room.

She was as sexless as a bee.

"Look at you," Hamilton accused her savagely. "For God's sake, look! Can't you *feel* it?"

Astonished, Marsha glanced down at herself. Her breasts were totally gone. Her body was smooth, slightly angular, without primary or secondary sex characteristics of any sort. Slim, hairless, she might have been a young boy. But she wasn't even that; she was nothing. Absolutely and unequivocally neuter.

"What . . ." she began, frightened. "I don't understand."

"We're not back," Hamilton said. "This isn't our world."

"But the angels," Miss Reiss said. "They disappeared."

Touching his normal-sized jaw, McFeyffe protested, "And my abscessed tooth's okay."

"This isn't Silvester's world, either," Hamilton told him. "It's somebody else's. Some third party's. Good Lord—we'll *never* get back." Agonized, he appealed to the stunned figures around him. "How many worlds are there? *How many times is this going to happen?*"

IX

STREWN across the floor of the Bevatron lay eight persons. None of them was fully conscious. Around them lay littered and smoking ruin, the charred metal struts and concrete that had been the observation platform, the confused tangle of material on which they had once stood.

Like snails, medical workers crept cautiously down ladders into the chamber. It would not be long before the eight bodies were reached, before the power of the magnet had died and the humming stream of protons had dimmed into silence.

Tossing and turning in his bed, Hamilton studied the unceasing tableau. Again and again he examined it; every aspect of the scene was scrutinized. As he moved toward wakefulness, the scene dimmed. As he sank restlessly back into sleep the scene reemerged, clear, sharp and totally distinct.

Beside Hamilton, his wife twisted and sighed in her sleep. In the town of Belmont, eight persons were tossing and shifting, alternating between wakefulness and sleep, seeing again and again the fixed outlines of the Bevatron, the sprawled, crumpled figures.

Struggling to learn every detail of the scene, Hamilton contemplated each figure inch by inch.

First—and most compelling—was his own physical body. It had landed last. Striking the cement with stunning force, it lay sprawled sickeningly, arms extended, one leg crumpled under it. Except for vague, shallow breathing, it made no movement. God, if there were only some way he could reach it . . . if he could shout at it, wake it up, bellow so loudly that it would rise out of the darkness of unconsciousness. But it was hopeless.

Not far off lay the slumped hulk of McFeyffe. The man's thick face bore an expression of furious amazement; one hand was still extended to grab futilely at a railing that no longer existed. A trickle of blood leaked down his fat cheek. McFeyffe was injured; there was no doubt of that. His breathing came hoarsely, unevenly. Under his coat his chest rose and fell painfully.

Beyond McFeyffe lay Miss Joan Reiss. Half buried in rubble, she lay panting for breath, arms and legs reflexively struggling to push away the layer of plaster and concrete. Her glasses were smashed. Her clothing was rumpled and torn, and an ugly welt was rising on her temple.

His own wife, Marsha, was not far off. At the fixed, unmoving sight, Hamilton's heart convulsed with sorrow. She like the rest, could not be aroused. Unconscious, she lay with one arm bent under her, knees drawn up in a quasi-fetal posture, head turned on one side, singed brown hair spilled around her neck and shoulders. A slow flutter of breath stirred her lips; beyond that there was no motion. Her clothing was on fire; gradually, inexorably, a line of dull sparks made its way toward her body. A cloud of acrid smoke hovered over her, partially obscuring her slender legs and feet. One high-heeled shoe had been torn completely off; it lay a yard or so away, forlorn and abandoned.

Mrs. Pritchet was a tubby mound of pulsing flesh, grotesque in her gaudy flowered dress now terribly burned. Her fantastic hat had been mashed to remnants by falling plaster. Her purse, torn from her hands by the impact, was strewn open; its contents lay in confusion on all sides of her.

Almost lost in the debris was David Pritchet. Once the boy groaned. Once he stirred. A section of twisted metal lay over his chest, preventing him from rising. It was toward him that the snail-paced medical teams were moving. What the hell was the matter with them? Hamilton wanted to scream, to bellow hysterically. Why didn't they hurry? Four nights had passed . . .

But not there. In that world, the real world, only a few terrible seconds had gone by.

Among heaps of tattered safety screen lay the Negro guide, Bill Laws. His lank body twitched; eyes open and glazed, he gazed sightlessly at a smoking heap of organic matter. The heap was the thin, brittle body of Arthur Silvester. The old man had lost consciousness . . . the pain and shock of his broken back had driven away the last spark of personality. Of them all, he was the most injured.

There they lay, eight singed and terribly crumpled bodies. A discouraging sight. But Hamilton, tossing and turning in his comfortable bed, beside his slim and lovely wife, would have given anything on earth to find himself back there. To return to the Bevatron and rouse his inanimate physical counterpart . . . and thereby pry his mental self out of the wandering rut in which it was lost.

In all possible universes, Monday was the same. At eight-thirty A.M., Hamilton was seated on the Southern Pacific commuters' train, a San Francisco *Chronicle* spread out on his lap, on his way up the coast to the Electronics Development Agency. Assuming, of course, that it existed. As yet, he couldn't tell.

Around him, listless white-collar workers smoked and read the comics and discussed sports. Hunched over in his seat, Hamilton moodily considered them. Did they know they were distorted figments of somebody's fantasy world? Apparently not. Placidly, they went about their Monday routine, unaware that every aspect of their existence was being manipulated by an invisible presence.

It wasn't hard to guess the identity of that presence.

Probably, seven of the eight members of the group had figured it out by now. Even his wife. At breakfast, Marsha had faced him solemnly and said, "Mrs. Pritchet. I thought about it all night. I'm *positive*."

"Why are you positive?" he had asked acidly.

"Because," Marsha answered, with absolute conviction, "she's the only one who would believe this sort of thing." She ran her hands over her flat body. "It's exactly the sort of silly, Victorian nonsense she'd put over on us."

If there was any doubt in his mind, it was resolved by a sight glimpsed as the train sped out of Belmont. Standing obediently in front of a small rural shack was a horse attached to a cart full of scrap iron: rusty sections of abandoned autos. The horse was wearing trousers.

"South San Francisco," the conductor brayed, appearing at the end of the swaying coach. Pocketing his paper, Hamilton joined the meager crowd of businessmen moving toward the exit. A moment later he was striding gloomily toward the sparkling white buildings that were the Electronics Development Agency. At least the company existed . . . that was a helpful start. Crossing his fingers, he prayed fervently that his job was a part of this world.

Doctor Guy Tillingford met him in his outer office. "Bright and early, I see," he glowed, shaking hands. "Off to a good start."

Relaxing considerably, Hamilton began removing his coat. EDA existed, and he still had a job. Tillingford, in this distorted realm, had hired him; that much carried over. One major problem was erased from his note pad of things to worry about.

"Darn decent of you to let me have a day off," Hamilton said warily, as Tillingford led him down the hall to the labs. "I appreciated it."

"How did you make out?" Tillingford inquired.

That was a stopper. In Silvester's world, Tillingford had sent him to consult the Prophet of the Second Bab. The chances were slight that this also carried over . . . in fact, it was out of the question. Stalling, Hamilton said, "Not bad, considering. Of course, it's a little out of my line."

"Any difficulty in finding the place?"

"None at all." Sweating, Hamilton wondered just what he *had* done, in this world. "It was—" he began. "It was darn nice of you. The first darn day, like that."

"Think nothing of it. Just tell me one thing." At the lab doorway, Tillingford halted briefly. "Who won?"

"W-won?"

"Did your entry take the prize?" Grinning, Tillingford slapped him warmly on the back. "By golly, I'll bet it did. I can tell by the expression on your face."

The portly Personnel Director came striding along the hall, a thick briefcase under his arm. "How'd he do?" he demanded, with a moist chuckle. Knowingly, he tapped Hamilton on the arm. "Got a little something to show us? A ribbon, maybe?"

"He's holding back," Tillingford confided. "Ernie, let's give it a write-up in the office bulletin; wouldn't the staff be interested?"

"You're darn right," the Personnel Director agreed. "I'll make a note of that." To Hamilton he said, "What did you tell us your cat's name is?"

"What?" Hamilton faltered.

"Friday, when we were talking about it. Darned if I can remember. I want to get the spelling right for the office bulletin."

In this universe, Hamilton had been given a day off—
his first working day at the new job—to enter Ninny
Numbcat in a pet show. Inwardly, he groaned. Mrs.
Pritchet's world, in some ways, was going to be more of
a trial than Arthur Silvester's.

After collecting all details about the pet show, the
Personnel Director hurried off, leaving Hamilton and
his boss standing face to face. The moment had come;
it couldn't be put off.

"Doctor," Hamilton said grimly, taking the bit in his
teeth, "I have a confession to make. Friday, I was so
darn excited about going to work for you that I—" He
grinned pleadingly. "Well, frankly I don't remember a
darn thing we said. It's all just a sort of vague blur in
my mind."

"I understand, my boy," Tillingford said soothingly,
giving him a paternal leer. "Don't fret about it . . .
plenty of opportunity to go over the details. I expect
you'll be here a good long time."

"In fact," Hamilton plunged on, "I don't even remember what my job is. Isn't that a laugh?"

They both had a good laugh over it.

"That's certainly amusing, my boy," Tillingford agreed
finally, wiping tears of merriment from his eyes. "I
thought I'd heard everything."

"You suppose maybe—" Hamilton tried to make his
voice sound light and casual. "Just a short briefer course,
before you leave me off?"

"Well," Tillingford said. Some of his humor faded; he
gained a solemn, important expression, a look of serious
thoughtfulness. A vacant, far-seeing glaze settled over
his face; he was contemplating the overall picture. "I
don't think it ever does any harm to go over fundamen-
tals. It's important, I always say, to return to basic pos-

tulates, now and then. So we don't get steered too far off our course."

"Check," Hamilton agreed, praying silently that whatever it was, he would be able to adjust to it. What in hell *was* Edith Pritchet's conception of the function of a gigantic electronics research combine?

"EDA," Tillingford began, "as you fully realize, is a major element in the national social structure. It has a vital task to fulfill. And it *is* fulfilling that task."

"Absolutely," Hamilton echoed.

"What we here at EDA are doing is more than a job. More, I dare say, than a mere economic venture. EDA was not founded with the idea of making money."

"I follow you," Hamilton assented.

"It would be a small and unworthy thing to boast of, that EDA is a financial success. Actually, it is. But that's of no importance. Our task here—and it is a great and rewarding task—goes beyond any concept of profit and gain. This is especially so, in your case. You, as a young and idealistic beginner, are motivated by the same kind of zeal that prompted me, once. Now I'm old. I've done my work. Someday, perhaps not too far in the future, I will be laying down my burden, turning my load over to more eager, more energetic hands."

His hand on Hamilton's shoulder, Doctor Tillingford led him proudly into EDA's vast network of research labs.

"Our purpose," he intoned grandly, "is to turn the immense resources and talents of the electronics industry to the task of raising the cultural standards of the masses. To bring art to the great body of mankind."

Violently, Hamilton yanked himself away. "Doctor Tillingford," he shouted, "can you look me squarely in the eye and say that?"

Astonished, Tillingford stood opening and shutting his mouth. "Why, Jack—" he muttered. "What—"

"How can you stand here reciting all this nonsense? You're an educated, intelligent man; you're one of the world's greatest research statisticians." Waving his arms wildly, Hamilton roared at the bewildered old man, "Don't you have a mind of your own? For God's sake— try to remember who you are. Don't let this happen to you!"

Backing away in dismay, Tillingford stuttered and clasped his hands timidly together. "Jack, my boy. What's come over you?"

Hamilton shuddered. It was no use; he was wasting his time. Suddenly a desire to laugh overcame him. The situation was absurd beyond belief; he might as well conserve his anger. It was not poor Tillingford's fault . . . Tillingford wasn't any more to blame than the trouser-clad horse pulling the junk wagon.

"I'm sorry," he said wearily. "I'm upset."

"Goodness," Doctor Tillingford gasped, beginning to recover. "Would you mind if I sat down a moment? I have a heart condition . . . nothing serious, an odd complaint called paroxysmal tachycardia. Makes the old ticker run fast sometimes. Excuse me." He ducked off into a side office; the door slammed shut and the sounds of medicine bottle being hurriedly opened and pills being taken filtered out into the hall.

Probably, he had lost his new job. Listlessly, Hamilton sank down on a hall bench and groped for his cigarettes. A fine start in his adjustment . . . he couldn't have made a worse beginning.

Slowly, cautiously, the door of the side office opened. Doctor Tillingford, eyes wide and fearful, peeped hesitantly out. "Jack," he said faintly.

"What?" Hamilton muttered, not looking up.

"Jack," Tillingford asked uncertainly, "you *do* want to bring culture to the masses, don't you?"

Hamilton sighed. "Sure, Doctor." Getting to his feet he turned to face the old man. "I love it. It's the greatest thing invented."

Relief flooded Tillingford's face. "Thank heaven." His confidence somewhat restored, he ventured out into the hall. "You believe you feel strong enough to begin work? I—ah—don't want to put too much of a strain on you.
. . ."

A world composed of and inhabited by Edith Pritchets. He could envision it now: friendly, helpful, saccharine sweet. Doing, thinking, believing nothing but the beautiful and the good.

"You're not going to fire me?" Hamilton demanded.

"Fire you?" Tillingford blinked. "What on earth for?"

"I grossly insulted you."

Tillingford chuckled weakly. "Think nothing of it. My boy, your father was one of my dearest friends. Sometime I'll have to tell you how furious we used to get at each other. Chip off the old block, eh, Jack?" Patting Hamilton cautiously on the shoulder, Doctor Tillingford conveyed him into the labs proper. Technicians and equipment stretched out in all directions; a humming, vibrant expanse of busily functioning electronic research projects.

"Doctor," Hamilton said, without conviction, "can I ask you one question? Just for the record?"

"Why, of course, my boy. What is it?"

"Do you remember Somebody named (Tetragrammaton)?"

Doctor Tillingford looked puzzled. "What was that?

(Tetragrammaton)? No, I don't think so. Not that I can recall."

"Thanks," Hamilton said drearily. "I just wanted to make sure. I didn't think you did."

From a worktable, Doctor Tillingford picked up a copy of the *Journal of Applied Sciences* for November, 1959. "There's an article in here that's circulating among our staff. It may interest you, although it's somewhat old stuff, these days. An analysis of the writings of one of the really significant men of our century, Sigmund Freud."

"Fine," Hamilton said tonelessly. He was prepared for anything.

"As you realize, Sigmund Freud developed the psycho-analytic concept of sex as a sublimation of the artistic drive. He showed how the basic, fundamental human urge toward artistic creativity, if given no valid means of expression, is transformed and altered into its surrogate form: sexual activity."

"Is that right?" Hamilton murmured, resigned.

"Freud showed that in the healthy, uninhibited human, there is no sexual drive and no curiosity or interest in sexuality. Contrary to traditional thought, sex is a wholly artificial preoccupation. When a man or woman is given a chance for decent, normal, artistic activity—painting, writing, music—the so-called sexual drive withers away. Sexual activity is the covert, hidden form under which the artistic talent operates when mechanistic society subjects the individual to unnatural inhibition."

"Sure," Hamilton said. "I learned that in high school. Or something like it."

"Fortunately," Tillingford continued, "the initial resistance to Freud's monumental discovery has been overcome. Naturally, he met terrific opposition. But, happily, that's all dying out. Nowadays you rarely find an educated person speaking of sex and sexuality. I use the terms merely in their clinical sense, to describe an abnormal clinical condition."

Hopefully, Hamilton asked, "You say there's some remnant of traditional thinking among the lower classes?"

"Well," Tillingford conceded, "it will take time to reach everybody." He brightened; enthusiasm returned. "And that's our job, my boy. That's the function of the electronics craft."

"Craft," Hamilton muttered.

"Not quite an art-form, I'm afraid. But not far from it. Our task, my boy, is to continue the search for the *ultimate communication medium*, the device which will leave no stone unturned. By which all living humans will be faced with civilization's cultural and artistic heritage. You follow me?"

"I'm there already," Hamilton answered. "I've had a high fidelity rig for years."

"High fidelity?" Tillingford was delighted. "I didn't realize you had an interest in music."

"Only in sound."

Ignoring him, Tillingford rushed on: "Then you'll have to join the company symphony orchestra. We're challenging Colonel T. E. Edwards' orchestra the early part of December. By golly, you'll have a chance to play against your old company. What instrument do you play?"

"The uke."

"Just a beginner, eh? What about your wife? Does she play?"

"The rebeck."

Puzzled, Tillingford let the matter drop. "Well, we

can discuss it later. I imagine you're anxious to get to your work."

At five-thirty that afternoon, Hamilton was permitted to lay down his schemata and put away the tools of his craft. Joining the other homeward-bound workers, he made his way gratefully from the plant, out onto the tree-lined gravel paths that led to the street.

He was just beginning to look around for the train station, when a familiar blue car drove up to the curb and came quietly to a halt beside him. Behind the wheel of his Ford coupé was Silky.

"I'll be damned," he said—or thought he said. Actually, it came out *darned.* "What are you doing here? I was about to start hunting you down."

Smiling, Silky pushed open the car door for him. "I got your name and address from the registration tag." She indicated the white slip on the steering column. "You were telling the truth, after all. What's the 'W.' stand for?"

"Willibald."

"You're impossible."

As he got warily in beside her, Hamilton observed, "It doesn't tell where I work, though."

"No," Silky admitted. "I called your wife and she told me where I could find you."

While Hamilton gazed at her in blank dismay, Silky shifted into low and gunned the car forward.

"You don't mind if I drive, do you?" she asked wistfully. "I just love your little car . . . it's so cute and neat, and easy to handle."

"Drive it," Hamilton said, still marveling. "You—called Marsha?"

"We had a long heart-to-heart talk," Silky informed him placidly.

"What about?"

"About you."

"What about me?"

"What you like. What you do. Oh, everything about you. You know the way women talk."

Reduced to impotent silence, Hamilton gazed sightlessly at El Camino Real and the streams of cars moving down the peninsula to the various suburban towns. Beside him, Silky drove happily, her small sharp face bright and contented. In this untarnished world, Silky had undergone a radical transformation. Her blond hair dangled down her back in two tight yellow braids. She wore a white middy blouse and a conservative dark blue skirt. On her feet were plain, unadorned loafers. She looked, in all respects, like a guileless young school girl. Make-up was lacking. Her coy, predatory expression was absent. And her figure, like Marsha's, totally undeveloped.

"How've you been?" Hamilton inquired drily.

"Just fine."

"Do you remember," he asked carefully, "when I saw you last? You remember what was happening?"

"Of course," Silky answered confidently. "You and I and Charley McFeyffe drove up to San Francisco."

"What for?"

"Mr. McFeyffe wanted you to visit his church."

"Did I?"

"I suppose so. You both disappeared inside."

"Then what?"

"I have no idea. Then I fell asleep in the car."

"You—didn't see anything?"

"What like?"

It would have sounded odd to say, "Two grown men rising to Heaven on an umbrella. So he didn't say it.

Instead, he asked, "Where are we going? Back to Belmont?"

"Of course. What else?"

"To my house?" Adjustment to this world was going to be a slow process. "You and I and Marsha—"

"Dinner's all ready," Silky told him. "Or will be, by the time we get there. Marsha phoned me at work, told me what she wanted from the store, and I picked it up."

"At work?" Fascinated, he asked, "What, ah, line of business are you in?"

Silky glanced at him, perplexed. "Jack, you're such a strange man."

"Oh."

Troubled, Silky continued to gaze at him until a muffled squeak of brakes ahead forced her to turn back to the highway.

"Honk," Hamilton instructed her. A mammoth oil truck on their right was crowding into their lane.

"What?" Silky asked.

Annoyed, Hamilton reached over and tapped the horn. Nothing happened; no sound came out.

"Why did you do that?" Silky asked curiously, slowing down to allow the truck clearance ahead of her.

Relapsing back into meditation, Hamilton filed away another piece of datum in his storehouse of wisdom. In this world, the category *car horn* had been abolished. And, in the thick homeward bound traffic, there should have been a constant din.

In cleaning up the ills of the world, Edith Pritchet eradicated, not merely objects, but whole classes of objects. Probably, at some remote time and place, she had been annoyed by a honking car. Now, in her pleas

ant fantasy version of the world, such things didn't exist.
They simply *weren't*.

Her list of annoyances was undoubtedly considerable.
And there was no way to tell what was included. He
couldn't help thinking of Koko's song in *The Mikado*:

. . . But it really doesn't matter whom you put upon the
*   list,*
For they'd none of 'em be missed—they'd none of 'em be
*   missed!*

Not an encouraging thought. Whatever thing, object,
or event had at any time in her fifty-odd years stirred
the smooth surface of her vapid enjoyment was gently
eased out of existence. He could guess a few. Garbage
men who rattled cans. Door-to-door salesmen. Bills and
tax forms of all kinds. Crying babies (perhaps *all* babies). Drunks. Filth. Poverty. Suffering in general.

It was a wonder anything was left.

"What's the matter?" Silky asked sympathetically.
"Don't you feel well?"

"It's the smog," he told her. "It always makes me a
little ill."

"What," Silky inquired, "is smog? What a funny word."

For a long time there was no conversation; Hamilton
simply sat and tried vainly to hang onto his reason.

"Would you like to stop somewhere along the way?"
Silky asked sympathetically. "For a glass of lemonade?"

"Will you shut up!" Hamilton shouted.

Blinking, Silky shot him a mute glance of fear.

"Sorry." Slumped over, Hamilton fumbled for a labored apology. "New job—tough going."

"I can imagine."

"You can?" He couldn't keep the icy cynicism out of
his voice. "By the way—you were going to tell me. What's
your racket, these days?"

"Same thing."

"And what the heck is that?"

"I'm still working at the Safe Harbor."

A measure of confidence returned to Hamilton. Some things, at least, endured. There was still a Safe Harbor. Some small segment of reality carried over for him to hang his assurance on. "Let's go there," he said greedily. "A couple of beers, before we go home."

When they reached Belmont, Silky parked across the street from the bar. Critically, Hamilton sat inspecting it. At a distance, the bar wasn't particularly changed. A trifle cleaner, perhaps. More spick and span. The nautical element was intensified; the allusions to alcohol seemed to have subtly diminished. In fact, he had trouble reading the *Golden Glow* sign. The bright red letters seemed to fuse together into a nondescript blur. If he didn't already know what the sign read . . .

"Jack," Silky said, in a soft, troubled voice, "I wish you could tell me what it is."

"What what is?"

"I—can't say." She smiled hesitantly up at him. "I feel so sort of *odd*. I seem to have a lot of mixed-up memories running around loose in my head; nothing I can put my finger on, just a bunch of vague impressions."

"About what?"

"About you and me."

"Oh." He nodded. "That. And McFeyffe?"

"Charley, too. And Billy Laws. It seems like it happened a long time ago. But it couldn't, could it? Didn't I just meet you?" She pressed her slender fingers achingly to her temples; idly, he noticed that she wore no nail polish. "It's so darn confusing."

"I wish I could help you." And he meant it. "But I've been a little perplexed the last few days, myself."

"Is everything all right? I feel as if I'm just about to step through the pavement. You know . . . as if, when I put my foot down, it'll sink on through." She laughed nervously. "It must be time to find myself another analyst."

"Another? You mean you've got one now?"

"Of course." She turned anxiously toward him. "That's what I mean. You say things like that and it makes me feel so uncertain. You shouldn't ask me things like that, Jack; it isn't right. It—hurts too much."

"I'm sorry," he said awkwardly. "It isn't your fault; no point needling you."

"My fault? About what?"

"Let it go." Pushing the car door open, he stepped down onto the dark sidewalk. "Let's get inside and have our beers."

Safe Harbor had undergone an internal metamorphosis. Small square tables, draped with starched, white cotton cloths, were neatly spaced here and there. A candle burned and dripped on each table. On the walls hung a series of Currier and Ives prints. A few middle-aged couples sat quietly eating tossed green salad.

"It's nicer in the back," Silky said, leading the way among the tables. Soon they were sitting in the dark shadows of a rear booth, menus open in front of them.

The beer, when it came, was about the best beer he had ever tried. Examining the menu, he discovered that it was the real McCoy: genuine German bock beer, the kind he could seldom locate. For the first time since entering this world, he began to feel optimistic, even cheerful.

"Here's a rat down your shirt," he said to Silky, lifting his mug.

Smiling, Silky did the same. "It's good to be sitting here with you again," she told him, sipping.

"Sure is."

Fussing with her drink, Silky asked, "Do you recommend any particular analyst? I've tried hundreds . . . I'm always going on to the next one in line. Trying to find the best. Everybody has one he recommends."

"Not me," Hamilton said.

"Really? How eccentric." She gazed past him at the Currier and Ives print on the wall behind the table; it showed a New England winter in 1845. "I guess I'll go over to the MMHA and see their consultant. They usually can help."

"What's the MMHA?"

"The Mobilized Mental Hygiene Association. Aren't you a member? Everybody's a member."

"I'm a marginal character."

From her purse, Silky got out her membership card and showed it to him. "They handle all your mental health problems. It's wonderful . . . an analysis any hour of the day or night."

"Regular medicine, too?"

"You mean psychosomatics?"

"I suppose so."

"They take care of that, too. And they have a twenty-four hour dietetics service."

Hamilton groaned. "(Tetragrammaton) was better."

"(Tetragrammaton)?" Silky was suddenly floundering. "Do I know that name? What's it mean? I have a kind of vague impression that—" Sadly, she shook her head. "I just can't fix it."

"Tell me about dietetics."

"Well, they take care of your diet."

"So I gathered."

"The correct food is very important. Right now I'm living on molasses and cottage cheese."

"Give me sirloin steak," Hamilton said feelingly.

Shocked, Silky gazed at him with horror. "Steak? Animal flesh?"

"You bet. And plenty of it. Smothered in onions, with baked potato, green peas, and hot black coffee."

Horror turned to revulsion. "Oh, *Jack!*"

"What's wrong?"

"You're a—*savage*."

Leaning across the table toward the girl, Hamilton said: "What do you say we get the heck out of here? Let's go park on some back road and have sexual intercourse."

The girl's face showed only puzzled indifference. "I don't understand."

Hamilton sagged. "Forget it."

"But—"

"Forget it!" Moodily, he gulped down the remains of his beer. "Come on, let's go home and have dinner. Marsha's probably wondering what happened to us."

X

MARSHA greeted them with relief as they filed into the bright little living room. "Just in time," she told Hamilton, standing on tiptoe to kiss him. In her apron and

print dress she was a pretty, slender shape, warm and
fragrant. "Go wash and sit down."

"Can I help with anything?" Silky asked politely.

"Not a thing. Jack, take her coat."

"That's all right," Silky said, "I'll just toss it in the
bedroom." She trotted off, leaving them briefly alone.

"This is the damndest thing," Hamilton said, following his wife into the kitchen.

"You mean her?"

"Yeah."

"When did you meet her?"

"Last week. Friend of McFeyffe's."

"She's cute." Bending down, Marsha lifted a steaming casserole from the oven. "So sweet and fresh."

"Darling, she's a whore."

"Oh." Marsha blinked. "Really? She doesn't look like
a—what you said."

"Of course she doesn't. They don't have them here."
Marsha brightened. "Then she isn't. She can't be."

Exasperated, Hamilton blocked her way, as she started into the living room with the casserole. "She *is*. In
the real world she's a barfly, a professional pick-up
hanging around bars soliciting men and drinks."

"Oh, really," Marsha said, unconvinced. "I don't believe it. We had a long talk over the phone. She's a
waitress or something. She's a charming child."

"Darling, when her apparatus was intact—" He broke
off, as Silky reappeared, pert and wholesome-looking in
her school girl's outfit.

"I'm surprised at you," Marsha said to her husband, as
she skipped back into the kitchen. "You ought to be
ashamed of yourself."

Lamely, he shambled off. "The hell with it." Picking
up the evening Oakland *Tribune*, he threw himself down

on the couch, opposite Silky, and began scanning the headlines.

Feinberg Announces New Discovery
Heralding Permanent Asthma Cure!

The article, on page one, showed a picture of a smiling, plump, balding, white-clad doctor, straight from a mouthwash ad. The article told about his world-shaking discovery. Column one, page one.

Column two, page one, was a lengthy article on recent archeological discoveries in the Middle East. Pots, dishes, and vases had been unearthed; an entire Iron Age city had been located. Mankind watched with bated breath.

A kind of morbid curiosity overcame him. What had become of the Cold War with Russia? For that matter, what had become of Russia? Rapidly, he scanned the remaining pages. What he discovered made the hackles of his neck rise.

Russia, as a category, had been abolished. It was just too painfully unpleasant. Millions of men and women, millions of square miles of land—*gone!* What was there, instead? A barren plain? A misty emptiness? A vast pit?

In a sense, there was no front section to the newspaper . . . It began with section two: the women's world. Fashions, social events, marriages and engagements, cultural activities, games. The comic section? Part of it was there—and part of it wasn't. The fun-loving joke comics remained, the kiddies' humor strips. But the detective, tough-guy, and girlie strips were absent. Not that it mattered, much. Except that the peculiar expanse of bare white newsprint seemed somehow unsatisfying.

That was probably what northern Asia looked like, now. A kind of titanic strip of blank newsprint, where once millions of lives had been lived, for better or worse. Worse—as far as an overweight, middle-aged woman named Edith Pritchet was concerned. Russia bothered her; like a buzzing gnat, it made her life unpleasant.

Come to think of it, he hadn't seen any flies or gnats. Or spiders. Or pests of any kind. By the time Mrs. Pritchet was done, this was going to be a mighty pleasant world to live in . . . if anything remained.

"Doesn't it bother you?" he said suddenly to Silky. "That there isn't any Russia?"

"Any what?" Silky asked, looking up from her magazine.

"Forget it." Throwing down his newspaper, he plodded moodily out of the living room and into the kitchen. "That's the part I can't stand," he said to his wife.

"What's that, darling?"

"They don't care!"

Gently, Marsha pointed out, "There never was any Russia. So how can they care?"

"But they should care. If Mrs. Pritchet abolished writing, they wouldn't care. They wouldn't miss it—they wouldn't notice it was gone."

"If they didn't notice it," Marsha said thoughtfully, "then what does it matter?"

He hadn't thought about that. While the two women set the dinner table he did so. "It's worse," he told Marsha. "That's the worst part of it. Edith Pritchet tampers with their world—she remakes their lives and they don't even notice. It's terrible."

"Why?" Marsha flared up. "Maybe it's not so terrible." Lowering her voice, she nodded toward Silky. "Is that terrible? Was she so much better before?"

"That's not the point. The point is—" He followed angrily after her. "Now it's not Silky. It's somebody else.

A wax dummy Mrs. Pritchet made up to take Silky's place."

"It looks like Silky to me."

"You never saw her before."

"Thank God," Marsha said fervently.

A slow, dreadful suspicion began to creep over him. "You like this," he said softly. "You actually *prefer* this."

"I wouldn't say that," Marsha said evasively.

"You do! You like these—these *improvements*."

At the kitchen door, Marsha halted, her hands full of spoons and forks. "I've been thinking about it today. In many ways everything is much cleaner and neater. Not so messy. Things are—well, so much simpler. More orderly."

"Well, there aren't so *many* things."

"What's wrong with that?"

"Maybe we'll turn out to be objectionable elements. Have you thought about that?" Gesturing, he continued: "It's not safe. Look at us—we've been remolded already. We're sexless—do you like that?"

There was no immediate answer.

"*You do*," Hamilton said, aghast. "You prefer it."

"We'll talk about it later," Marsha said, going off with the silverware.

Grabbing hold of her arm, Hamilton roughly pulled her back. "Answer me! You like it her way, don't you? You like the idea of a great, fat, fussy old lady cleaning sex and nastiness out of the world."

"Well," Marsha said thoughtfully, "I think the world could use some cleaning up, yes. And if you men haven't been able to, or don't *want* to do it—"

"I'm going to let you in on something," Hamilton told her fiercely. "As fast as Edith Pritchet abolishes categories, I'm going to restore them. The first category I'm

going to restore is sex. As of tonight, I'm going to rein-
troduce sex into this world."

"Yes, you would, wouldn't you? That's something you
want; that's something you've been mulling about con-
stantly."

"That girl in there." Hamilton jerked his head toward
the living room; Silky was happily arranging napkins
around the dinner table. "I'm going to haul her downstairs and go to bed with her."

"Darling," Marsha said practically, "you can't."

"Why not?"

"She's—" Marsha gestured. "She's not equipped."

"Don't you care a damn bit?"

"But it's absurd. It's like talking about purple os-
triches. There just isn't any such thing."

Striding into the living room, Hamilton took firm hold
of Silky's hand. "Come along," he ordered her. "We're
going down to the audiophile room and listen to Beethoven quartets."

Astonished, Silky came stumbling involuntarily after
him. "But what about dinner?"

"The hell with dinner," he answered, pulling open the
door to the stairs. "Let's get down there before she
abolishes music."

The basement was cold and damp. Hamilton turned
on the electric heater and pulled down the window
blinds. As the room warmed to cheery friendliness, he
opened the doors of the record cabinet and began dragging out armloads of LP's.

"What do you want to hear?" he demanded belligerently.

Frightened, Silky lingered by the door. "I want to eat.
And Marsha fixed such a lovely dinner—"

"Only animals eat," Hamilton muttered. "It's unpleasant. Not nice. I've abolished it."

"I don't understand," Silky protested mournfully.

Clicking on his amplifier, Hamilton adjusted the elaborate network of controls. "What do you think of my rig?" he inquired.

"Very—attractive."

"Push-pull parallel output. Flat up to thirty thousand cps. Four fifteen-inch woofers. Eight theater horns: tweeters. Cross-over network at four hundred cps. Transformers wound by hand. Diamond styli and gold liquid-torque cartridge." As he placed an LP on the turntable, he added, "Motor able to spin a weight of ten tons without slowing below thirty-three and a third. Not bad, eh?"

"W-wonderful."

The music was *Daphnis and Chloë.* A good half of his LP collection was mysteriously absent; mostly modern atonal and experimental percussive works. Mrs. Pritchet preferred the good standard classics; Beethoven and Schumann, the heavy orchestral stuff familiar to the bourgeois concert-goer. Somehow the loss of his precious Bartok collection drove him into more of a frenzy than anything else so far. It had an intimate quality, a meddling with the deepest layers of his personality. There was no living in Mrs. Pritchet's world; she was even worse than (Tetragrammaton).

"How's that?" he asked automatically, as he turned down the lamp almost to nil. "Not in your eyes, now, eh?"

"It never was, Jack," Silky said, troubled. A dim fragment of recollection seeped into her purified mind. "Golly, I can hardly see my way around . . . I'm afraid I'll fall."

"Not very far," Hamilton retorted sardonically. "What do you want to drink? It just so happens that I have a fifth of Scotch somewhere around here."

Whipping open the liquor cabinet, he groped expertly inside. His fingers closed around the neck of a bottle; rapidly drawing it forth, he bent to locate glasses. Oddly, the bottle didn't feel right. A closer examination confirmed it; he wasn't holding a fifth of Scotch, after all.

"Let's make it creme de menthe," he corrected, resigned. In some ways, it was better. "Okay?"

Daphnis and Chloë swelled out luxuriantly into the darkened room as Hamilton conveyed Silky to the couch and sat her down. Obediently, she accepted her drink and dutifully sipped, a blank and humble expression on her face. Prowling intently around, Hamilton made the various fine adjustments of the connoisseur, straightening a wall print here, turning up the amplifier a trifle, lowering the lamp still more, fluffing up a pillow on the couch, assuring himself that the door to the stairs was closed and locked. Upstairs, he could hear Marsha stirring around. Well, she had asked for it.

"Just close your eyes and relax," he ordered wrathfully.

"I'm relaxed." Silky was still afraid. "Isn't this enough?"

"Sure," he muttered morbidly. "That's great. Here's an idea—try taking off your shoes and putting your feet up on the couch. You get a different impression of Ravel when you do that."

Silky obediently kicked off her white loafers and lifted her bare feet up and under her. "That's nice," she said wanly.

"A lot better, isn't it?"

"Much."

All at once a vast, overwhelming sorrow overcame

Hamilton. "It's no use," he said, defeated. "It can't be done."

"What can't be done, Jack?"

"You wouldn't understand."

For a time the two of them were silent. Then, slowly, quietly, Silky reached out and touched his hand. "I'm sorry."

"So am I."

"It's my fault, isn't it?"

"Sort of. In a way. A very diffuse and abstract way."

After a hesitant pause, Silky asked, "Can—I ask you something?"

"Sure. Anything."

"Would—" Her voice was so faint that he could hardly hear it. She was gazing up at him, eyes large and dark in the dim light of the room. "Jack, would you kiss me? Just once?"

Putting his arms tightly around her, he pulled her to him and, lifting up her small, sharp face, kissed her on the mouth. She clung to him, fragile and light, and so terribly, humiliatingly thin. Clutching her, holding her with all his strength, he sat for an endless interval, until at last she moved away from him, a tired, forlorn figure, almost lost in the murky gloom.

"I feel so darn bad," she faltered.

"Don't."

"I feel so—empty. I ache all over. *Why*, Jack? What is it? Why should I feel so bad?"

"Let it go," he said tightly.

"I don't want to feel this way. I want to give you something. But I don't have anything I can give you. *I'm* nothing but an emptiness, aren't I? A sort of vacant place."

"Not totally."

In the darkness there was a flicker of motion. She had gotten to her feet; now she stood in front of him, blurred and indistinct in a sudden rapidness of motion. When he looked again, he found that she had slid hastily out of her clothing; it was piled up by him in a small, neat heap.

"Do you want me?" she asked hesitantly.

"Well, in a sort of theoretical way."

"You can, you know."

He smiled ironically. "Can I?"

"You may, then."

Hamilton lifted up her bundle of clothes and handed them to her. "Get dressed and let's go upstairs. We're wasting our time and dinner's getting cold."

"It's no use?"

"No," he answered achingly, trying not to see the barren plainness of her body. "No use at all. But you did your best. You did what you could."

As soon as she had dressed, he took her hand and led her to the door. Behind them, the phonograph still blared out the futile, lush tangle of sound that was *Daphnis and Chloë*. Neither of them heard it as, unhappily, they toiled up the stairs.

"I'm sorry I let you down," Silky said.

"Forget it."

"Maybe I can make it up, some way. Maybe I can . . ."

The girl's voice faded out. And in his hand, the presence of her small, dry fingers ebbed into nothingness. Shocked, he spun and squinted down into the darkness.

Silky was gone. She had dimmed out of existence.

Baffled, incredulous, he was still standing rooted to the spot when the door above him opened and Marsha appeared at the top of the stairs. "Oh," she said, surprised. "There you are. Come on up—we have company."

"Company," he muttered.

"Mrs. Pritchet. And she's brought all kinds of people with her—it looks like a regular party. Everybody laughing and excited."

In a stupefied haze, Hamilton climbed the remaining steps and entered the living room. A babble of voices and motion greeted him. Looming over the group of people stood the great lump of a woman in her tawdry fur coat, ornate hat flapping its feathered grotesqueness, peroxide blond hair clinging in metallic piles to her plump neck and cheeks.

"There you are," Mrs. Pritchet cried happily, as she caught sight of him. "Surprise! Surprise!" Lifting up a bulging square pasteboard carton, she confided loudly, "I brought over the dearest little cakes you ever saw— regular treasures. And the most wonderful glazed fruit you ever—"

"What did you do with her?" Hamilton demanded hoarsely, advancing toward the woman. "Where is she?"

For a moment, Mrs. Pritchet was perplexed. Then the mottled wads of flesh that were her features relaxed into a smile of crafty slyness. "Why, I abolished her, dear. I eliminated that category. Didn't you know?"

XI

As HAMILTON stood, staring fixedly at the woman, Marsha came quietly over beside him and grated in his ear, "Be careful, Jack. *Be careful.*"

He turned to his wife. "You were in on it?"

"I suppose so." She shrugged. "Edith asked me where you were, and I told her. Not the details . . . just the general outline."

"What category did Silky fall into?"

Marsha smiled. "Edith put it very well. Little snit of a girl, I think she called her."

"There must be quite a lot of them," Hamilton said. "Is it worth it?"

Behind Edith Pritchet came Bill Laws and Charley McFeyffe. Both were loaded down with armfuls of groceries. "Big celebration," Laws revealed, with a cautious, half-apologetic nod at Hamilton. "Where's the kitchen? I want to put this stuff down."

"How's it going, friend?" McFeyffe said craftily, with a broad wink. "Having a good time? I've got twenty cans of beer in this sack; we're all set."

"Great," Hamilton said, still dazed.

"All you have to do is snap your fingers," McFeyffe added, his broad face flushed and perspiring. "I mean, all *she* has to do."

After McFeyffe came the small, humorless figure of Joan Reiss. The boy, David Pritchet, walked beside her. Taking up the rear hobbled the sour, dignified war veteran, his wrinkled face an expressionless mask.

"Everybody?" Hamilton inquired, sick with dismay.

"We're going to play charades," Edith Pritchet informed him joyously. "I dropped over this afternoon," she explained to Hamilton. "Your cute little wife and I had a good, long, heart-to-heart chat."

"Mrs. Pritchet—" Hamilton began, but Marsha quickly cut him off.

"Come on in the kitchen and help me get things ready," she said to him in a clear, commanding voice.

Reluctantly, he followed after her. In the kitchen, McFeyffe and Bill Laws stood around, awkward and clumsy, not certain how to occupy themselves. Laws grinned fleetingly, a brief grimace touched with apprehension and what might have been guilt. Hamilton couldn't tell; Laws turned hastily away and busied himself unwrapping endless cold cuts and sandwich spreads. Mrs. Pritchet liked hors d'oeuvres.

"Bridge," Mrs. Pritchet was saying emphatically in the other room. "But we'll need at least four people. Can we count on you, Miss Reiss?"

"I'm afraid I'm not much good at bridge," Miss Reiss' colorless voice answered. "But I'll do the best I can."

"Laws," Hamilton said, "you're too smart for this. I can see McFeyffe, but not you."

Laws didn't look directly at him. "You worry about yourself," he said huskily, "I'll worry about me."

"Don't you have enough sense to—"

"Massa Hamilton," Laws burlesqued, "Ah jes' strings along wit' what Ah finds. Iffen Ah do, Ah lives longah."

"Cut it out," Hamilton said, flushing resentfully. "Don't turn that junk on me."

Dark eyes mocking, hostile, Laws turned his back. But he was shaking; his hands trembled so badly that Marsha had to take the pound of smoked bacon from him. "Leave him alone," she chastised her husband. "It's his life."

"That's where you're wrong," Hamilton said. "It's *her* life. Can you live on cold cuts and sandwich spreads?"

"It's not so bad," McFeyffe said, philosophically. "Wake up, friend. This is the old lady's world—correct? She runs this place; she's the boss."

Arthur Silvester appeared in the doorway. "Could I have a glass of warm water and bicarbonate of soda, please? My stomach's a bit acid, today."

Putting his hand on Silvester's frail shoulder, Hamilton said to him, "Arthur, your God doesn't hang around this place; you won't like it here."

Without a word, Silvester brushed past him and over to the sink. There, he received his glass of warm water and soda from Marsha; going off in a corner he concentrated on it, excluding all else.

"I still can't believe it," Hamilton said to his wife.

"Believe what, darling?"

"Silky. She's gone. Absolutely. Like a moth you slap between your hands."

Marsha shrugged indifferently. "Well, she's around somewhere, in some other world. Back in the *real* world she's still cadging drinks and strutting her stuff." The way she said the word "real" made it sound smutty and contaminated.

"Can I help?" Edith Pritchet, fluttering coyly, appeared in the doorway, a great mass of wobbling flesh encased in an outrageously garish flowered silk dress. "Goodness, where can I find an apron?"

"Over in the closet, Edith," Marsha said, showing her where.

With instinctive aversion, Hamilton drew away from the creature as she waddled past him. Mrs. Pritchet smiled fatuously at him, a knowing expression on her face. "Now, don't you sulk, Mr. Hamilton. Don't spoil our party."

When Mrs. Pritchet had waddled back out of the kitchen and into the living room, Hamilton cornered Laws. "You're going to let that monster control your life?"

Laws shrugged. "I never had a life. You call guiding people around the Bevatron a life? People who don't understand anything about it, people who wandered in off the streets, a bunch of tourists without technical training—"

"What are you doing, now?"

A shudder of defiant pride passed over Laws. "I'm in charge of research for the Lackman Soap Company, down in San Jose."

"I never heard of it."

"Mrs. Pritchet invented it." Not quite looking at Hamilton, he explained, "It makes those fancy perfumed bath soaps."

"Christ," Hamilton said.

"That isn't much, is it? Not for you. You wouldn't be caught dead with a job like that."

"I wouldn't manufacture perfumed soaps for Edith Pritchet, no."

"I tell you what," Laws said, in a low, unsteady voice. "You try being colored awhile. You try bowing and saying, 'Yes, sir,' to any piece of white trash that happens to come along, some Georgia cracker so ignorant he blows his nose on the floor, so moronic he can't find the men's room without somebody to guide him there. *Me* to guide him there. I practically have to show him how to let down his pants. Try that awhile. Try putting yourself through six years of college washing white men's dishes in a two-bit hash house. I've heard about you;

your Dad was a big shot physicist. You had plenty of money; you weren't working in any hash house. Try getting a degree the way I did. Try carrying that degree around in your pocket a few months, looking for a job. Winding up guiding people around with an arm band on your sleeve. Like one of those Jews in a concentration camp. Then maybe you won't mind operating the research end of a perfumed soap plant."

"Even if the soap plant doesn't exist?"

"It exists *here*." Laws' dark, lean face was bleak with defiance. "And that's where I am. As long as I'm here, I'm going to make the best of it."

"But," Hamilton protested, "this is an illusion."

"Illusion?" Laws grinned sarcastically; with his hard fist he thumped the wall of the kitchen. "It feels real enough to me."

"It's in Edith Pritchet's mind. A man of your intelligence—"

"Save that," Laws broke in brutally. "I don't want to hear it. Back there, you weren't so concerned with my intelligence. You didn't particularly mind if I was a guide; you didn't act very bothered."

"Thousands of people are guides," Hamilton said uncomfortably.

"People like me, maybe. But not people like you. Want to know why I'm better off here? Because of *you*, Hamilton. It's your fault, not mine. Think that over. If you'd made some attempt, back there . . . but you didn't. You had your wife and house and cat and car and job. You had it fine . . . naturally, *you* want to go back. But not me; I didn't have it so fine. And I'm not going back."

"You are if this world ceases," Hamilton said.

A cold, vitriolic hate appeared on Laws' face. "You'd break this up?"

"Bet your life."

"You want me back with an arm band, don't you? You're like the others—you're no different. Never trust a white man; that's what they told me. But I thought you were my friend."

"Laws," Hamilton said, "you're the most neurotic sonofabitch I've ever met."

"If I am, it's your fault."

"I'm sorry you feel that way."

"It's the truth," Laws said emphatically.

"Not exactly. Part of it is true. There's a hard kernel of truth down in it, somewhere. Maybe you're right; maybe you ought to stay here. Maybe this would be the better place for you—Mrs. Pritchet will take care of you, if you get down on all fours and make the right noises. If you walk the proper distance behind her and don't annoy her. If you don't mind perfumed soap and cold cuts and asthma cures. Back in the real world you'd have to keep fighting it out with everybody. Maybe it's time you had a rest. You probably couldn't have won, anyhow."

"Stop pestering him," McFeyffe said, listening. "It's a waste of time—he's nothing but a coon."

"You're wrong," Hamilton said to McFeyffe. "He's a human being and he's tired of losing. But he won't win here, and neither will you. Nobody wins here but Edith Pritchet." To Laws, he said: "This will be worse than being pushed around by white men . . . in this world you'll be in the hands of a fat, middle-aged white woman."

"Dinner's ready," Marsha called sharply from the living room. "Everybody come and get it."

One by one they filed into the living room. Hamilton

emerged just in time to see Ninny Numbcat, attracted by
the smell of food, appear in the doorway. Rumpled from
having slept in a shoe box in the closet, Ninny wandered
across Edith Pritchet's line of march.

Crossly, half-stumbling, Mrs. Pritchet said, "Goodness." And Ninny Numbcat, getting ready to hop up on
somebody's lap, disappeared. Mrs. Pritchet went on her
way without noticing, a tray of petits fours gripped in
her lumpy pink fingers.

"She took your cat," David Pritchet spoke up shrilly,
in a loud, accusing voice.

"Don't worry about it," Marsha said absently. "There're
plenty more."

"No," Hamilton corrected thickly. "There aren't. Remember? There goes the whole class of cats."

"What was that?" Mrs. Pritchet asked. "What was that
term? I didn't catch it."

"Never mind," Marsha said quickly, seating herself at
the table and beginning to serve. The others took their
places. The last to appear was Arthur Silvester. Having
finished his glass of warm water and baking soda, he
entered from the kitchen, carrying a pitcher of tea.

"Where'll I put this?" he asked querulously, hunting
for a place on the crowded table, the glass pitcher large,
slippery, and shiny, in his withered hands.

"I'll take it," Mrs. Pritchet said, smiling vacantly. As
Silvester came toward her, she reached up for the pitcher. Silvester, without a change of expression, raised the
pitcher and brought it down on the woman's head with
all his atrophied strength. A gasp of disbelief rose from
the table; everybody was on his feet.

An instant before the pitcher struck, Arthur Silvester
faded out of existence. The pitcher itself, falling from
his dissolved hands, dropped to the carpet, shattering

and rolling. Tea spilled everywhere, an ugly, urine-colored stain.

"Oh, dear," Mrs. Pritchet said, vexed. Along with Arthur Silvester, the smashed pitcher, the pool of steaming tea, ceased to exist.

"How unpleasant," Marsha managed, after awhile.

"I'm glad that's over," Laws said thinly, his hands shaking. "That—was close."

Abruptly, Joan Reiss rose from the table. "I'm not feeling well. I'll be back in a moment." Turning quickly, she hurried out of the living room, down the hall, and disappeared into the bedroom.

"What's wrong?" Mrs. Pritchet inquired anxiously, gazing around the table. "Is there something upsetting the girl? Perhaps I can—"

"Miss Reiss," Marsha called, in an urgent, penetrating voice, "please come back here. We're eating dinner."

"I'll have to go see what's troubling her," Mrs. Pritchet sighed, beginning to struggle to her feet.

Hamilton was already out of the room. "I'll handle it," he said, over his shoulder.

In the bedroom Miss Reiss sat, her hands folded in her lap, her coat, hat, and purse beside her. "I told him not to," she said quietly to Hamilton. She had taken off her horn-rimmed glasses; they rested loosely between her fingers. Her eyes, exposed, were pale and weak, almost colorless. "That's not the way to do it."

"Then it was *planned?*"

"Of course. Arthur, the boy, and myself. We met today. That's all we can count on. We were afraid to approach you, because of your wife."

"You can count on me," Hamilton said.

From her purse, Miss Reiss took a small bottle and

laid it on the bed beside her. "We're going to put her to sleep," she said tonelessly. "She's old and worn-out."

Sweeping up the bottle, Hamilton held it to the light. It was a liquid preparation of cholorform, used in biological specimen fixing. "But this'll kill her."

"No, it won't."

David, the boy, appeared anxiously in the doorway. "You better come back—Mother's getting fretful."

Rising to her feet, Miss Reiss took back the bottle and stuffed it in her purse. "I'm all right, now. It was the sudden shock. He had promised not to do it . . . but these old soldiers—"

"I'll do the job," Hamilton told her.

"Why?"

"I don't want you to kill her. And I know you will."

For a moment they faced each other. Then, with a brief, impatient twitch, Miss Reiss fished out the bottle and pushed it in his hands. "Do a good job, then. And do it tonight."

"No. Sometime tomorrow. I'll get her outdoors—on a picnic. We'll take her up into the mountains, early in the day. As soon as it's light."

"Don't get frightened and back out."

"I won't," he said, pocketing the bottle.

He meant it.

XII

OCTOBER sunlight hung cold and sparkling. A faint trace of frost still lay over the lawns; it was early morning and the town of Belmont steamed quietly in a dull cloud of blue-white mist. Along the highway, a steady stream of cars moved up the peninsula toward San Francisco, bumper-to-bumper.

"Oh dear," Mrs. Pritchet said, distressed. "All that traffic."

"We won't be taking that rout," Hamilton told her, as he turned the Ford coupé from Bayshore Freeway, onto a side road. "We're going down toward Los Gatos."

"And then what?" Mrs. Pritchet asked, with avid, almost childish expectancy. "Goodness, I've never been over *that* way."

"Then all the way to the ocean," Marsha said, flushed with excitement. "We're going to drive down Highway One, the coast highway, down to Big Sur."

"Where's that?" Mrs. Pritchet asked doubtfully.

"That's in the Santa Lucia Mountains, just below Monterey. It won't take too long and it's a lovely place for a picnic."

"Fine," Mrs. Pritchet agreed, settling back against the car seat and folding her hands in her lap. "It certainly is sweet of you to suggest a picnic."

"Not at all," Hamilton said, giving the coupé a vicious spurt of gas.

"I don't see what's wrong with Golden Gate Park," McFeyffe said suspiciously.

163

"Too many people," Miss Reiss said logically. "Big Sur is part of a Federal Preserve. It's still wild."

Mrs. Pritchet looked apprehensive. "Will we be safe?"

"Absolutely," Miss Reiss assured her. "Nothing will go wrong."

"Shouldn't you be at work, Mr. Hamilton?" Mrs. Pritchet asked. "This isn't a holiday, is it? Mr. Laws is at work."

"I took the morning off," Hamilton said sardonically. "So I could pilot you around."

"Why, how sweet," Mrs. Pritchet exclaimed, her pulpy hands fluttering on her lap.

Puffing moodily on his cigar, McFeyffe said, "What's going on, Hamilton? Are you trying to put something over on somebody?" A tendril of sickening cigar smoke drifted to the back seat where Mrs. Pritchet sat. Frowning, she abolished cigars. McFeyffe found himself clutching empty air; for an instant his face turned beet-red, then, gradually, the color faded. "Uh," he muttered.

"What were you saying?" Mrs. Pritchet urged.

McFeyffe failed to answer; he was clumsily searching his pockets, hoping that by some miracle one cigar had been overlooked.

"Mrs. Pritchet," Hamilton said casually, "has it ever occurred to you that the Irish have made no contribution to culture? There are no Irish painters, no Irish musicians—"

"Jesus God," McFeyffe said, stricken.

"No musicians?" Mrs. Pritchet asked, in surprise. "Dear, dear, is that so? No, I hadn't realized that."

"The Irish are a barbaric race," Hamilton continued, with sadistic pleasure. "All they do is—"

"George Bernard Shaw!" McFeyffe howled fearfully. "The greatest playright in the world! William Butler

Yeats, the greatest poet. James Joyce, the—" He broke off quickly. "Also a poet."

"Author of *Ulysses*," Hamilton added. "Banned for years because of its lewd and vulgar passages."

"It's great art," McFeyffe croaked.

Mrs. Pritchet reflected. "Yes," she agreed finally, her decision made. "That judge decided it was art. No, Mr. Hamilton, I think you're quite wrong. The Irish have been very talented in the theater and in poetry."

"Swift," McFeyffe whispered encouragingly. "Wrote *Gulliver's Travels*. Sensational work."

"All right," Hamilton agreed amiably. "I lose."

Almost unconscious with terror, McFeyffe lay gasping and perspiring, his face a mottled gray.

"How could you?" Marsha said accusingly, lips close to her husband's ear. "You—beast."

Amused, Miss Reiss contemplated Hamilton with new respect. "You came close."

"As close as I wanted to," Hamilton answered, a little shocked at himself, now that he thought it over. "Sorry, Charley."

"Forget it," McFeyffe muttered hoarsely.

To the right of the road lay an expanse of barren fields. As he drove, Hamilton searched his mind; hadn't something been here? Finally, after considerable effort, he recalled. This was supposed to be a roaring, hammering industrial section of factories and refining plants. Ink, tallow, chemicals, plastics, lumber . . . now it was gone. Only the open countryside remained.

"I was by here once before," Mrs. Pritchet said, seeing the expression on his face. "I abolished all those things. Nasty, bad-smelling, noisy places."

"Then there aren't any more factories?" Hamilton inquired. "Bill Laws must feel disappointed, without his soap works."

"I left soap plants," Mrs. Pritchet said sanctimoniously. "The ones that smell nice, at least."

In a kind of depraved way, Hamilton was almost beginning to enjoy himself. It was so completely faulty, so ramshackle and precarious. With a wave of her hand, Mrs. Pritchet wiped out whole industrial regions, the world over. Surely this fantasy couldn't last. Its basic substructure was breaking down, crumbling away. Nobody was born, nothing was manufactured . . . entire vital categories simply didn't exist. Sex and procreation were a morbid condition, known only to the medical profession. This fantasy, of its own innate logic, was tumbling.

That gave him an idea. Perhaps he was tugging at the wrong end. Perhaps there was a quicker, easier way to pull the fur off the cat.

Only, there weren't any cats. At memory of Ninny Numbcat a miserable, baffled fury rose up and choked him. Because the tomcat had accidentally strolled in her way . . . but, at least, cats existed back in the real world. Arthur Silvester, Ninny Numbcat, gnats, ink factories, and Russia, still muddled on in the real world. He felt cheered.

Ninny wouldn't have liked it here, anyhow. Mice and flies and gophers had already been eliminated. And, in this distorted existence, there wasn't any back-fence carnality.

"Look," Hamilton said, as an initial experiment. They had entered a run-down slum highway town. Pool halls, shoeshine parlors, slatternly hotels. "A disgrace," he declared. "I'm outraged."

Pools halls, shoeshine parlors, and slatternly hotels

ceased to exist. All over the world, more blank spaces opened up in the fabric of reality.

"That's better," Marsha said, a triffe uneasily. "But Jack, maybe it would be better if—I mean, let Mrs. Pritchet decide for herself."

"I'm trying to help," Hamilton said. genially. "After all, I'm helping to bring culture to the masses, too."

Miss Reiss was not long in catching on. "Look at that policeman," she observed. "Giving that poor motorist a ticket. How can he do such a thing?"

"I pity that motorist," Hamilton agreed heartily. "Falling into the clutches of that beefy savage. Probably another Irishman. They're all that way."

"He looks more like an Italian to me," Mrs. Pritchet said critically. "But don't the police do good, Mr. Hamilton? It was always my impression—"

"The police, yes," Hamilton agreed. "But not the traffic cops. That's different."

"Oh," Mrs. Pritchet said, nodding. "I understand." Traffic cops, including the one on their left, ceased to exist. Everybody, except McFeyffe, breathed more easily.

"Don't blame me," Hamilton said. "Blame Miss Reiss."

"Let's abolish Miss Reiss," McFeyffe said sullenly.

"Now, Charley," Hamilton said, grinning. "That isn't a proper humanistic spirit."

"Yes," Mrs. Pritchet agreed severely. "I'm surprised at you, Mr. McFeyffe."

Lapsing into smoldering withdrawal, McFeyffe turned to glare out the car window. "Somebody ought to get rid of those marshes," he announced. "They smell to high heaven."

The mud flats ceased to smell. In fact, there were no longer any mud flats there. Instead, a kind of vague depression hung along the edge of the road. Peering at it,

Hamilton wondered how far down it went. Probably not more than a few yards . . . the mud flats hadn't been very deep. Stalking morosely up onto the road came a handful of wild birds: inhabitants of the ex-marshes.

"Say," David Pritchet said, "this is sorta fun."

"Join in," Hamilton said expansively. "What are you tired of?"

Speculatively, David said, "I'm not tired of anything. I want to see all this stuff."

That sobered Hamilton. "You're all right," he told the boy. "And don't let anybody change your mind."

"How can I be a scientist if there's nothing to examine?" David wanted to know. "Where'm I going to get pond water for my microscope? All the stagnant ponds are gone."

"Stagnant ponds," Mrs. Pritchet repeated, with an effort. "What is that, David? I'm not sure—"

"And there aren't any more broken bottles lying around in fields," David complained resentfully. "And I can't find any more beetles for my beetle collection. And you took all the snakes so I can't set out my snake trap. What am I going to do instead of watching them load coal down at the railroad? There isn't any more coal. And I used to go through the Parker Ink Company . . . now it's gone. Aren't you going to leave *anything?*"

"Nice things," his mother said reprovingly. "There'll be all kinds of nice things for you to think about. You don't want to play with dirty, unpleasant things, do you?"

"And," David continued vigorously, "Eleanor Root, the girl who moved in across the street, was going to show me something she had that I didn't have, if I went out back to the garage with her, and I did, and she didn't have it after all. And I don't think much of that."

Scarlet, Mrs. Pritchet struggled for words. "David

Pritchet," she cried, "you're a filthy-minded little pervert. What in the name of heaven is the matter with you? How did you get this way?"

"Got it from his father," Hamilton conjectured. "Bad blood."

"It must be." Breathing with difficulty, Mrs. Pritchet rushed on, "He certainly didn't get it from me. David, when I get you home I'm going to give you the whipping of your life. You won't be able to sit down for a week. Never in all my life have I—"

"Abolish him," Miss Reiss said philosophically.

"Don't you abolish me!" David roared belligerently. "You just better not; that's all I have to say."

"I'll speak to you later," his mother snapped, chin up, eyes blazing. "Right now I don't have another word to address to you, young man."

"Gee whiz," David complained, despairing.

"I'll talk to you," Hamilton told him.

"I'd prefer it if you wouldn't," Mrs. Pritchet said tightly. "I want him to learn that he can't associate with decent people if he's going to take up filthy ways."

"I have a few filthy ways myself," Hamilton began, but Marsha kicked him on the ankle and he lapsed into silence.

"If I were you," Marsha said thinly, "I wouldn't boast."

Disturbed and upset, Mrs. Pritchet gazed mutely out the window of the car and systematically abolished various categories. Old farmhouses with tottering windmills ceased to be. Ancient rusty automobiles vanished from this version of the universe. Outhouses disappeared, along with dead trees, shabby barns, rubbish heaps, and poorly-dressed itinerant fruit-pickers.

"What's that over there?" Mrs. Pritchet demanded irritably.

To their right was a squat, ugly building of concrete. "That," Hamilton stated, "is a Pacific Gas and Electric Company power station. It relays high voltage cables."

"Well," Mrs. Pritchet conceded, "I suppose that's useful."

"Some people think so," Hamilton said.

"They could make it more attractive," Mrs. Pritchet objected. As they passed the building, its plain lines flowed and wavered. By the time they had left it, the power station had become a quaint, tile-roofed cottage, with nasturtiums tangled up its pastel walls.

"Lovely," Marsha murmured.

"Wait until the electricians show up to check the cable," Hamilton said. "They'll be surprised."

"No," Miss Reiss corrected, with a humorless smile. "They won't notice a thing."

It was not quite noon when Hamilton drove the Ford from Highway One into the chaotic green wilderness that was the Los Padres Forest. Massive redwoods towered on all sides of them; glades of frigid gloom lay forebodingly on either side of the narrow road that led deep into Big Sur Park and up the slope of Cone Peak itself.

"It's scary," David pronounced.

The road climbed. Presently they had reached a broad slope of bright bushes and shrubbery, with rocks scattered here and there among the slender evergreens. And Edith Pritchet's favorite flowers, California golden poppies, grew by the millions. Mrs. Pritchet, at the sight, gave a delighted cry.

"Oh, it's so beautiful! Let's have our picnic here!"

Obligingly, Hamilton left the road and drove the Ford

out onto the meadow itself. Bump-bump went the car, before Mrs. Pritchet had a chance to abolish ruts. A moment later they came to a halt and Hamilton turned off the car engine. There was no sound but the faint steaming of the radiator, and the echoing cry of birds.

"Well," Hamilton said, "here we are."

They piled eagerly out of the car. The men hauled the baskets of food from the luggage compartment. Marsha carried the blanket and the camera. Miss Reiss brought the thermos bottle of hot tea. David, leaping and scampering around, slashed at bushes with a long stick, flushing a whole family of quail.

"How cute," Mrs. Pritchet noticed. "Look at the baby ones go."

No other people were visible. Only the expanse of tumbling green forest leading down to the ribbon of the Pacific Ocean, the endless lead-gray body of unroad far below, and, beyond that, the mighty surface of moving water that awed even David.

"Gosh," he whispered. "It's sure big."

Mrs. Pritchet selected the exact spot for the picnic, and the blanket was scrupulously spread out. Baskets were opened. Napkins, paper plates, forks and cups were passed jovially around.

Off in the shadows of the nearby evergreens, Hamilton stood preparing the chloroform. Nobody paid any attention to him, as he unfolded his handkerchief and began saturating it. The cool mid-day wind whipped the fumes away from him. No danger to anybody else: only one person's nose, mouth and breathing apparatus were going to be menaced. It would be quick, safe, and effective.

"What are you doing, Jack?" Marsha said suddenly in

his ear. Startled, he leaped guiltily, almost dropping the bottle.

"Nothing," he told her shortly. "Go back and start cracking the hard-boiled eggs."

"You're doing something." Frowning, Marsha peered over his broad shoulder. "Jack! Is that—rat poison?"

He grinned shakily. "Cough medicine. For my catarrh."

Brown eyes large, Marsha said, "You're going to do something. I can tell; you always have a sort of shifty way, when you're up to something."

"I'm going to put an end to this ridiculous business," Hamilton said fatalistically. "I've had all I can stand."

Marsha's firm, sharp fingers closed around his arm. "Jack, for my sake—"

"You like it here so much?" Bitterly, he jerked away from her. "You and Laws and McFeyffe. Having a fine time, wish you were here. While that hag abolishes people and animals and insects—everything her limited imagination fixes itself on."

"Jack, *don't do anything*. Please, don't. Promise me!"

"Sorry," he told her. "It's all decided. The wheels have started turning."

Peering near-sightedly across the meadow at the two of them, Mrs. Pritchet called, "Come on, Jack and Marsha. Cold cuts and yogurt. Hurry, while there's still some left!"

Blocking his way, Marsha said swiftly, "I won't let you. You just can't, Jack. Don't you understand? Remember Arthur Silvester; remember—"

"Get out of the way," he broke in testily. "This stuff evaporates."

Suddenly, to his amazement, tears filled her eyes. "Oh Christ, darling. What'll I do? I couldn't stand it if she abolished you, I'd die."

Hamilton's heart softened. "You donkey."

"It's true." Tears rolled helplessly down her cheeks; clutching at him, she tried to push him back. It was, naturally, a waste of effort. Miss Reiss had successfully maneuvered Edith Pritchet around so that her back was to Hamilton. David, talking excitedly, was holding his mother's attention, waving a curious rock he had excavated and pointing off into the distance at the same time. The situation was set up and waiting; his chance wouldn't come again.

"Go stand over there," Hamilton said gently. "Turn your back if you can't watch." Firmly, he pried loose her fingers and shoved her away. "It's for your sake, too. For you, Laws, Ninny, all the rest of us. For the sake of McFeyffe's cigars."

"I love you, Jack," Marsha quavered wretchedly.

"And I'm in a hurry," he answered. "Okay?"

She nodded. "Okay. Good luck."

"Thanks." As he moved toward the picnic site, he said to her, "I'm glad you've forgiven me about Silky."

"Have you forgiven me?"

"No," he said stonily. "But maybe I will when I see her again."

"I hope you do," Marsha said pitifully.

"Just keep your fingers crossed." Striding over the spongy ground, he left her and rapidly made his way toward the sloping, shapeless back of Edith Pritchet. Mrs. Pritchet was in the process of downing a paper cupful of hot orange-blossom tea. Gripped in her left hand was half of a hard-boiled egg. On her extensive lap lay a plate of potato salad and stewed apricots. As Hamilton approached and hurriedly bent down, Miss Reiss said firmly to the old woman, "Mrs. Pritchet, would you pass me the sugar?"

"Why, certainly, dear," Mrs. Pritchet replied civilly, setting down the remains of her hard-boiled egg and groping intently for the waxed paper bundle that was the sugar. "Goodness," she went on, wrinkling her nose, "whatever is that distressing odor?"

And, in Hamilton's trembling hands, the cholorofrm-impregnated cloth faded away. The bottle, pressing against his hip, ceased to trouble him; he had been relieved of it. Mrs. Pritchet politely placed the sugar bundle in Miss Reiss' nerveless hands and returned to her hard-boiled egg.

It was over. The strategy had collapsed, quietly and completely.

"Very delicious tea," Mrs. Pritchet exclaimed, as Marsha came slowly over. "You're to be congratulated, my dear. You're a natural-born cook."

"Well," Hamilton said, "that's that." Settling down on the ground he rubbed his hands briskly together and surveyed the assortment of food. "What do we have here?"

Wide-eyed, David Pritchet gaped at him. "The bottle's gone!" he wailed. "She took it!"

Ignoring him, Hamilton began collecting a lapful of food. "I guess I'll have some of everything," he said heartily. "It sure looks good."

"Help yourself," Mrs. Pritchet gushed, her mouth stuffed with egg. "Do try some of this marvelous celery and cream cheese. It's really incredible."

"Thanks," Hamilton acknowledged. "I'll do that."

David Pritchet, hysterical with despair, leaped to his feet, pointed his finger at his mother, and shrieked, "You wicked old frog—you took our chloroform! You made it disappear. Now what'll we do?"

"Yes, dear," Mrs. Pritchet said matter-of-factly. "It was a nasty, foul-smelling chemical, and I frankly don't know what you can do. Why don't you finish your meal and then go see how many kinds of ferns you can identify?"

In a funny, strained little voice Miss Reiss said, "Mrs. Pritchet, what are you going to do with us?"

"Gracious," Mrs. Pritchet declared, helping herself to more potato salad, "what kind of a question is that? Eat your food, dear. You're really too thin; you should have more flesh on your bones."

Mechanically, the group of people ate. Only Mrs. Pritchet seemed to enjoy her meal; she ate with relish . . . and she ate quite a lot.

"It's so peaceful up here," she observed. "Only the sound of the wind rustling through the pines."

Off in the distance, a plane buzzed faintly, a Coast Guard patrol craft on its way up the shore line.

"Dear me," Mrs. Pritchet said, her brows drawing pettishly together. "What an unwelcome intrusion." The plane, and all other members of the genus *plane*, ceased to be.

"Well," Hamilton said, with mock carelessness, "there goes that. I wonder what next."

"Dampness," Mrs. Pritchet answered emphatically.

"I beg your pardon?"

"Dampness." Uncomfortably, the woman squirmed around on her cushion. "I can feel the dampness of the ground. It's very annoying."

"Can you abolish an abstraction?" Miss Reiss inquired.

"I can, my dear." The ground, under the six of them, became as warm and dry as toast. "And the wind; it's a trifle chill, don't you think?" The wind became a glowing caress. "How do you find it, now?"

A crazed abandon overcame Hamilton. What did he have to lose? There was nothing left; they had reached the end. "Isn't that ocean a disgusting color?" he announced. "I find it offensive."

The ocean ceased to be a dull, leaden gray. It became a gay, pastel green.

"Much better," Marsha managed. Sitting close beside her husband she clutched convulsively at his hand. "Oh, darling—" she began hopelessly.

Pulling her close against him, Hamilton said, "Look at that sea gull flapping around out there."

"It's looking for fish," Miss Reiss comented.

"Evil-minded bird," Hamilton declared. "Killing helpless fish."

The gull vanished.

"But fish deserve it," Miss Reiss pointed out thoughtfully. "They prey on small water life; simple, one-celled protozoa."

"Vicious, filthy-minded fish," Hamilton said spiritedly.

A faint ripple seemed to stir the water. Fish, as a category, had ceased to exist. In the middle of the picnic cloth, their small wad of smoked herring faded out.

"Oh dear," Marsha said. "That was imported from Norway."

"Must have cost quite a bit," McFeyffe muttered sickly. "All that imported stuff costs."

"Who wants money?" Hamilton demanded. Getting out a handful of change, he scattered it down the hillside. The bits of bright metal lay sparkling in the early-afternoon sun. "Dirty stuff."

The glowing dots vanished. In his pocket, his wallet gave a queer thump; the paper bills had left it.

"This is charming," Mrs. Pritchet giggled. "It's so

sweet of you all to help me. I run out of things, now and then."

Far down the slope a cow was visible, making its way slowly along. As they watched, the cow did something unmentionable. "Abolish cows!" Miss Reiss cried, but it was unnecessary. Edith Pritchet had already felt displeasure; the cow was gone.

And so, Hamilton noted, was his belt. And his wife's shoes. And Miss Reiss' purse. All were made from hide. And on the picnic cloth, the yogurt and cream cheese had left, too.

Leaning over, Miss Reiss tugged at an annoying clump of dry, ragged weeds. "What offensive plants," she complained. "One of them stuck me."

The weeds vanished. So did most of the dry grass on the fields where the former cows had grazed. Instead, only barren rock and dirt were visible.

Racing around in an hysterical circle, David shouted, "I found some poison oak! Poison oak!"

"The woods are full of it," Hamilton revealed. "And nettles. And treacherous vines."

To their right, the grove of trees shuddered. All around them the forest gave a faint, almost invisible twitch. A thinness of vegetation became evident.

Gravely, Marsha removed the remnants of her shoes. Only the cloth stitching and the metal staples remained. "Isn't this sad?" she said mournfully to Hamilton.

"Banish shoes," Hamilton suggested.

"That would be a good idea," Mrs. Pritchet agreed, bright-eyed with enthusiasm. "Shoes cramp the feet." The remnants in Marsha's hands disappeared, along with the various shoes of the group. McFeyffe's great loud socks waggled starkly in the sunlight. Embarrassed, he dragged them under him and out of sight.

On the horizon, the smoke of an ocean tramp steamer was faintly visible. "Crass commercial freighter," Hamilton stated. "Wipe it off the map."

The haze of dark smoke vanished. Commercial shipping had come to an end.

"A much cleaner world," Miss Reiss commented.

Along the highway, a car moved. Its radio blared up tinnily. "Abolish radios," Hamilton said. The noise ceased. "And TV sets and movies." No visible change occurred, but it had been consummated, nevertheless. "And cheap musical instruments—accordions and harmonicas and banjos and vibraharps."

All over the world, those instruments were gone.

"Advertisements," Miss Reiss cried, as a heavy oval truck moved along the highway, its painted sides gleaming with words. The words disappeared. "Trucks, too." The truck itself disappeared, hurtling the driver into the drainage ditch at the edge of the pavement.

"He's hurt," Marsha said feebly. The struggling driver was immediately gone.

"Gasoline," Hamilton said., "That's what the truck was carrying."

All over the world, gasoline vanished.

"Oil and turpentine," Miss Reiss added.

"Beer, rubbing alcohol and tea," Hamilton said.

"Pancake syrup, honey and cider," Miss Reiss said.

"Apples, oranges, lemons, apricots and pears," Marsha said faintly.

"Raisins and peaches," McFeyffe muttered grumpily.

"Nuts, yams and sweet potatoes," Hamilton said.

Obligingly, Mrs. Pritchet abolished those various categories from the face of the earth. Their cups of tea became empty. The supply of picnic food markedly dwindled.

"Eggs and frankfurters," Miss Reiss cried, leaping to her feet.

"Cheese, doorknobs and coat hangers," Hamilton added, joining her.

Giggling, Mrs. Pritchet added the categories. "Really," she gasped, heaving with merriment, "aren't we going too far?"

"Onions, electric toasters and toothbrushes," Marsha said clearly.

"Sulphur, pencils, tomatoes and flour," David chimed in, getting into the swing of it.

"Herbs, automobiles, and plows," Miss Reiss shouted. Behind them, the Ford coupé quietly vanished. On the rolling hills and slopes of Big Sur Park, the vegetation again thinned.

"Sidewalks," Hamilton suggested.

"Drinking fountains and clocks," Marsha added.

"Furniture polish," David screamed, dancing up and down.

"Hairbrushes," Miss Reiss said.

"Comic books," McFeyffe mentioned. "And that gooey pastry with all the writing on it. That French stuff."

"Chairs," Hamilton said suddenly, dazed by his daring. "And couches."

"Couches are immoral," Miss Reiss agreed, stepping on the thermos bottle in her excitement. "Away with them. And glass. Everything glass."

Obligingly, Mrs. Pritchet abolished her spectacles, and all related items throughout the universe.

"Metal," Hamilton cried in a weak, astonished voice. The zipper of his trousers disappeared. What was left of the thermos bottle—a metal husk—vanished. Marsha's tiny wrist watch, the fillings in their teeth; the staves and hooks of the women's underclothing, ceased to be.

In a frenzy, David scampered off, screaming, "Clothes!" Instantly, they were all mother-naked. But it scarcely mattered; sex had long ago disappeared.

"Vegetation," Marsha said, scrambling up to stand fearfully beside her husband. This time, the change was startling. The hills, the vast expanse of mountain, became as bald as a slab of stone. Nothing remained but the brown earth of autumn, baking under the cold, pale sun.

"Clouds," Miss Reiss said, face twitching. The few puffs of delicate white that drifted overhead were gone. "And haze!" Instantly, the sun blazed furiously.

"Oceans," Hamilton said. The pastel green expanse winked out abruptly; all that remained was an incredibly deep pit of dry sand that extended as far as the eye could see. Appalled, he hesitated for an instant, giving Miss Reiss time to cry:

"Sand!"

The titanic pit deepened. The bottom was lost from sight. A low, ominous rumble shook the ground under them; the basic balance of the earth had been shifted.

"Hurry," Miss Reiss panted, her face distorted with passion. "What next? What's left?"

"Cities," David suggested.

Impatiently, Hamilton waved him aside. "Gullies," he bellowed. At once, they were standing on a uniform plain; all depressions had been ironed out. Six naked, pale figures of assorted weights and shapes, they stood gazing fervently around them.

"All animals but man," Miss Reiss gasped breathlessly. It was done.

"All *life forms* but man," Hamilton topped her.

"Acids!" Miss Reiss shouted, and instantly sank down to her knees, face contorted with pain. All of them writhed in an ecstasy of discomfort; basic body chemistry had been radically altered.

"Certain metallic salts!" Hamilton screamed. Again, they were convulsed by internal agony.

"Specific nitrates!" Miss Reiss added shrilly.

"Phosphorus!"

"Sodium chloride!"

"Iodine!"

"Calcium!" Miss Reiss sank semi-conscious onto her elbows; all of them lay strewn about in postures of helpless suffering. The bloated, palpitating body of Edith Pritchet wriggled in spasms; saliva dribbled from her slack lips as she fought to concentrate on the enumerated categories.

"Helium!" Hamilton croaked.

"Carbon dioxide!" Miss Reiss whispered faintly.

"Neon," Hamilton managed. Everything around him wavered and faded; he was spinning in a chaos of infinite, gloomy darkness. "Freon. Gleon."

"Hydrogen," Miss Reiss' pale lips formed, swimming in the shadows close by.

"Nitrogen," Hamilton summoned, as the swirl of nonbeing closed around him.

In a last feeble burst of energy, Miss Reiss raised herself up and quavered, "Air!"

The world's layer of atmosphere swept out of existence. His lungs totally empty, Hamilton descended into a crashing blur of death. As the universe ebbed away, he saw the inert form of Edith Pritchet roll over in a reflexive spams: her consciousness and personality had fled.

They had won. Her grip on them was gone. They had put an end to her—they were finally, agonizingly free.

. . .

He lived. He lay outstretched, too drained of energy to stir, his chest rising and falling, his fingers clutching at the ground. But where the hell was he?

With tremendous effort, he managed to open his eyes.

He was not in Mrs. Pritchet's world. Around him, the dull pulse of darkness pounded and throbbed. An ugly undercurrent that drifted and swelled and pressed ominously against him. But dimly, he could make out other shapes, other bodies sprawled here and there.

Marsha, inert and silent, lay not far off. Beyond her lay the hulk of Charley McFeyffe, mouth open, eyes glazed. And, vaguely, in the swirl of drifting gloom, he could identify Arthur Silvester, David Pritchet, the limp form of Bill Laws, and the vast, clumsy shape of Edith Pritchet, still unconscious.

Were they back in the Bevatron? A brief, thrilling flicker of joy touched him . . . and then it slipped away. No. This was not the Bevatron. In his throat, a slow bubbling wail formed, forcing its way up and out of his mouth. Desperately, feebly, he struggled to creep away from the thing that loomed over him, the slender, bone-like shell of life that gradually crumpled into itself until it was bending down close to him.

In his ear, its dry, plucking whisper began. Vibrating dully, the sound drummed and echoed at him, coming again and again until he had stopped trying to scream it down, had stopped his futile effort to push it away.

"Thank you," it breathed metallically. "You did your part very well. It happened just as I planned."

"Get away!" he shrieked.

"I'll get away," the voice promised. "I want you to get up and go about your business. I want to watch you. All of you are very interesting. I've been watching you a long time, but not the way I want. I want to watch you close up. I want to watch you every minute. I want to see everything you do. I want to be around you, right inside you, where I can get at you when I need to. I want to be able to touch you. I want to be able to make you do things. I want to see how you react. I want. I want . . ."

Now he knew where he was; he knew whose world they were in. He recognized the calm, metallic whisper that beat relentlessly into his ears and brain.

It was the voice of Joan Reiss.

XIII

"THANK HEAVEN," a voice was saying, slowly and methodically. A woman's crisp voice. "We're back. We're back in the real world."

The pools of gloom were gone. The familiar scene of forest and ocean lay spread out everywhere; the green expanse of Big Sur Park and the ribbon of highway at the foot of Cone Peak had seeped back into existence.

Overhead hung the crisp blue sky of afternoon. The California golden poppies sparkled in the autumn moisture. There lay the picnic spread, the jars and dishes and paper plates and cups. To Hamilton's right rose the cool grove of evergreens. The Ford coupé, bright and shiny, glinted in a friendly, metallic way from where he had parked it, not far off, at the end of the meadow.

A sea gull flapped through the haze gathered along the horizon. A Diesel truck rumbled noisily along the highway, trailing clouds of black smoke. In the dry shrubbery halfway down the slope, a ground squirrel zigzagged toward his crumbling dirt burrow.

On all sides of Hamilton the others were stirring. They were seven in all: Bill Laws was somewhere at San Jose, lamenting the loss of his soap factory. Through a pain-wracked blur, Hamilton could make out the form of his wife; Marsha had risen shakily to her knees and was gazing blankly around her. Not far off was the still-inert Edith Pritchet. Beyond were Arthur Silvester and David Pritchet. At the edge of the picnic spread, Charley McFeyffe had begun to feebly twitch.

Close by Hamilton sat the trim, sparse figure of Joan Reiss. Methodically, the woman was gathering together her purse and glasses; her face was almost expressionless as she circumspectly patted at her tight bun of hair.

"Thank heaven," she repeated, climbing skillfully to her feet. "That's over."

It was her voice that had aroused him.

McFeyffe, from where he lay, gazed at her vacantly, his face blank with shock. "Back," he echoed, without comprehension.

"We're back in the real world," Miss Reiss said, in a matter-of-fact voice. "Isn't that wonderful?" To the large, unmoving shape stretched out in the moist grass beside her, she said: "Get up, Mrs. Pritchet. You don't have any hold over us, now." Bending over, she pinched the woman's great bloated arm. "Everything's the way it used to be."

"Thank God," Arthur Silvester muttered piteously, as
he struggled to get up. "Oh, God, that awful voice."

"Is it over?" Marsha breathed, her brown eyes misty
with doubt and relief. Shuddering, she tottered up and
stood swaying. "That awful nightmare at the end . . . I
only caught a glimpse of it—"

"What was it?" David Pritchet pleaded, trembling with
fright. "That place and that voice talking to us—"

"It's gone," McFeyffe said weakly, with prayerful
avidity. "We're safe."

"I'll help you up, Mr. Hamilton," Miss Reiss said, approaching him. Extending her slender, bony hand, she
stood smiling her pale, colorless smile. "How does it feel
to be back in the real world?"

He could say nothing. He could only lie, petrified with
terror.

"Come now," Miss Reiss said calmly. "You're going to
have to get up sooner or later." Pointing to the Ford, she
explained, "I want you to drive us back to Belmont. The
sooner everybody is back home safe and sound, the hap-
pier I'll be." Sharp faced without a trace of sentiment,
she added, "I want to see you all back the way you
were, back where you belong. I won't be satisfied until
then."

His driving, like everything else, was mechanical, rigid,
a thing done reflexively, without volition. Ahead of them
the state highway spread out, smooth and carefully
tended, between the rolling gray hills. Now and then
other cars passed them; they were nearing Bayshore
Freeway.

"It won't be long," Miss Reiss said with anticipation.
"We're almost back to Belmont."

"Listen," Hamilton said hoarsely. "Stop pretending; stop playing this sadistic game."

"What game is that?" Miss Reiss inquired mildly. "I don't follow you, Mr. Hamilton."

"We're not back in the real world. We're in your world, your paranoiac, vicious—"

"But I've *created* the real world for you," Miss Reiss said simply. "Don't you see? Look around you. Haven't I done a good job? It was all planned out in advance, a long time ago. You'll find everything as it should be; I haven't overlooked anything."

His hands white as they gripped the steering wheel, Hamilton demanded, "You were waiting? You knew it would come around to you after Mrs. Pritchet?"

"Of course." Quietly, with controlled pride, Miss Reiss explained, "You just haven't used your head, Mr. Hamilton. Remember why Arthur Silvester had control first, before any of the rest of us? Because he never lost consciousness. And why did Edith Pritchet follow him?"

"She was stirring," Marsha said, stricken. "There, on the floor of the Bevatron. I—we could see her, at night, when we dreamed."

"You should have paid more attention to your dreams, Mrs. Hamilton," Miss Reiss observed. "You could have looked down the line and seen who lay ahead. After Mrs. Pritchet, I was the closest to consciousness."

"And after you?" Hamilton demanded.

"It doesn't matter what comes after me, Mr. Hamilton, because I'm the last. You're back . . . you've come to the end of your trip. Here's your little world; isn't it lovely? And it belongs to all of you. That's why I created it—so you'd have things as you wanted them. You'll find everything intact . . . I hope you'll begin living as you were before."

"I guess," Marsha said presently, "we'll have to. We don't have any other choice."

"Why don't you let us go?" McFeyffe demanded futilely. .

"I can't let you go, Mr. McFeyffe," Miss Reiss answered. "I'd have to stop existing, to do that."

"Not completely," McFeyffe pointed out, in an eager, stuttering voice. "You could let us use something on you. That chloroform—something to knock you out. Something to—"

"Mr. McFeyffe," Miss Reiss interrupted calmly, "I've worked very hard on this. I've been planning it for a long time, since the accident at the Bevatron. Since I first found out that my turn would come. Wouldn't it be a shame to let all this go to waste? We may never have another chance . . . No, this is too valuable an opportunity to miss. Much too valuable."

After awhile, David Pritchet pointed and said, "There's Belmont."

"It'll be nice to be back," Edith Pritchet said, in a wavering, uncertain voice. "It's such a sweet little town."

One by one, under Miss Reiss' directions, Hamilton let them off at their homes. The last were himself and Marsha. The two of them sat in the parked coupé in front of Miss Reiss' apartment house as Miss Reiss collected her things and climbed nimbly out onto the sidewalk.

"You go on home," she told them helpfully. "A hot bath and then bed would be the best thing in the world for you."

"Thanks," Marsha said, almost inaudibly.

"Try to relax and enjoy yourselves," Miss Reiss instructed. "And please, try to forget all the things that have happened. They're behind you, now. Try to remember that."

"Yes," Marsha repeated, mechanically responding to the dry, dispassionate, school-teacher tone. "We'll remember."

As she crossed the sidewalk toward the apartment house steps, Miss Reiss paused a moment. Her long corduroy coat pulled around her, she was an unimposing, not particularly striking figure. With her armload of purse, gloves, and a copy of the *New Yorker* she had picked up at a drugstore, she might have been any middle-class secretary returning home from a day at the office. The cold wind of evening ruffled her sand-colored hair. Behind her horn-rimmed glasses, her eyes were enlarged and distorted as she gazed perceptively at the two people in the car.

"Maybe I'll drop over and visit you in a few days," she said tentatively. "We might have a quiet evening, just sitting and chatting."

"That—would be fine," Marsha managed.

"Good night," Miss Reiss said, concluding the matter. With a brisk nod, she turned and tripped up the stairs, unlocked the massive front door, and disappeared into the dim, carpeted lobby of her apartment building.

"Get us home," Marsha said, in a low, jangling voice. "Jack, get us home. Please, get us home."

He did, as quickly as possible. Bouncing the coupé up into their driveway, he yanked on the parking brake, snapped off the motor, and savagely kicked open the door.

"Here we are," he told her. Marsha sat beside him unmoving, her skin as pale and cold as wax. Gently but firmly, he took hold of her and lifted her from the car; picking her up in his arms he strode along the path, around the side of the house and onto the front porch.

"Anyhow," Marsha said shakily, "Ninny Numbcat will be back. And sex, that's back, too. Everything will be back, won't it? Won't this be just as good?"

He said nothing. Busily, he concentrated on getting the front door open.

"She wants power over us," Marsha went on. "But that's all right, isn't it? We have our world; she did create the real world for us. It looks the same to me; do you see any difference? Jack, for God's sake, *say something*."

With his shoulder, he pushed the door aside and shoved on the living room light.

"We're home," Marsha said, glancing timidly around as he set her unceremoniously on her feet.

"Yes, we are." He slammed the door behind them.

"It's our old place, isn't it? Just like it used to be before—this all started." Starting to unbutton her coat, Marsha paced around their living room, examining the drapes, the books, the prints on the walls, the furnishings. "It feels good, doesn't it? Such a relief . . . all the familiar things. Nobody dropping snakes on us, nobody abolishing categories . . . isn't it fine?"

"It's sensational," Hamilton said bitterly.

"Jack." She came up quietly beside him, her coat over her arm. "We can't put anything over on her, can we? It won't be like Mrs. Pritchet; she's too smart. She's a long way ahead of us."

"A million years ahead of us," he agreed. "She had all this planned out. Thinking, meditating, plotting, scheming . . . waiting for her chance to get control of us." In his pocket was a hard, round cylinder; with a furious jerk he yanked it out and hurled it across the room, against the wall. The empty bottle of chloroform bounced against the rug, rolled a short distance, and came silently to rest, unbroken.

"That won't do any good here," he said. "We might as well give up. This time we really are licked."

From the closet, Marsha got a hanger and began pulling her coat around it. "Bill Laws is going to feel bad."

"He ought to slaughter me."

"No," Marsha disagreed. "It isn't your fault."

"How can I look him in the face? How can I look any of you in the face? You wanted to stay back in Edith Pritchet's world; I brought you here—I fell for that psychotic's strategy."

"Don't worry about it, Jack. It won't do any good."

"No," he admitted. "It won't do any good."

"I'll fix us some hot coffee." At the kitchen door, Marsha turned wanly. "You want brandy in yours?"

"Sure. Swell."

With a forced smile, Marsha disappeared into the kitchen. For an interval there was silence.

Then her screams began.

Hamilton was on his feet in an instant; sprinting down the hall he emerged at the doorway of the kitchen. At first he failed to see it; Marsha, leaning against the kitchen table, partly blocked his view.

It was as he moved forward to grab hold of her that he saw it. The scene imprinted itself on his brain, and then cut off as he closed his eyes and dragged his wife away. One hand over her mouth, he stood forcing back her moaning screams, trying not to join with her, trying, with all his will, to control his own emotions.

Miss Reiss had never liked cats. She had been afraid of cats. Cats were her enemies.

The thing on the floor was Ninny Numbcat. He had

been turned inside out. But he was still alive; the tangled mess was a still-functioning organism. Miss Reiss had seen to that; she was not going to let the animal get away.

Quivering, palpitating, the moistly-shining blob of bones and tissue was undulating sightlessly across the kitchen floor. Its slow, steady progress had been going on for some time, probably since Miss Reiss' world had come into existence. The grotesque mass, in three and a half hours, had managed to drag itself in a kind of peristaltic wave, halfway across the kitchen.

"It can't," Marsha wailed. "It *can't* be alive."

Getting a shovel from the back yard, Hamilton scooped the mess up and carried it outside. Praying that it could be killed, he filled a zinc bucket with water and slid the quivering heap of organs, bones and tissue into it. For a time the remnants lay half-swimming, oozing and clinging, seeking to find some way out of the bucket. Then, gradually, with a final shudder of animation, the thing sank under and died.

He burned the remains, dug a hasty grave, and buried it. Washing his hands and putting away the shovel, he returned to the house. It had taken only a few minutes . . . it seemed longer.

Marsha was sitting quietly in the living room, her hands pressed together, gazing steadily ahead of her. She didn't look up as he entered the room. "Darling," he said.

"Is it over?"

"All over. He's dead. We can be glad of that. She can't do anything more to him."

"I envy him. She hasn't even begun on us."

"But she hated cats. She doesn't hate us."

Marsha turned slightly. "Remember what you said to

her that night? You scared her. And she remembers it."

"Yes," he admitted. "She probably does. She probably doesn't forget anything." Returning to the kitchen, he began fixing the coffee. He was pouring it into the cups when Marsha came quietly in and began getting out the cream and sugar.

"Well," she said, "that's our answer."

"To what question?"

"To the question, can we live? The answer is no. Worse than no."

"There's nothing worse than no," he said, but even to his own ears his voice lacked conviction.

"She's insane, isn't she?"

"Apparently. A paranoiac, with delusions of conspiracy and persecution. Everything she sees has some significance, part of the plot directed against her."

"And now," Marsha said, "she doesn't have to worry. Because, for the first time in her life, she's in a position to combat it."

As he sipped the scalding black coffee, Hamilton said, "I think she really believes this is a replica of the real world. Of *her* real world, at least. Good God, her real world will be so far beyond any of the fantasies of the rest of us—" He was silent a moment and then finished: "That thing she made Ninny into. She probably imagines that's what we would do to her. She probably thinks that goes on all the time."

Getting to his feet, Hamilton began moving around the house, pulling down the blinds. It was evening; the sun had sunk into oblivion. Outside the house, the streets were dark and chill.

From the locked desk drawer, he got his .45 caliber automatic and began fitting shells into the chamber.

"Just because she runs this world," he said to his tensely-watching wife, "doesn't mean she's omnipotent."

He pushed the gun away in his inside coat pocket. There it made a lumpy, conspicuous bulge. Marsha smiled wanly. "You look like a criminal."

"I'm a private eye."

"Where's your bosomy secretary?"

"That's you," Hamilton said, smiling back at her.

Self-consciously, Marsha raised her hands. "I wondered if you'd notice that I'm—back again."

"I do notice."

"Is it all right?" she asked shyly.

"I'm willing to tolerate you. For old time's sake."

"Such a strange thing . . . I feel almost gross. So sort of non-ascetic." Lips pressed tight together, she wandered around in a little circle. "Don't you think I'll get used to it again? But it does feel odd . . . I must still be under Edith Pritchet's influence."

Ironically, Hamilton said, "That was the last place. We're on a different treadmill, now."

In her shy pleasure, Marsha chose not to hear him. "Let's go downstairs, Jack. Down in the audiophile room. Where we can sort of—relax and listen to music." Coming toward him, she lifted her small hands to his shoulders. "Can we? Please?"

Pulling roughly away, he said, "Some other time."

Dismayed, Marsha stood hurt and surprised. "What's the matter?"

"You don't remember?"

"Oh." She nodded. "That girl, that waitress. She disappeared, didn't she? While you and she were down there."

"She wasn't a waitress."

"I guess not." Marsha brightened. "Anyhow, she's back now. So it's all right. Isn't it? And"—she gazed hopefully up into his face—"I don't mind about her. I understand."

He wasn't sure whether to be annoyed or amused. "You understand about what?"

"How you felt. I mean, it didn't really have anything to do with her; she was just a way for you to assert yourself. You were *protesting*."

Putting his arms around her, he pulled her close to him. "You're an incredibly broad-minded person."

"I believe in looking at things in a modern way," Marsha said stoutly.

"Glad to hear it."

Disengaging herself, Marsha tugged coaxingly at his shirt collar. "Could we? You haven't played records for me in months . . . not like you used to. I was so jealous when you two went down there. I'd like to hear some of our old favorites."

"You mean Tchaikowsky? That's what you usually want when you talk about 'our old favorites.'"

"Go turn on the light and the heater. Get it all nice, all lit up and inviting. So it'll be that way when I come down."

Bending forward, he kissed her on the mouth. "I'll have it radiating eroticism."

Marsha wrinkled her nose at him. "You scientists."

The stairs were dark and cold. Feeling his way with care, Hamilton descended into the gloom, one step at a time. A measure of good feeling returned to him, brought by the familiar routine of love. Soundlessly humming to himself, he advanced farther into the shadowy depths of the basement, making his way with the automatic reflex of long experience. . . .

Something coarse and slimy brushed his leg and stuck there. A heavy, ropy strand, sticky with damp ooze. Violently, he jerked his leg away. And beneath him, at the bottom of the steps, something hairy and ponderous scuttled off into the audiophile room and became still.

Not moving his body, Hamilton clung to the wall of the stairwell. Extending his arm, he groped for the light switch below. His probing fingers touched it; with a sweeping surge, he flicked it on and straightened himself out. The light winked fitfully into existence, a sputtering yellow puddle in the murkiness.

Across the basement stairs hung a crude bundle of strands, some of them broken, many of them wound together in a shapeless cable of gray. A web, a clumsy and brutal job of spinning, done hurriedly, without finesse, by something immense and squat and bestial. Underfoot, the steps were coated with dust. The ceiling was stained with vast streaks of filth, as if the web spinner had crawled and crept everywhere, exploring each corner and crack.

Drained of strength, Hamilton sank down on the step. He could sense her there, below him, waiting in the audiophile room, in the fetid darkness. He had, by blundering into her half-completed web, frightened her off. The web was not strong enough to hold him; he was still free to struggle—to pull himself loose.

He did so, slowly, with painstaking care, disturbing the web as little as possible. The strands came away and his leg was free. His trouser was coated with a thick blob of gummy substance, as if a giant slug had squirmed across him. Shuddering, Hamilton grasped the railing and began to climb back upstairs.

He had gone only two steps when his legs, of their own volition, refused to carry him farther. His body comprehended what his mind refused to accept. He was going back down. Down, toward the audiophile room.

Dazed, terrified, he spun around and scrambled in the opposite direction. And again the monstrous thing happened—the ragged, clinging nightmare. Still he was going down . . . beneath him the dark shadows stretched out, the strewn filth and debris.

He was trapped.

As he crouched staring in hypnotized fascination at the descent below him, there was a sound. Above and behind him, at the top of the stairs, Marsha had appeared.

"Jack?" she called hesitantly.

"Don't come down," he snarled, turning his head slightly, until he could dimly make out the illuminated shape of her body. "Keep off the stairs."

"But—"

"Stay where you are." Breathing heavily, he clung to the step, his fingers wrapped tightly around the railing, trying to collect his wits. He had to proceed slowly; he had to keep from leaping up and scrambling mindlessly toward the bright doorway above him, and the slender image of his wife.

"Tell me what it is," Marsha said sharply.

"I can't."

"Tell me, or I'll come down." She meant it; the decision was there in her voice.

"Darling," he said huskily, "I can't seem to get back upstairs."

"Are you hurt? Did you fall?"

"I'm not hurt. Something's happened. When I try to come back up . . ." He took a deep, shuddering breath. "I find myself going down."

"Is—there anything I can do? Won't you turn toward me? Must you have your back to me?"

Hamilton laughed wildly. "Sure I'll turn toward you."

Gripping the railing, he made a cautious about-face—
and found himself still facing the gloomy cave of dust
and shadows.

"Please," Marsha begged. "Please turn and look at me."

Anger surged up in him . . . impotent fury that
could not be expressed. With a baffled curse, he slid
to his feet. "The hell with you," he snapped. "The hell
with—"

From a long way off came the peal of the door chimes.

"Somebody's at the door," Marsha said frantically.

"Well, go let them in." He was past caring; he had
given up.

For a moment Marsha struggled. Then, with a swirl
of her skirts, she was gone. The hall light flooded starkly
down behind him, casting a long, foreboding shadow
into the stairwell. His own shadow, elongated and immense . . .

"Good God," a voice said, a man's voice. "What are
you doing down there, Jack?"

Peering over his shoulder, he made out the grim,
upright figure of Bill Laws. "Help me," Hamilton said
quietly.

"Certainly." Promptly, Laws turned to Marsha, who
had come up beside him. "Stay up here," he ordered
her. "Hold onto something so you won't fall." Grabbing
her hand, he fastened her fingers around the corner of
the wall. "Can you hang on?"

Mutely, Marsha nodded. "I—think so."

Taking the woman's other hand, Laws stepped gingerly onto the stairs. Step by step he descended, still holding onto Marsha's hand. When he had gone as far as
possible, he squatted down and reached for Hamilton.

"Can you get hold?" he grunted.

Hamilton, without turning around, held his arm back

and stretched with all his strength. He could not see Bill Laws, but he could sense him there, could hear the harsh, rapid breathing of the Negro as he sat perched above him, trying to get hold of his groping fingers.

"No dice," Laws said dispassionately. "You're down too far."

Giving up, Hamilton pulled his aching arm back and settled down on the step.

"Wait where you are," Laws said. "I'll be back." With a series of crashing noises, he bolted back up the stairs to the hallway, dragged Marsha with him, and was gone.

When he returned, he had David Pritchet with him.

"Take hold of Mrs. Hamilton's hand," he instructed the boy. "Don't ask questions; do as I say."

Gripping the corner of the wall at the top of the stairs, Marsha closed her fingers around the boy's small hand. Laws herded the boy down the stairs, as far as he could go. Then, taking hold of David's other hand, he himself descended.

"Here I come," he grunted. "You ready, Jack?"

Clutching at the railing, Hamilton extended his other hand into the invisibility behind him. Laws' harsh breathing sounded near by; now he could feel the stairs quake as Laws came lower and lower. Then, incredibly, Laws' hard, sweat-slippery hand closed around his own. With a furious tug, Laws wrenched him loose from his position at the railing and forcibly dragged him up the stairs.

Panting, gasping, Hamilton and Laws sprawled into the cheery hallway. David scrambled off in fright; Marsha, climbing unsteadily to her feet, reached quickly to take hold of her trembling husband.

"What happened?" Laws demanded, when he could talk. "What was going on down there?"

"I—" He could hardly speak. "I couldn't get back up.

No matter which way I turned." After a minute he added, "Both ways were down."

"There's something down there," Laws said. "I saw it."

Hamilton nodded. "She was waiting for me."

"*She?*"

"That's where I left her. She was on the stairs when Edith Pritchet abolished her."

Marsha moaned sharply. "He means the waitress."

"She's back," Hamilton said methodically. "But she's not a waitress. Not in this world."

"We can board up the stairwell," Laws suggested.

"Yes," Hamilton agreed. "Board it up. Close her off, so she can't get me."

"We will," Laws assured him; both he and Marsha hung tightly onto Hamilton as he stood staring back down into the gloomy, web-ridden depths of the stairwell. "We'll board it up. We won't let her get you."

XIV

"WE'VE got to get hold of Miss Reiss," Hamilton said, as the balance of the group filed up the front walk of the house and into the living room. "And then we've got to kill her. Quickly and completely. Without hesitation. As soon as we can physically reach her."

"She'll destroy us," McFeyffe muttered.

"Not all of us. Most of us, maybe."

"But it would be better," Laws said.

"Yes," Hamilton said. "It would be a lot better than sitting here waiting. This world has to come to an end."

"Does anybody disagree?" Arthur Silvester inquired.

"No," Marsha said. "Nobody disagrees."

"How about you, Mrs. Pritchet?" Hamilton asked. "What do you say?"

"Of course she must be put to sleep," Mrs. Pritchet said. "The poor creature—"

"Poor?"

"This is the world she's always lived in. This awful, insane world. Imagine it . . . year after year. A world of predatory horrors."

Eyes fixed on the boarded-up door to the basement, David Pritchet asked nervously, "Can that thing get up here?"

"No," Laws told him. "It can't. It'll stay down there until it starves. Or until we destroy Miss Reiss."

"Then we all agree," Hamilton said with finality. "That's something, at least. This is one world none of us wants to stay in."

"All right," Marsha said, "we've decided what we want to do. Now how do we do it?"

"A good question," Arthur Silvester said. "It's going to be hard."

"But not impossible," Hamilton said. "We succeeded with you; we succeeded with Edith Pritchet."

"Have you noticed," Silvester said thoughtfully, "that each time it becomes more difficult? Now we wish we were back in Mrs. Pritchet's world—"

"And when we were in her world," McFeyffe finished glumly, "we wished we were back in his."

"What are you trying to say?" Hamilton demanded
uneasily.

"Maybe we'll wish it again," Silvester said, "when we
get to the next world."

"The next world should be the real world," Hamilton
said. "Sooner or later we're going to be out of this rat
race."

"But not yet," Marsha objected. "There are eight of
us, and we've only gone through three. Do we have five
till ahead?"

"We've been in three fantasy worlds," Hamilton said.
"Three closed worlds that don't touch on reality at any
point. Once we're in them we're stuck—there's no way
out. So far, we've had bad luck." Thoughtfully, he said,
"But I'm not so sure the rest of us live in total fantasies."

After a moment, Laws said, "You smug sonofabitch."

"It could be true."

"Possibly."

"It includes you."

"No thanks!"

"You," Hamilton said, "are neurotic and cynical, but
you're also a realist. So am I. So is Marsha. So is Mc-
Feyffe. So is David Pritchet. I think we're almost out of
the fantasy realms."

"What do you mean, Mr. Hamilton?" Mrs. Pritchet
asked, troubled. "I don't understand."

"I didn't expect you to," Hamilton said. "It isn't necessary."

"Interesting," McFeyffe commented. "You may be
right. I'll agree about you and myself and Laws and the
boy. But not about Marsha. Sorry, Mrs. Hamilton."

Pale, Marsha said, "You haven't forgotten that, have
you?"

"That's my idea of a fantasy world."

"It's my idea of a fantasy world, too." White-lipped, Marsha said, "Your kind of person—"

"What are they talking about?" Laws asked Hamilton.

"It isn't important," Hamilton said impatiently.

"Maybe it is. What's this all about?"

Marsha glanced at her husband. "I'm not afraid to drag it out in the open. McFeyffe has already made an issue of it."

"We have to make an issue of it," McFeyffe said soberly. "Our whole lives depend on it."

"Marsha has been accused of being a Communist," Hamilton explained. "McFeyffe brought up the charges. They're absurd, of course."

Laws considered. "This could be serious. I wouldn't want to wind up in that kind of fantasy."

"You won't," Hamilton assured him.

A cold, bitter grimace touched Laws' dark face. "You let me down once, Jack."

"I'm sorry."

"No," Laws disagreed, "you were probably right. I wouldn't have liked the smell of perfumed soap very long. But—" He shrugged. "As it stands, you're wrong as hell. Until we can get ourselves out of this mess—" He broke off. "Let's forget the past and deal with the here-and-now. There's plenty of it."

"One more thing," Hamilton said. "Then we can forget it."

"What's that?"

"Thanks for pulling me up those stairs."

Fleetingly, Laws smiled. "That's okay. You sure looked little and sad, crouched down there. I think I would have gone down, even if I couldn't have got back out

There wasn't enough of you, there on that step. Not with what I saw at the bottom."

Turning toward the kitchen, Marsha said, "I'll put the coffee back on. Does anybody want anything to eat?"

"I'm plenty hungry," Laws said alertly. "I came directly up from San Jose when the soap factory disappeared."

"What showed up in its place?" Hamilton asked, as they moved down the hall after Marsha.

"Something I wasn't able to figure out. Some kind of factory that made instruments. Tongs and pincers, stuff that clamped, like surgical tools. I picked up a couple and took a good look at them but they weren't really anything."

"No such product?"

"Not in the real world. It's probably something Miss Reiss saw at a distance. Something she never made sense out of."

"Torture instruments," Hamilton guessed.

"Very possibly. I got the hell out of there, naturally, and grabbed the bus up the peninsula."

Getting up on a little stepladder, Marsha opened the cupboards over the kitchen sink. "How about some canned peaches?" she asked.

"Fine," Laws said. "Anything that's handy."

As Marsha reached into the cupboard, the can slipped from its stack, rolled forward, and dropped with a sickening crunch on her foot. Gasping with pain, Marsha jumped away. A second can rattled forward, hung on the up of the cupboard for an instant, and then dropped straight down. Twisting to one side, Marsha barely managed to avoid it.

"Close the cupboards," Hamilton ordered sharply,

stepping forward. Without using the ladder, he managed to reach up and slam the wooden doors shut. The dull bump of heavy metal cans striking the door was audible. For an interval the sound continued; then, reluctantly, it died.

"Accident," Mrs. Pritchet said lightly.

"Let's try to work this out rationally," Laws said. "It happens all the time."

"But this isn't the regular world," Arthur Silvester pointed out. "This is Miss Reiss' world."

"And if this happened to Miss Reiss," Hamilton agreed, "she wouldn't think it was an accident."

"Then it was intentional?" Marsha asked faintly, huddled over and rubbing her injured foot. "That can of peaches—"

Hamilton scooped up the can and carried it to the wall opener. "We'll have to be careful. From now on we're accident-prone. With a vengeance."

At the first bite from his dish of canned peaches Laws made a face and immediately set the dish down on the drainboard. "I see what you mean."

Warily, Hamilton tasted. Instead of the usual blandness of canned fruit, his tongue was curled by an acrid metallic taint that made him retch and quickly spit his mouthful into the sink.

"Acid," he choked.

"Poison," Laws said calmly. "We'll have to be careful of that, too."

"Maybe we ought to take an inventory," Mrs. Pritchet said uncomfortably. "We should try to find out how things are acting."

"Good idea," Marsha agreed, with a shiver. "So we won't be surprised." Painfully, she put her shoe back on and limped over to her husband. "Everything with

life of its own, vicious and hateful, trying to do harm.
. ."

As they were starting back down the hall, the light in
the living room quietly winked off. The living room
plunged into darkness.

"Well," Hamilton said mildly, "there's another accident. Bulb burned out. Who wants to go in and change
it?"

Nobody volunteered.

"We'll leave it," Hamilton decided. "It's not worth it.
Tomorrow, when it's daylight, I'll take care of it."

"What happens," Marsha asked, "if they all go out?"

"Good question," Hamilton admitted. "I can't answer
it. Then we try like hell, I guess, to find candles. Inde-
pendent power sources like flashlights, cigarette lighters."

"The poor insane thing," Marsha murmured. "Just
think—every time there's a blown-out power line, she
sits in the dark waiting for the monsters to descend on
her. Thinking, all the time, that it's part of an elaborate
plot."

"Like we're thinking now," McFeyffe said sourly.

"But it is," Laws said. 'This is her world. Here, when
the lights go out—"

In the darkness of the living room the phone began
to ring.

"And that, too," Hamilton said. "What do you suppose she thinks when the phone rings? We better try
to figure it out in advance; what does a ringing phone
mean to a paranoiac?"

"I suppose it depends on the paranoiac," Marsha answered.

"Obviously, in this case it's to lure her into the dark
living room. So we won't go."

They waited. Presently, the phone ceased ringing. The seven of them began to breathe more easily.

"We better stay here in the kitchen," Laws said, turning around and starting back. "It won't hurt us; it's nice and cozy."

"A sort of fortress," Hamilton said morbidly.

When Marsha tried to put the second can of peaches into the refrigerator, the door refused to open. She stood holding the can foolishly, plucking at the inoperative handle until her husband came and gently urged her away.

"I'm just nervous," she murmured. "It's probably perfectly all right. It always sort of stuck."

"Did anybody turn this toaster on?" Mrs. Pritchet asked. On the little kitchen table the toaster was humming away. "It's as hot as a stove."

Hamilton came over and inspected it. After struggling futilely with the thermostat he finally gave up and yanked out the cord. The heating element of the toaster faded into darkness.

"What can we trust?" Mrs. Pritchet asked fearfully.

"Nothing," Hamilton told her.

"It's so—grotesque," Marsha protested.

Thoughtfully, Laws opened the drawer by the sink. "We may need protection." He began rummaging through the silverware until he found what he wanted, a heavy-handled, steel steak-knife. As his fingers closed around it, Hamilton stepped forward and tugged his arm away.

"Be careful," he warned. "Remember the can of peaches."

"But we need this," Laws said irritably. Evading Hamilton, he snatched up the knife. "I've got to have some thing; you've got that damn gun there, bulging out like a brick."

For an instant the knife lay resting in the palm of his hand. Then, with a determined squirm, it forced itself around, quivering skillfully, and plunged itself directly at the Negro's stomach. Agilely, Laws eluded it; the knife buried itself in the wooden panel of the sink. Quick as a flash, Laws raised his heavy shoe and tramped down on the handle. With a metallic tinkle, the handle broke off, leaving the severed blade embedded in the wood. There it remained, struggling uselessly.

"See?" Hamilton said drily.

Weak and fainting, Mrs. Pritchet sank down on a chair by the table. "Oh dear," she murmured. "Whatever will we do?" Her voice trailed off in an indistinct moan. "Oh . . ."

Quickly taking a glass from the drainboard, Marsha reached for the water faucet. "I'll get you a drink of cold water, Mrs. Pritchet."

But the fluid that poured from the tap wasn't water. It was warm, thick, red blood.

"The house," Marsha said faintly, shutting off the flow. In the white enamel sink, an ugly pool of blood sluggishly, dribbled reluctantly down the drain. "The house itself is alive."

"Absolutely," Hamilton agreed. "And we're inside it."

"I think we all agree," Arthur Silvester said, "that we're going to have to get outdoors. The question is, *can we?*"

Going to the back door, Hamilton tried the bolt. It was firmly in place; tugging with all his strength he failed to budge it. "Not that way," he answered.

"That always stuck," Marsha said. "Let's try the front door."

"But that means going through the living room," Laws pointed out.

"You have a better suggestion?"

"No," Laws conceded. "Except that whatever we do, we better do it right away."

In single file, the seven of them moved cautiously through the dark hall toward the pool of blackness that was the living room. Hamilton led the procession; realization that, after all, it was his house, gave him a measure of courage. Perhaps—a dim hope—he could expect some special dispensation.

From the furnace vent in the hall came a rhythmic wheezing. Halting, Hamilton stood listening. The air that billowed out was warm—and fragrant! Not the dead, stale air of a mechanical appliance, but the personal, body-warmed breath generated by a living organism. Down in the basement the furnace was breathing. Back and forth the air moved, as the house-creature inhaled and exhaled.

"Is it—male or female?" Marsha asked.

"Male," McFeyffe said. "Miss Reiss is afraid of men."

The air that billowed out smelled pungently of cigar smoke, stale beer and masculine perspiration. The tough composite odors that Miss Reiss must have encountered on buses, in elevators, in restaurants. The harsh, garlic laden scent of middle-aged men.

"That's probably how her boy friend smells," Hamilton said, "when he breathes down her neck."

Marsha shuddered. "And to come home and smell it all around her . . ."

Probably, by now, the electrical wiring of the house was a neurological system, carrying the nervous impulse of the house-creature. Why not? The water pipes carried its blood; the furnace pipes carried air to its basement lungs. Through the living room window Hamilton could make out the shape of the trailing ivy vines that Marsha had painstakingly induced to climb to the roof. In the night darkness, the ivy was no longer green: it was a dull brown.

Like hair. Like the thick, dandruff-clouded hair of a middle-aged businessman. The ivy blew slightly in the wind, an ominous shudder that sent bits of dirt and stem showering down to the lawn outside.

Under Hamilton's feet the floor stirred. At first he failed to notice; it wasn't until Mrs. Pritchet began to wail that he identified the faint undulation.

Bending down, he touched the asphalt tile with the palm of his hand. The tile was warm—like human flesh.

The walls, too, were warm. And not hard. Not the firm, unyielding surface of paint, paper, plaster and wood—but a soft surface that gave slightly under his fingers.

"Come on," Laws said tightly. "Let's move."

Warily, like trapped animals, the seven of them made their way forward into the darkness of the living room. Under their feet, the carpet stirred restlessly. They could hear it all around them, the uneasy living presence, rippling and fretting, struggling into irritable animation.

It was a long trip across the dark living room. On all sides, lamps and books stirred sullenly. Once, Mrs. Pritchet gave a mindless squeak of terror; the cord of the television set had craftily wrapped itself around her ankle. Bill Laws, with a swift yank of his hand, snapped the cord and pulled her loose. Behind them, the severed cord lashed furiously, impotently.

"We're almost there," Hamilton said to the indistinct

shapes behind him. He could make out the door and the doorknob; already, he was reaching for it. Praying silently, he groped closer: three feet, two feet, only one single foot left. . . .

He seemed to be going uphill.

Astonished, he drew his hand back. He was on a slant, a rising expanse of material down which he was already beginning to slide. Suddenly, he was rolling and falling; arms flailing, he fought to get up. All seven of them slipped and bumped back toward the center of the living room, toward the hall itself. The hall was utterly dark; even the kitchen light had gone off. There was only the dim flicker of stars beyond the windows, tiny spots of brilliance a long way off.

"It's the carpet," Bill Laws was saying, in a muted, unbelieving whisper. "It—licked us back."

Under them, the carpet stirred violently. A warm, spongy surface, it was already becoming moist. Stumbling up, Hamilton collided with a wall—and recoiled. The wall dripped a thick ooze of wetness, an avid, leaking sheet of anticipatory saliva.

The house-creature was getting ready to feed.

Cringing against the wall, Hamilton tried to edge past the carpet. The tip of it reached cunningly around, groping for him as he advanced, sweating and trembling, toward the front door. One step. Two. Three. Four. Behind him, other shapes came—but not all.

"Where's Edith Pritchet?" Hamilton demanded.

"Gone," Marsha said. "Rolled back into the—hall."

"The throat," Laws' voice came.

"We're in its mouth," David Pritchet said faintly.

The warm wet flesh of the creature's mouth billowed and pushed against Hamilton. The pressure of it sent shudders of revulsion through him; struggling forward, he groped again for the doorknob, concentrating on the small orb of faintly glimmering metal. This time he managed to catch hold of it; with one great tug he flung the door wide. The shapes behind him gasped as the night became abruptly visible. Stars, the street, dark houses on the far side, trees swaying in the uneven wind . . . and cold, crisp air.

That was all. Without warning, the square outline began to fold up. The doorway became smaller as the walls squeezed it shut. Only a tiny slot remained; like lips, the walls had pressed together, closing it out of existence.

From behind them, the garlicky, rancid breath of the creature billowed out of the hall. The tongue rippled greedily. The walls sweated saliva. In the gloom around Hamilton, human voices shrilled in hopeless fear; ignoring them, he fought to get his hands and arms into the dwindling cavity that had been the front door. Beneath him, the floor began to rise. And the ceiling, slowly and inexorably, was coming down. With rhythmical precision, the two were coming together; in a moment they would meet.

"Chewing," Marsha gasped, beside him in the darkness.

Hamilton kicked with all his strength. Putting his shoulder against the compressed door, he shoved, fought, scratched and tore at the soft flesh. Tatters of organic substance came away in his hands; gouging, he dug away great gobs of it.

"Help me!" he shouted to the shapes struggling around him. Bill Laws and Charley McFeyffe rose up from the ooze of saliva and began tearing at the door in frenzy. An opening appeared; with Marsha and David

Pritchet helping, they managed to tear a circular gap in the flesh.

"Out," Hamilton snarled, pushing his wife through. Marsha sprawled on the front porch and rolled away. "You next," Hamilton said to Silvester. The old man was shoved roughly through; after him came Laws, and then McFeyffe. Glaring around, Hamilton saw no other shapes but himself and David Pritchet. The ceiling and floor had virtually met; there was no time to worry about anybody else.

"Get through there," he grunted, and heaved the boy bodily through the palpitating gap. Then, twisting and shuddering, he got himself through. Behind, within the mouth of the creature, the ceiling and floor came together. A sharp crunch was audible as hard surfaces met. Again and again the crunching sound came.

Mrs. Pritchet, who had not gotten out, was being chewed up.

The surviving members of the group collected in the front yard, safely away from the house. None of them spoke as they stood watching the creature methodically contract and expand. Digestive processes were taking place. Finally, the movement ebbed away. A last ripple of spasmodic activity passed through it, and then the creature was silent.

With a dull whir, the window shades came down, forming opaque shadows that remained in place.

"It's sleeping," Marsha said distantly.

Idly, Hamilton wondered what the garbage men would say when they came to pick up the garbage. A neat heap of bones would lie resting on the back porch, a glistening pile that would have been expertly picked, sucked, and then cast out. And, perhaps, a few buttons and metal hooks.

"That's that," Laws observed.

Hamilton started toward the car. "It's going to be a real pleasure to kill her," he stated.

"Not the car," Laws warned. "We can't trust it."

Halting, Hamilton considered. "We'll go over to her apartment on foot. I'll try to get her to come outside; if we can catch her in the open, without going indoors—"

"She's probably already outdoors," Marsha said. "This would be working against her, too. Maybe she's already dead; maybe her apartment house devoured her as soon as she went inside."

"She's not dead," Laws pointed out sardonically. "Or we wouldn't still be here."

From the dark shadows by the garage, a slim shape emerged. "That's right," it said, in a quiet, colorless voice. A familiar voice. "I'm still alive."

From his coat pocket, Hamilton got the .45. As his fingers probed for the safety catch, a bizarre realization came to him. He had never in his life used the gun before—or even seen it. In the real world, he owned no .45. The gun had appeared with Miss Reiss' world; it was part of his personality and existence in this feral, pathological fantasy.

"You escaped?" Bill Laws asked Miss Reiss.

"I was wise enough not to go upstairs," the woman's answer came. "I realized what you had planned as soon as I set foot on the lobby carpet." There was a touch of frantic triumph in Miss Reiss' voice. "You're not as clever as you thought."

"My God," Marsha said. "But we never—"

"You're going to try to kill me, aren't you?" Miss Reiss inquired. "All of you, the whole group. You've been conspiring for some time, haven't you?"

"That's true," Laws admitted suddenly. "It really is."

Harshly, metallically, Miss Reiss laughed. "I knew it. And you're not afraid to come right out and say it, are you?"

"Miss Reiss," Hamilton said, "of course we're conspiring to kill you. But we can't. There isn't a human being in this insane world that could lay a finger on you. It's these horrors you've dreamed up that—"

"But," Miss Reiss broke in, "you're not human beings."

"What?" Arthur Silvester demanded.

"Of course not. I knew that when I first saw you, that day at the Bevatron. That's why you all survived the fall; it was an obvious attempt to get me out there and push me to my death. But I didn't die." Miss Reiss smiled. "I have a few resources of my own."

Very slowly, Hamilton said, "If we're not human beings, then what are we?"

At that moment Bill Laws stirred. Whirring up from the moist grass, he glided directly toward the small, thin shape of Joan Reiss. Unfolded wings, dusty and parchment-like, flapped and rustled in the night gloom. His aim was absolutely correct; he was on top of her before she could move or cry out.

What had seemed to be a human being was a multi-jointed, chitinous entity that buzzed and fluttered as it folded itself around Miss Reiss' feebly protesting body. The elongated rear portion of the creature twisted; with a sharp jab, it stung the woman, held its poisonous tail deep in her body for an interval, and then, satiated, withdrew. Gradually, the creature's clicking, scrabbling claws released her. Swaying, Miss Reiss pitched onto her hands and knees and lay stunned, face down and gasping in the wet grass.

"She'll crawl away," Arthur Silvester said quickly.

Running forward, he sprang on the shrinking body and turned it over. Rapidly, efficiently, he squirted quick-drying cement in a continuous trail around the woman's bony hips; revolving her, he wound her tightly in a thick net of tough fibers. When he had finished, the elongated insect that had been Bill Laws grappled her up in his claws; supporting the feebly quivering cocoon, he held it in place while Silvester spun a long strand and tossed it over the limb of a tree. In a moment, the half-paralyzed shape of Joan Reiss hung head downward in her sack of gummy webs, eyes glazed, mouth half-open, swaying slightly with the night wind.

"That should hold her," Hamilton said, with satisfaction.

"I'm glad you kept her alive," Marsha said avidly. "We can take our time with her . . . There's nothing she can do."

"But we've got to kill her eventually," McFeyffe pointed out. "After we have our pleasure."

"She killed my mother," David Pritchet said, in a small, vibrating voice. Before any of them could catch him, he sprinted forward, crouched, and leaped up onto the swaying cocoon. Extending a protruding feeding-tube, he pushed aside the strands of the cocoon, tore away the woman's dress, and greedily drilled into her pale flesh. Very shortly, he had probed deep into the moistures of her body. After a time he dropped back to the ground, bloated and dizzy leaving behind him a withered, dehydrated husk.

The husk was still alive, but it was dying rapidly. Pain-blurred eyes gazed sightlessly down at them. Joan Reiss was past comprehension; only a vague, dull spark of personality remained. The members of the group watched appreciatively, conscious that the final seconds of her agony were drifting away.

"She deserved it," Hamilton said hesitantly. Now that the job had been accomplished, he was beginning to have doubts.

Beside him, the tall, multi-pointed chitinous insect that was Bill Laws nodded in agreement. "Of course she did." His voice was a thin, buzzing rasp. "Look what she did to Edith Pritchet."

"It'll be good to get out of this world," Marsha said. "Back to our own world."

"And our own shapes," Hamilton added, with an uneasy glance at Arthur Silvester.

"What do you mean?" Laws demanded.

"He doesn't understand," Silvester said, with a trace of cold amusement. "These *are* our shapes, Hamilton. But they haven't appeared before." He added: "At least, not where you could see them."

Laws laughed brittlely. "Listen to him. Listen to what he thinks. Hamilton, you're so very interesting."

"Maybe we should see what else he thinks," Arthur Silvester suggested.

"Let's watch him," Laws agreed. "Let's get up close where we can see what he has to say. Let's find out what he can do."

Aghast, Hamilton said, "Kill her and let's end this— you're part of her insanity and you don't know it."

"I wonder how fast he can run," Arthur Silvester conjectured, slowly approaching Hamilton.

"Keep away from me," Hamilton said, reaching for his gun.

"And his wife," Silvester said. "Let's give her a go-around, too."

"I want her," David Pritchet said greedily. "Let me

ave her. You can hold her for me if you want. You
in keep her from trying to—"

Hanging silently in her cocoon, Miss Reiss quietly
ied. And, without a sound, the world around them ex-
ired into random particles.

Weak with relief, Hamilton pulled the dim shape of
is wife to him and stood holding her. "Thank God," he
iid. "We're out of there."

Marsha hung on tight to him. "It was just in time,
asn't it?" Swirling shadows drifted around them; pa-
ently, Hamilton stood waiting. There was going to be
ain ahead, as they emerged on the litter-strewn con-
rete floor of the Bevatron. All of them were injured;
iere would be a period of suffering and slow recovery,
ing empty days in the hospital. But it would be worth
. Well worth it.

The shadows cleared. They were not in the Bevatron.

"Here we go again," Charley McFeyffe said heavily.
Ie rose from the moist lawn and stood gripping the
orch railing.

"But it can't be," Hamilton said stupidly. "There
ren't any left. We've been through all of them."

"You're wrong," McFeyffe said. "Sorry, Jack. But I told
ou. I warned you about her and you wouldn't listen."

Parked at the curb in front of Hamilton's house was an
minous black car. The doors had been pushed open;
om the back seat stepped a vast waddling figure that
alked rapidly across the dark yard and up to Hamilton.
ehind it came hulking, grim-faced men in overcoats
nd hats, hands thrust menacingly in their pockets.

"There you are," the corpulent man grunted. "Okay,
famalton. Come along."

At first, Hamilton didn't recognize him. The man's face
as a mass of doughy flesh, corrupted by a weak chin

and ugly little eyes set deep in the fat. His fingers, as
they closed roughly over Hamilton's arm, were fleshy
talons; he gave off a foul odor of rancid but expensive
cologne and—blood.

"Why weren't you at work today?" the heavy-set man
grunted. "I'm sorry for you, Jack. I knew your father."

"We found out about the picnic," one of his company
toughs added.

"Tillingford," Hamilton said, dazed. "Is it really you?"

With an ugly leer, Doctor Guy Tillingford, the
bloated, blood-smeared capitalist, turned and shambled
back toward his parked Cadillac. "Bring him along," he
ordered his gang of men. "I have to get back to the Epi-
demic Development Agency labs. We've got some new
bacterial poisons we want to try. He'll make a good
subject."

XV

DEATH lay heavily in the chill night darkness. In the
gloom ahead of them, a great corroded organism was
dying. Cracked and broken, the crumpled shape painfully oozed body fluids onto the curb and sidewalk;
around it a growing pool of shiny moisture formed,
expanding and bubbling.

For a moment Hamilton failed to identify it. The shape ᵻivered slightly as it settled onto one side. Starlight ᵻlsed weakly from its shattered windows. Like rotten ᵼod, the bulging hull of the car sagged and collapsed. ᵼen as he watched, the hood split open like an egg; ᵻsting parts dribbled from it and lay spread out, half-ᵻbmerged in the puddle of oil, water, gasoline and brake ᵻid.

Momentarily, a flicker of solidity played through the ᵼr's massive frame. Then, with a protesting groan, the ᵼmains of the engine settled down through the corroded ᵼpports and onto the pavement. The motor block ᵼoke in half and began a slow, methodical collapse into ᵼnfused, blunted particles.

"Well," Tillingford's driver said, resigned, "there goes ᵼat."

Glumly, Tillingford gazed at the wreck that had been ᵼs Cadillac. Gradually, infuriated outrage crept visibly ᵼrough him. "Everything's collapsing," he said. Vicious-ᵻ, he gave the remains of the car a kick; the Cadillac ᵻttled further into a shapeless blob of metal that faded ᵻf into the night shadows.

"That won't do any good," one of his men pointed out. ᵼfight as well leave it alone."

"We're going to have trouble getting back to the ᵼlant," Tillingford said, shaking ugly drops of oil from ᵼs trouser cuff. "There's a working class district sepa-ᵼting us."

"They may have the highway barricaded," his driver ᵼgreed. In the semi-gloom, the company toughs were in-ᵼistinguishable from one another; to Hamilton each was ᵼ vague, heavy-set Germanic giant, brutal-faced and ᵻmotionless.

"How many men do we have here?" Tillingford de
manded.

"Thirty," the answer came.

"Better light a flare," another company tough sug
gested, without particular conviction. "It's too dark t
see them when they start moving."

Shouldering his way to Doctor Tillingford, Hamilto
said harshly, "Is this all serious? Do you people reall
believe—"

He broke off, as a brick crashed against the remains o
the Cadillac. Off in the gathering shadows, dim shape
raced and crouched.

"I see," he said, filled with dread. And with compre
hension.

"Oh my God," Marsha said thinly. "How can we liv
through it?"

"Maybe we won't," Hamilton answered.

A second brick came singing through the darknes:
With a shudder of fright, Marsha ducked and made he
way to Hamilton. "It almost hit me. We're right in th
middle; they're going to kill each other right here."

"Too bad it didn't hit you," Edith Pritchet said quietl
"Then we'd be out of this."

Aghast, Marsha gave a little despairing cry. Aroun
her, the hard, unsympathetic faces of the group wer
stark white in the uncompromising flicker of the com
pany flare. "You all believe it. You think I'm a—*Com
munist.*"

Tillingford turned quickly. An almost hysterical terr
appeared on his brutal, corrupt face. "That's right;
forgot. You were all out on a Party picnic."

Hamilton started to deny it. Then weariness overcam
him. What did it matter? Probably, in this world, the
had been out on a Communist picnic, a Progressive ra

with folk dances, songs of Loyalist Spain, slogans and speeches and petitions. "Well," he said mildly to his wife, "we've come a long way. Through three worlds to get here."

"What do you mean?" Marsha faltered.

"I wish you had told me."

Her eyes blazed. "Don't you believe me, either?" In the darkness, her slim, pale hand flashed upward; a stinging pain burst against his face and shattered around him in a blinding turmoil of sparks. Then, almost immediately, the resentment drained out of her. "It's not true," she said hopelessly.

Rubbing his swollen, burning cheek, Hamilton said, "It's interesting, though. We were saying we wouldn't know until we could get into people's minds. Well, here we are. We were in Silvester's mind; we were in Edith Pritchet's mind; we were in Miss Reiss' insane mind—"

"If we kill her," Silvester said evenly, "we'll be out of here."

"Back in our own world," McFeyffe said.

"Keep away from her," Hamilton warned them. "Keep your hands off my wife."

Around them stood the tight, hostile circle of the group. For a time none of them moved; the six figures were stiff with tension, arms rigid at their sides. Then Laws shrugged and relaxed. Turning his back he walked slowly off. "Forget it," he said over his shoulder. "Let Jack take care of her. She's his problem."

Marsha began breathing in rapid, shallow gasps. "This is so damn awful . . . I don't understand it." Miserably, she shook her head. "It just doesn't make sense."

More stones had fallen around them. In the eddying shadows, sounds were audible, faint and rhythmic, swelling until they had become drifting chants. Tillingford, his heavy features cruel and bitter, stood listening.

"Hear them?" he said to Hamilton. "They're out there, hiding in the darkness." His coarse face twisted in a spasm of loathing. "Beasts."

"Doctor," Hamilton protested, "you can't believe this. You must know this isn't you."

Without looking at him, Tillingford said, "Go join your Red friends out there."

"Is that the situation?"

"You're a Communist," Tillingford said tonelessly. "Your wife's a Communist. You're human debris. You have no place at my plant, no place in decent human society. Get out and *stay* out!" After a moment he added, "Go back to your Communist picnic."

"Are you going to fight it out?" Hamilton asked him.

"Naturally."

"You're actually going to start shooting? You're going to kill those men out there?"

"If we don't," Tillingford said logically, "they'll kill us. That's the way it is; it's not my fault."

"This stuff can't last," Laws said disgustedly to Hamilton. "They're dummy actors in a cheap Communist play. This is a shoddy parody—Life in America. You can damn near see the real world showing through."

A burst of staccato gunfire broke out wildly. On the roofs of nearby houses, workmen had silently mounted a machine gun. Puffs of luminous gray cement dust billowed up as the line of bullets rattled closer. Tillingford dropped awkwardly down on his hands and knees behind the ruin of his Cadillac. His own men, squatting and running, began to fire back. A hand grenade was tossed through the darkness; Hamilton hunched over, rocking with the concussion as a column of exploding flame leaped searingly into his eyes and face. When the fury had settled, a deep pit lay spread out, half-filled with littered rubble. Several of Tillingford's henchmen were visible among the debris, their bodies distorted into impossible postures.

As Hamilton dully watched their broken struggles, Laws said in his ear, "Do they look familiar? Look close."

In the billowing darkness, Hamilton could not make out the sight with clarity. But one of the shattered, inert figures had a familiar appearance. Baffled, he stared down at it. Who was the person stretched out among the littered ruin, half-buried by sections of torn-up pavement and still-smouldering chunks of ash?

"It's you," Laws said softly.

So it was. The dim outlines of the real world wavered and ebbed, visible behind this distorted fantasy. As if even the creator of the scene around them had developed certain fundamental doubts. The rubble-littered pavement was not the street; it was the floor of the Bevatron. Here and there lay other familiar figures. Stirring faintly, they were beginning to creep back to life.

Among the smoking ruins, a few technicians and medical workers inched cautiously forward. They picked their way with care, moving with agonizing slowness, step by step, careful not to expose themselves. Descending from nearby houses to ground level, they dropped stealthily to the gutted street . . . or was it a street? Now it seemed more like the walls of the Bevatron, and the safety catwalks leading to the floor. And the red arm bands of the workmen seemed more like Red Cross arm bands. Confused, Hamilton gave up trying to unscramble the montage of places, shapes.

"It won't be long," Miss Reiss said quietly. With the break-up of her world she had reemerged, exactly as before, in her long corduroy coat, wearing her usual horn-rimmed glasses and clutching her precious purse. "This particular conspiracy isn't very successful. Not nearly so well constructed as the last."

"You found the last one convincing?" Hamilton inquired icily.

"Oh, yes. At first I was almost taken in. I thought—" Miss Reiss smiled with fanatical intensity. "So very clever, really. I almost believed it was *my* world. But, of course, when I started into the lobby of my apartment building, I realized the truth. When I found the usual threatening letters on the hall table."

Shivering and kneeling down beside her husband, Marsha said, "What's wrong with it? Everything seems so hazy."

"It's almost over," Miss Reiss said remotely.

In an ecstasy of hope, Marsha clutched convulsively at her husband. "Is it? Are we going to wake up?"

"Maybe," Hamilton answered. "Some say so."

"That's—wonderful."

"Is it?"

Panic fluttered across her face. "Of course it is. I hate this place—I can't stand it. It's so—bizarre. So mean and dreadful."

"We'll talk about it later." His attention was fixed on Tillingford; the ponderous capitalist boss had assembled his gang of men and was talking with them in low measured tones.

"These goons," Laws said softly, "are by no means done. Before we're out of here, we're going to see a fight."

Tillingford had finished his discussion. Jerking his thumb toward Laws, he said, "String him up. That's one out of the way."

Laws grinned starkly. "Another nigger about to be lynched. The capitalists do it all the time."

Incredulous, Hamilton almost laughed out loud. But Tillingford meant it; he was in deadly earnest. "Doctor," Hamilton said thickly, "this only exists because Marsha believes in it. You, all this fighting, this whole demented fantasy—she's already letting it fall apart. It's not real—it's her illusion. Listen to me!"

"And that Red," Tillingford said wearily. He mopped his bloody, grimy forehead with a silk handkerchief. "And his Red floozy. Douse them with gasoline when they're through kicking. I wish we'd stayed at the plant. We were safe there for awhile, at least. And we could have set up a better formula of defense."

Like ghostly shadows, the workmen were creeping through the rubble. More grenades exploded; the air was heavy with indistinct bits of ash and fragments of debris that rained silently down.

"Look," David Pritchet said, awed.

Across the dark night sky, huge letters were forming. Hazy, uncertain, luminous blurs that gradually burgeoned themselves into words. Already partially disintegrated slogans of comfort, written shakily across the black emptiness, for their benefit.

> We Are Coming.
> Hold Out.
> Fighters Of Peace.
> Arise.

"Very comforting," Hamilton said, revolted.

From the darkness, the dull chanting had risen in pitch. The cold wind swirled phrases of shouted song to the half-concealed group. "Maybe they'll save us yet," Mrs. Pritchet said uncertainly. "But those awful words up there . . . they make me feel so strange."

Here and there, Tillingford's men moved, gathering rubble, collecting odds and ends, building up fortified positions. Almost lost in the swirling clouds of mist and smoke, they were only dimly visible. Now and then, a harsh, bony face was illuminated, rising momentarily into sight and then sinking back into the nebulous gloom. Who did they remind him of? Hamilton tried to think. The pulled-down hats, the beaked noses . . .

"Gangsters," Laws reminded him. "Chicago gangsters of the 'thirties."

Hamilton nodded. "That's it."

"Everything according to the book. She must have memorized it perfectly."

"Leave her alone," Hamilton told him, without much conviction.

"What comes next?" Laws said ironically to the huddled shape of Marsha Hamilton. "The capitalist bandits become crazed with desperation? Is that it?"

"They look desperate already," Arthur Silvester commented in his somber way.

"Such unpleasant-looking men," Mrs. Pritchet fluttered apprehensively. "I didn't realize such men existed."

At that moment, one of the fiery slogans in the sky exploded. Bits of flaming word cascaded down, setting the heaps of rubble on fire. Cursing, beating at his clothing, Tillingford reluctantly retreated; a section of burning rubbish had fallen on him, setting his coat on fire. To his right, his group of company toughs were half-buried under a vast, incandescent outline-portrait of Bulganin that had come loose from the sky and fallen directly on top of them.

"Buried alive," Laws said, with satisfaction.

More words were falling now. A gigantic sizzling *Peace* had landed on Hamilton's tidy little house; the roof was ablaze, as well as the garage and clothesline. Wretchedly, he watched it flare up brilliantly and send flickering tongues of flame high into the night. There was no responding wail of sirens from the dark town; the streets and houses lay stretched silently out, closed and hostile to the incineration.

"Good Lord," Marsha said fearfully. "I think that big *Coexistence* is coming loose."

Crouched with his men, Tillingford had lost control of the situation. "Bombs and bullets," he was repeating, over and over again, in a low, monotonous voice. Only a few of his gang of toughs survived. "Bombs and bullets won't stop them. They're starting to march."

In the flickering darkness, a line of shapes was moving forward. The singing chant had risen to an orgy of feverish excitement; dark and harsh it swelled out, preceding the stern men making their way through the burning piles of rubble.

"Come on," Hamilton said. Grabbing his wife's limp hand, he led her swiftly off into the settling chaos around them.

Finding his way by instinctive memory, Hamilton led his wife around the side of their burning house, along the cement path and into the back yard. A section of fence had charred through and disintegrated; pulling Marsha along, he shoved his way among the smoking fragments and into the dark yard beyond. The houses were opaque forms that loomed ominously. Now and then, a transient vision of running men appeared ahead; faceless, interchangeable workmen quietly making their way to the scene of the fighting. Gradually, the shapes and the sound of gunfire died. The sputter of flames receded. They were out of the immediate battle.

"Wait." Laws and McFeyffe appeared behind them, panting for breath. "Tillingford has gone berserk," Laws gasped. "God, it's a mess."

"I can't believe it," McFeyffe muttered, his thick face shiny and contorted. "They're down on all fours. Matted with filth and blood. Fighting like animals."

Ahead of them, lights winked and glowed.

"What's that?" Laws demanded suspiciously. "We better keep off the main drag."

It was the business section of Belmont that lay spread out. But not as they remembered it.

"Well," Hamilton said acidly, "we should have expected it."

It was a sprawling slum that winked and glowed in the night darkness. Seedy, slatternly shops rose up like unwholesome mushrooms, ugly and blatant. Bars, pool halls, bowling alleys, houses of prostitution, gun shops . . . and over everything came a metallic screech. The blaring din of American jazz, projected by speaker horns mounted over tawdry pinball arcades. Neon signs flashed and winked. Armed soldiers wandered aimlessly, picking over the stale choices in this crumbling expanse of moral depravity.

In a store window, Hamilton saw a strange sight. Rows of knives and guns displayed in plush cases.

"Why not?" Laws said. "The Communist idea of America—gangster cities, full of vice and crime."

"And the rural areas," Marsha said drably. "Indians, wild killings and lynchings. Bandits, massacres, bloodshed."

"You seem pretty well informed," Laws observed.

Dejected, despairing, Marsha sank down on the curb. "I can't go any farther," she informed them.

The three men stood awkwardly, not knowing what

to do. "Come on," Hamilton told her roughly. "You'll freeze."

Marsha said nothing. Shivering, she hunched over, face down, arms clasped together, body small and frail against the cold.

"We better get her inside," Laws said. "Maybe one of these restaurants."

"There's no point in going on," Marsha said to her husband. "Is there?"

"I suppose not," he answered simply.

"You don't care if we get back."

"No."

"Is there anything I can say?"

Hamilton, standing behind her, indicated the world around them. "I can see it; that's about all there is."

"I'm sorry," McFeyffe said clumsily.

"It's not your fault," Hamilton answered.

"But I feel responsible."

"Forget it." Bending down, Hamilton placed his hand on his wife's trembling shoulder. "Let's go, honey. You can't stay here."

"Even if there's no other place to go?"

"That's right. Even if there's no other place to go. Even if we've reached the end of the world."

"Which you have," Laws commented brutally.

Hamilton had no answer. Crouching down, he pulled his wife firmly to her feet. Listlessly, she permitted him to drag her up. In the cold and darkness, she was an unimposing collection of matter that followed obediently after him. "It seems like a long time ago," Hamilton reflected, holding onto her hand. "That day I met you in the lounge and told you Colonel T. E. Edwards wanted me."

Marsha nodded.

"The day we visited the Bevatron."

"Just think," McFeyffe said harshly, "if you hadn't visited it, you wouldn't have found out."

The restaurants were too lavish, too ostentatious. Uniformed servants bowed and scraped, rat-like obsequious men who scuttled about among the ornate tables. Hamilton and his group roamed aimlessly, with no particular destination in mind. The sidewalks were almost deserted; now and then a ragged shape pushed past them, a bent-over figure hunched against the wind.

"A yacht," Laws said spiritlessly.

"What?"

"A yacht." Laws nodded toward a block-long illuminated display window. "Lots of them. Want to buy one?"

In other windows, expensive furs and jewelry were displayed. Perfumes, imported foods . . . and the eternal rococo restaurants with their bowing servants and luxurious hangings. Occasional clusters of ragged men and women stood gazing in, without the means to buy. Once, moving glumly along the street, came a horse-drawn cart. In the back of the cart, a dull-eyed family sat clutching its lump of belongings.

"Refugees," Laws conjectured. "From drought-starved Kansas. From the Dust Bowl. Remember?"

Ahead of them stretched the vast red-light district.

"Well," Hamilton said presently, "what do you say?"

"What have we got to lose?" Laws agreed. "We've gone as far as we can; there's nothing left."

"We might as well enjoy ourselves," McFeyffe muttered. "While we still can. Before this unholy ruin breaks down completely."

Wordlessly, the four of them made their way toward the mass of glaring neon lights, beer signs, blaring horns

and flapping, tattered awnings. Toward the old familiar
Safe Harbor.

Weary and grateful, Marsha sank down at a table in
the corner. "It feels good," she commented. "Nice and
warm."

Hamilton stood absorbing the dim friendliness of the
room, the bedraggled comfortableness of the heaped
ashtrays, the collections of exhausted beer bottles, the
tinny jangle of the jukebox. Safe Harbor hadn't changed.
At the bar sat the usual group of workmen, vacant-faced
shapes hunched moodily over their beers. The wooden
floor was littered with cigarette butts. The bartender,
languidly wiping the surface of the bar with his dirty
rag, nodded to McFeyffe as the three of them seated
themselves around Marsha.

"Good to get off my feet," McFeyffe sighed.

"Everybody want beer?" Laws asked. They signified
their assent and he wandered off to the bar.

"We've come a long way," Marsha said wanly, slipping out of her coat. "I don't believe I've ever been here
before."

"Probably not," Hamilton agreed.

"Is this a place you come to?"

"This is where we all used to go for beer. When I was
working for Colonel Edwards."

"Oh," Marsha said. "I remember, now. You used to
mention it."

Carrying four bottles of Golden Glow beer, Laws appeared and cautiously seated himself. "Help yourselves,"
he told them.

"You notice something?" Hamilton said, as he sipped
his beer. "Look at the kids."

Here and there in the dim recesses of the bar were

teenagers. Fascinated, he watched a young girl, certainly no older than fourteen, make her way to the bar. That was new; he didn't recall that. In the real world . . . it seemed a long way behind them. And yet, this Communist fantasy wavered around him, insubstantial and hazy. The bar, the rows of bottles and glasses, extended into an indistinct blur. The drinking youths, the tables, the litter of beer bottles, faded off into cloudy darkness; he couldn't locate the rear of the room. The familiar red neon signs reading *Men* and *Women* were not visible.

Squinting, he shaded his eyes and peered. A long way off, past the tables and drinkers, was a nondescript streak of red light. Was that the signs?

"What does that read?" he asked Laws, pointing.

Lips moving, Laws said, "It looks like *Emergency Exit.*" After a moment he added, "It's up on the wall of the Bevatron. In case there's a fire."

"It looks more like *Men* and *Women* to me," McFeyffe said. "That's what it always said, before."

"Habit," Hamilton told him.

"Why are those kids drinking?" Laws asked. "And taking dope. Look at them—they've got weed there, sure as hell."

"Coca-cola, dope, liquor, sex," Hamilton said. "The moral depravity of the system. They probably work in uranium mines." He couldn't erase the bitterness from his voice. "And they'll grow up to be gangsters and carry sawed-off shotguns."

"Chicago gangsters," Laws amplified.

"Then into the Army to slaughter peasants and burn their huts. That's the kind of system we have; that's the kind of country this is. Breeding ground for killers and exploiters." Turning to his wife, he said, "Right, honey? The kids taking dope, capitalists with blood on their hands, starving bums scavenging through garbage cans—"

"Here comes a friend of yours," Marsha said quietly.

"Of mine?" Surprised, Hamilton turned dubiously around in his chair.

Hurrying through the shadows toward them came a slim, willowy blonde, lips breathlessly apart, hair tumbled over her shoulders. At first he didn't recognize her. She wore a drawstring blouse, low-cut and rumpled. Her face glowed with layers of make-up. Her tight skirt was slit almost to her thighs. She had on no stockings and her bare feet were thrust into untidy, low-heeled loafers. Her breasts were immense. As she came up to the table, a cloud of perfume and warmth drifted around him . . . a complicated mixture of scents that brought back equally complicated memories.

"Hello," Silky said, in a low, husky voice. Bending over him, she briefly touched her lips to his temple. "I was waiting for you."

Rising, Hamilton offered her a chair. "Sit down."

"Thanks." Seating herself, Silky glanced around the table. "Hello, Mrs. Hamilton," she said to Marsha. "Hello, Charley. Hello, Mr. Laws."

"May I ask you one question?" Marsha said curtly.

"Certainly."

"What size bra do you wear?"

Without self-consciousness, Silky slipped down her blouse until her magnificent breasts were visible. "Does that answer your question?" she asked. She wore no bra.

Blushing, Marsha retreated. "Yes, thanks."

Gazing with unabashed awe at the girl's distended, almost mystically up-raised bosom, Hamilton said, "I guess the bra is a capitalist trick, designed to deceive the masses."

"Talk about masses," Marsha said halfheartedly, but

the sight had robbed her of any real spirit. "You must have trouble finding things you've dropped," she said to Silky.

"In a Communist society," Laws announced, "the proletariat never drops anything."

Silky smiled absently. Touching her breasts with her long, tapering fingers, she sat for a time, deep in thought. Then, with a shrug, she lifted her blouse around her, smoothed down her sleeves, and folded her hands on the table. "What's new?"

"Big battle over our way," Hamilton said. "Bloodsucking vampire of Wall Street versus heroic, clear-eyed, joyfully-singing workmen."

Silky eyed him uncertainly. "Who seems to be winning?"

"Well," Hamilton conceded, "the lying fascist jackalpack is pretty much buried in flaming slogans."

"Look," Laws said suddenly, pointing. "See that over there?"

In the corner of the bar stood the cigarette dispensing machine.

"Remember that?" Laws asked Hamilton.

"I sure do."

"And there's the other one." Laws pointed to the candy dispensing machine, in the opposite corner of the bar, almost lost in the drifting shadows. "Remember what we did to that?"

"I remember. We had that thing spouting top-quality French brandy."

"We were going to change society," Laws said. "We were going to alter the world. Think what we could have done, Jack."

"I'm thinking."

"We could have turned out everything anybody ever

wanted. Food, medicine, whiskey, comic books, plows, contraceptives. What a principle that was."

"The Principle of Divine Regurgitation. The Law of Miraculous Fission." Hamilton nodded. "That would have worked out fine in this particular world."

"We could have outdone the Party," Laws agreed. "They have to build the dams and heavy industries. All we needed was a U-no bar."

"And a length of neon tubing," Hamilton reminded him. "Yes, it would have been a lot of fun."

"You sound so sad," Silky said. "What's wrong?"

"Nothing," Hamilton answered shortly. "Nothing at all."

"Is there anything I can do?"

"No." He grinned a little. "Thanks anyhow."

"We could go upstairs and go to bed." Willingly, she stroked aside the fabric that covered her loins. "I always wanted you to have me."

Hamilton patted her wrist. "You're a good girl. But that won't help."

"You're sure?" Appealingly, she showed him her bare, moistly luminous thighs. "It'll make us both feel better . . you'd enjoy it . . . ."

"Maybe once, but not now."

"Isn't this a sweet little conversation?" Marsha murmured, her face pinched and drawn.

"We were just kidding," Hamilton told her gently. "No harm intended."

"Death to monopolistic capitalism," Laws interjected, with a solemn belch.

"All power to the working class," Hamilton responded dutifully.

"For a people's democracy of the United States," Laws stated.

"For a Soviet of Socialistic Americas."

Around the dim bar, a few of the workmen had looked up from their beers. "Keep your voice down," McFeyffe warned uneasily.

"Hear, hear," Laws cried, banging on the table with his pocketknife. Opening the knife, he laid it out menacingly. "I'm going to skin one of the carrion-eaters of Wall Street," he explained.

Hamilton studied him suspiciously. "Negroes don't carry pocketknives. That's a bourgeois stereotype."

"I do," Laws said flatly.

"Then," Hamilton decided, "you're not a Negro. You're a crypto-Negro who's betrayed his religious group."

"Religious group?" Laws echoed, hypnotized.

"The concept race is a fascistic concept," Hamilton confided. "The Negro is a religious and cultural group, nothing more."

"I'll be damned," Laws said, impressed. "Say, this stuff isn't bad at all."

"Would you like to dance?" Silky said to Hamilton with sudden intensity. "I wish I could do something for you . . . there's such an awful despair about you."

"I'll recover," he told her briefly.

"What can we do for the revolution?" Laws demanded eagerly. "Who do we kill?"

"It doesn't matter," Hamilton said. "Anybody you see. Anybody who can read and write."

Silky and some of the attentive workmen exchanged glances. "Jack," Silky said, in a worried voice, "this isn't a joking matter."

"Absolutely not," Hamilton agreed. "We were almost lynched by that mad dog of monopolistic finance, Tillingford."

"Let's liquidate Tillingford," Laws cried.

"I'll do it," Hamilton said. "I'll dissolve him and pour him down the drain."

"It seems so funny to hear you talk this way," Silky said, eyes still fixed doubtfully on him. "Please, Jack, don't talk this way. It scares me."

"Scares you? Why?"

"Because—" She gestured hesitantly. "I think you're being sarcastic."

Marsha gave a thin, frantic bark of hysteria. "Oh, God, not *her*, too."

Some of the workmen had slid from their stools; edging their way among the tables, they were approaching quietly. The noise of the bar had faded away. The jukebox was deathly still. In the rear, the teen-agers had slipped away into the eddying gloom.

"Jack," Silky said apprehensively, "be careful. For my sake."

"Now I've seen everything," Hamilton said. "You, politically active. You! An honest, home-loving girl, is that it? Corrupted by the system?"

"By capitalist gold," Laws said moodily, rubbing his dark forehead and upturning his empty beer bottle. "Seduced by a bloated entrepreneur. A minister, probably. Has her maidenhead mounted on the wall of his library, over the fireplace."

Gazing around the room, Marsha said, "This isn't really a bar, is it? It just looks like a bar."

"It's a bar in front," Hamilton pointed out. "What more do you want?"

"But in back," Marsha said unsteadily, "it's a Communist cell. And this *girl* here—"

"You work for Guy Tillingford, don't you?" Silky said to Hamilton. "I picked you up there, that day."

"That's right. But Tillingford fired me. Colonel T. E.

Edwards fired me, Tillingford fired me . . . and I guess we're not done, yet." With vague interest, Hamilton noticed that the circle of workmen around them were armed. In this world, everybody was armed. Everybody was on one side or the other. Even Silky. "Silky," he said aloud, "is this the same person I used to know?"

For a moment the girl faltered. "Of course. But—" She shook her head uncertainly; tides of blond hair spilled down around her shoulders. "Everything's so darn mixed-up. I can hardly keep it straight."

"Yeah," Hamilton agreed. "It has been a mess."

"I thought we were friends," Silky said unhappily. "I thought we were on the same side."

"We are," Hamilton said. "Or were, once. Somewhere else, in some other place. A long way from here."

"But—didn't you want to exploit me?"

"My dear," he said sadly, "I have eternally wanted to exploit you. Throughout time. In all lands and places, in all worlds. Everywhere. I'll want to exploit you until the day I die. I would like to take hold of you and exploit you until that titanic chest of yours rattles like an aspen in the wind."

"I thought so," Silky said brokenly. For an interval she leaned against him, her cheek resting against his necktie. Clumsily, he toyed with a strand of blond hair that had fallen across her eye. "I wish," she said distantly, "that things had worked out better."

"So do I," Hamilton said. "Maybe—I could drop by and have a drink with you, once in awhile."

"Colored water," Silky said. "That's all it is. And the bartender gives me one chip."

A little sheepishly, the circle of workmen had drawn their rifles out. "Now?" one of them asked.

Disengaging herself, Silky got to her feet. "I suppose,

she murmured, almost inaudibly. "Go ahead. Get it over with."

"Death to the fascist dogs," Laws said hollowly.

"Death to the wicked," Hamilton added. "Can we stand up?"

"Certainly," Silky said. "Whatever you want. I wish— I'm sorry, Jack. I really am. But you're not with us, are you?"

"Afraid not," Hamilton agreed, almost good-humoredly.

"You're against us?"

"I must be," he admitted. "I can't very well be anything else. Isn't that so?"

"Are we just going to let them murder us?" Marsha protested.

"They're your friends," McFeyffe said, in a sick, defeated voice. "Do something; say something. Can't you reason with them?"

"It wouldn't do any good," Hamilton said. "They don't reason." Turning to his wife, he gently raised her to her feet. "Close your eyes," he told her. "And relax. It won't hurt much."

"What—are you going to do?" Marsha whispered.

"I'm going to get us out of here. By the only method that seems to work." As the circle of rifles clicked and lifted around him, Hamilton drew back his fist, took careful aim, and hit his wife cleanly on the jaw.

With a faint shiver, Marsha collapsed in Bill Laws' arms. Hamilton took hold of her limp body and stood foolishly clutching her. Foolishly, because the dispassionate workmen were still very tangible and real, as they loaded and adjusted their guns.

"My God," Laws said wonderingly. "They're still here. We're not back at the Bevatron." Stunned, he helped

Hamilton support his inert, totally unconscious wife. "This isn't Marsha's world after all."

XVI

"BUT it doesn't make sense," Hamilton said woodenly, holding onto the unstirring, warmly yielding body of his wife. "It must be Marsha's world. If it isn't, then whose world is it?"

And then, with overwhelming relief, he noticed it.

Charley McFeyffe had begun to change. It was involuntary; McFeyffe could not control it. The transformation stemmed from his deepest, most profound layer of beliefs. Part of and hub to his over-all view of the world.

McFeyffe was visibly growing. As they watched, he ceased to be a squat, heavy-set little man with a potbelly and pug nose. He became tall. He became magnificent. A god-like nobility descended over him. His arms were gigantic pillars of muscle. His chest was massive. His eyes flashed righteous fire. His square, morally inflexible jaw was set in a stern and just line as he gazed severely around the room.

The resemblance to (Tetragrammaton) was startling McFeyffe had clearly not been able to shed all his religious convictions.

"What is it?" Laws demanded, fascinated. "What's he turning into?"

"I don't feel so good," McFeyffe boomed, in ringing, god-like tones. "I think I'll go take a bromo."

The burly workmen had lowered their guns. Awed, trembling, they gaped at him with reverence.

"Comrade Commissar," one of them muttered. "We didn't recognize you."

Sickishly, McFeyffe turned to Hamilton. "Damn fools," he boomed in his great authoritative voice.

"Well, I'll be goddammed," Hamilton said softly. "The little Holy Father himself."

McFeyffe's noble mouth opened and closed, but no sound came.

"That explains it," Hamilton said. "When the umbrella got up there and (Tetragrammaton) had a good look at you. No wonder you were shocked. And no wonder He gave you a blast."

"I was surprised," McFeyffe admitted, after pause. "I didn't really believe He was up there. I thought it was a fake."

"McFeyffe," Hamilton said, "you're a Communist."

"Yeah," McFeyffe boomed wretchedly. "Aren't I, though?"

"How long?"

"Years. Since the Depression."

"Kid brother shot by Herbert Hoover?"

"No. Just hungry and out of work and tired of taking it on the chin."

"You're not a bad guy, in a way," Hamilton said. "But you certainly are twisted around inside. You're more insane than Miss Reiss. You're more of a Victorian than Mrs. Pritchet. You're more of a father-worshiper than Silvester. You're the worst parts of all of them rolled in together. And a lot more. But other than that, you're all right."

"I don't have to listen to you," the magnificent golden deity declared.

"And on top of everything else, you're a heel. You're a subversive, a conscienceless liar, a power-hungry crook, and you're a heel. How could you do that to Marsha? How could you make up all that stuff?"

After a moment, the radiant creature answered him. "The end, it's said, justifies the means."

"Party tactics?"

"People like your wife are dangerous."

"Why?" Hamilton asked.

"They don't belong to any group. They fool around with everything. As soon as we turn our back—"

"So you destroy them. You turn them over to the lunatic patriots."

"The lunatic patriots," McFeyffe said, "we can understand. But not your wife. She signs Party peace petitions and she reads the Chicago *Tribune*. People like her—they're more of a menace to Party discipline than any other bunch. The cult of individualism. The idealist with his own law, his own ethics. Refusing to accept authority. It undermines society. It topples the whole structure. Nothing lasting can be built on it. People like your wife just won't take orders."

"McFeyffe," Hamilton said, "you're going to have to forgive me."

"Why?"

"Because I'm going to do something fruitless and futile. Because, even though I realize it's useless, I'm going to kick the living Jesus out of you."

As he flung himself on McFeyffe, Hamilton saw the massive, iron-hard muscles tense. It was too uneven; he couldn't even begin to dent the great visage. McFeyffe stepped back, caught himself, and grimly responded.

Closing his eyes, Hamilton hugged McFeyffe tightly, refusing to let go. Bruised, missing teeth, dribbling blood from a cut over his eye, his clothing in tatters, he hung on like a delapidated rat. A kind of religious frenzy overcame him; clutching McFeyffe in an ecstasy of loathing, he began systematically battering the noble head against the wall. Fingers tore and pried at him, but he could not be ripped loose.

It was virtually over; his fitful little assault had dissipated itself uselessly. Laws lay stretched out with a cracked skull, not far from the crumpled, abandoned figure of Marsha Hamilton. She lay where he had discarded her. Hamilton himself, still on his feet, identified the gathering rifle butts; his time had come.

"Come right in," he invited them, panting. "It doesn't make a bit of difference. Even if you batter us to splinters. Even if you grind us up and build barricades out of us. Even if you use us for mortar. This isn't Marsha's world, and that's all I—"

A rifle butt crashed down on him; closing his eyes, he huddled against the pain. One of the Party workmen kicked him in the groin; another methodically smashed in his ribs. Dimly, Hamilton felt the massive body of McFeyffe melt away from him. From the swirls of darkness, the shapes of workmen came and went; then he was down on all fours, grunting and creeping, trying to find McFeyffe through the haze of his own blood. And trying to get away from the attackers.

Shouts. The hammering rifle butts against his skull. He shuddered, pawed at the confusion around him, made out the form of a sprawled, inert figure and dragged himself toward it.

"Let go of him," they were saying. He ignored them and went on pawing for McFeyffe. But the inert and damaged figure was not McFeyffe; it was Joan Reiss.

After an interval he located McFeyffe. Weak, feeble, he searched among the litter for something to kill him with. As his hands closed over a chunk of concrete, a stunning kick sent him sprawling. The unmoving form of McFeyffe receded; he was alone, floundering in the debris and chaos, lost in the drifting particles of random ash that were settling everywhere.

The litter around him was the strewn wreckage of the Bevatron. The cautiously advancing figures making their way forward were Red Cross workers and technicians.

In the indiscriminate hail of rifle butts, McFeyffe had been knocked down. In the general murder he had not received special dispensation. Fine nuances had not been observed.

To Hamilton's right lay the inert body of his wife, clothes smoking and singed. One arm was bent under her; knees drawn up, she was a small, pathetic bundle on the charred concrete surface. And, not far off, lay McFeyffe. Reflexively, Hamilton crawled toward him. Halfway there, a medical team pushed him back and tried to get a stretcher under him. Numbed, bewildered, but still grimly motivated, Hamilton shoved the men off and pulled himself up to a sitting position.

McFeyffe, knocked senseless by his own Party hatchetmen, wore an expression of outraged fury. His lumpy, battered face was contorted with anger and dismay. The expression had not faded as he returned painfully to consciousness. His breathing came hoarsely, unevenly. Muttering, he flopped and struggled, thick fingers closing over nothing.

Half-buried in rubble, Miss Reiss was already beginning to stir. Rising unsteadily to her knees, she groped feebly for the shattered remains of her glasses. "Oh," she said faintly, weak eyes blind, blinking, streaming tears of fright. "What—" Defensively, she gathered her torn, charred coat and hugged it around her.

A group of technicians had reached Mrs. Pritchet; rapidly, they scooped aside the rubbish spread across her heaving, smoking body. Struggling painfully to his feet, Hamilton crept over to his wife and began beating out the smouldering line of sparks traveling across her tattered, carbonized dress. Marsha shuddered and twitched reflexively.

"Don't move," he warned her. "You may have broken something."

She lay obediently still, eyes shut, body rigid. In the distance, lost in the swirling clouds of fire-darkened cement ash, sounded the frightened wail of David Pritchet. All of them were stirring; all of them were returning to life. Bill Laws groped aimlessly as white-faced workmen collected around him. Yells, shouts, the blare of emergency alarms . . .

The harsh din of the real world. Acrid fumes of burning, half-ruined electronic equipment. The clumsy attempts at first aid by the nervous medical teams.

"We're back," Hamilton told his wife. "Can you hear me?"

"Yes," Marsha said. "I hear you."

"Are you glad?" he demanded.

"Yes," Marsha said quietly. "Don't shout, darling. I'm very glad."

Colonel T. E. Edwards listened patiently, without comment, while Hamilton gave his statement. After the resumé of Hamilton's charges, the long, efficient confer-

ence room was quiet. The only sounds were the dull
rhythm of cigars being smoked and stenographic notes
being taken.

"You're accusing our security officer of being a member of the Communist Party," Edwards said, after a period of frowning contemplation. "Is that it?"

"Not exactly," Hamilton said. He was still a little
shaky; slightly over a week had passed since the accident at the Bevatron. "I'm saying McFeyffe is a disciplined Communist who's using his position to further the
aims of the Communist Party. But whether that discipline is internal or external—"

Turning briskly to McFeyffe, Edwards said, "What do
you say to this, Charley?"

Without looking up McFeyffe answered, "I'd say it's a
fairly obvious smear."

"You maintain Hamilton is merely trying to impugn
your motives?"

"That's right." Mechanically, McFeyffe rattled the
phrases off. "He's seeking to cast doubt on the validity of
my motives. Instead of defending his wife he's attack-
ing me."

Colonel Edwards turned back to Hamilton . "I'm afraid
I'll have to agree. It's your wife, not Charley McFeyffe,
who's under fire. Try to keep your defense pertinent."

"As you realize," Hamilton said, "I cannot now and
could under no circumstances prove that Marsha isn't a
Communist. But I can show you why McFeyffe brought
those charges against her. I can show you what he's doing
and what this whole business is really about. Look at
the position he's in; who would suspect him? He has free
access to security files; he can bring charges against
anybody he wants . . . an ideal position for a Party
thug. He can pick off anybody the Party dislikes, any-

body who stands in its way. Systematically, the Party weeds out its opponents."

"But this is all so indirect," Edwards pointed out. "A hatful of logic—where's the proof? Can you prove that Charley's a Red? As you said yourself, he's not a member of the Communist Party."

"I'm not a detective agency," Hamilton said. "I'm not a police force. I have no way to gather information against him. I presume he has some kind of contact with the CP-USA or with Party front organizations . . . he must get his instructions somewhere. If the FBI will take him into surveillance—"

"No proof, then," Edwards broke in, chewing on his cigar. "Correct?"

"No proof," Hamilton admitted. "No proof of what goes on in Charley McFeyffe's mind. Any more than he had proof of what goes on in my wife's mind."

"But there was all that derogatory material against your wife. All those petitions she signed; all the pinko meetings she showed up at. You show me one petition Charley has signed. One front meeting he's been at."

"No real Communist is going to expose himself," Hamilton said, realizing, as he said it, how absurd it sounded.

"We can't fire Charley on grounds like that. Even you must see how tenuous all this is. Fire him because he *hasn't* gone to pinko meetings?" The trace of a smile appeared on Colonel Edwards' face. "I'm sorry, Jack. You just haven't got a case."

"I know," Hamilton agreed.

"You know?" Edwards was astonished. "You *admit* it?"

"Of course I admit it. I never thought I had." Without particular emotion, Hamilton explained, "I merely thought I'd bring it to your attention. For the record."

Sullen and pudgy, sunk down in his chair, McFeyffe

said nothing. His stumpy fingers were knotted tensely together; concentrating on them, he didn't look directly at Hamilton.

"I'd like to help you," Edwards said uneasily. "But hell, Jack. We'd have everybody in the country classed as a security risk, using your logic."

"You will anyhow. I just wanted the method extended to McFeyffe. It seems a shame that he's exempt."

"I think," Edwards said stiffly, "that the integrity and patriotism of Charley McFeyffe is beyond reproach. You understand, don't you, that this man fought in the Second World War in the Army Air Corps? That he's a devout Catholic? That he's a member of the Veterans of Foreign Wars?"

"And probably a Boy Scout," Hamilton agreed. "And he probably decorates a tree every Christmas."

"Are you trying to say Catholics and Legionnaires are disloyal?" Edwards demanded.

"No, I'm not. I'm trying to say that a man can be all those things and still be a dangerous subversive. And a woman can sign peace petitions and subscribe to *In Fact*, yet love the very dirt this country is made of."

"I think," Edwards said coldly, "that we're wasting our time. This is errant nonsense."

Pushing back his chair, Hamilton got to his feet. "Thanks for hearing me out, Colonel."

"Not at all." Awkwardly, Edwards said, "I wish I could do more by you, boy. But you see my situation."

"It's not your fault," Hamilton agreed. "In fact, in a sort of perverse way, I'm glad you won't pay any attention to me. After all, McFeyffe is innocent until proven guilty."

The meeting had broken up. The Directors of California Maintenance began strolling out into the corridor, glad to return to their routines. The trim stenographer collected her stenotype machine, cigarettes and purse. McFeyffe, with a cautiously malevolent glance at Hamilton, pushed brusquely past him and disappeared.

In the doorway, Colonel Edwards stopped Hamilton. "What are you going to do?" he inquired. "Going to take a run up the peninsula? Give Tillingford and EDA a try? He'll take you on, you know. He and your Dad were good friends."

In this, the real world, Hamilton hadn't yet approached Guy Tillingford. "He'll take me on," he said thoughtfully, "partly for that reason, and partly because I'm a top-notch electronics expert."

Embarrassed, Edwards began to bluster. "Sorry, boy. I didn't mean to insult you; I meant merely—"

"I understand what you meant." Hamilton shrugged, being careful of a cracked and tightly-taped rib. In his mouth, his two new front teeth felt loose and odd, as did the bald patch above his right ear, where two stitches had been taken in his scalp. The accident, the ordeal, had, in many ways, made an old man out of him. "I'm not trying out Tillingford," he stated. "I'm striking out on my own."

Hesitating, Edwards asked, "You feel any resentment toward us, here?"

"No. I've lost this job, but it doesn't matter. In a way it's a relief. I probably would have gone on here indefinitely if this hadn't happened. Completely unbothered by the security system, hardly aware that it existed. But now my nose has been rubbed in it; I've been forced to face it. I've had to wake up, whether I like it or not."

"Now, Jack—"

"I always had it pretty easy. My family had plenty of

money and my father was well-known in his field. Normally, people like me aren't touched by people like McFeyffe. But times are changing. The McFeyffes are out to get us; we're beginning to meet head on. So it's time we started noticing their existence."

"That's all very well," Edwards said. "Very noble and stirring. But you're going to have to earn a living; you're going to have to get a job and support your family. Without a security clearance you won't be designing missiles here or anywhere else. Nobody with a Government contract will hire you."

"Maybe that's a good thing, too. I'm a little tired of building bombs."

"Monotony got you?"

"I like to call it awakening conscience. Some of the things that have happened to me have changed my ways of thinking. Jarred me out of my rut, as they say."

"Oh, yes," Edwards said vaguely. "The accident."

"I've seen a lot of aspects of reality I didn't realize existed. I've come out of this with an altered perspective. Maybe it takes a thing like this to break down the walls of the groove. If so, it makes the whole experience worth it."

Behind him in the corridor came the sound of sharp, staccato heel-taps. Marsha, breathless and glowing, hurried up and took hold of his arm. "We're ready to go," she told him eagerly.

"And the important thing," Hamilton said to Colonel T. E. Edwards, "has been settled. Marsha was telling the truth; that's what I care about. I can always get another job, but wives are scarce."

"What do you think you'll do?" Edwards persisted, as Hamilton and his wife started down the corridor.

"I'll drop you a card," Hamilton said, over his shoulder. "On Company letterhead."

"Darling," Marsha said excitedly, as they descended the front steps of the California Maintenance Building and started along the concrete walk, "the trucks are starting to show up already. They're beginning to unload."

"Fine," Hamilton said, gratified. "That'll make a good showing when we go to work on the old bat."

"Don't talk like that," Marsha said anxiously, squeezing his arm. "I'm ashamed of you."

Grinning, Hamilton helped her into the car. "From now on I'm going to be perfectly honest with everybody, say exactly what I think, do exactly what I feel like. Life's too short for anything else."

Exasperated, Marsha complained, "You and Bill—I'm beginning to wonder where this will wind up."

"We'll be rich," Hamilton told her gaily, as he drove out onto the highway. "Mark my words, sweetheart. You and Ninny will be lapping up dishes of cream and sleeping on silk pillows."

Half an hour later, the two of them stood on a rise of uncleared ground, critically studying the small corrugated-iron shed that Hamilton and Laws had leased. Equipment was heaped up in gigantic plywood cartons; a string of ponderous-moving trucks were backed up at the rear loading platform.

"One of these days," Hamilton said reflectively, "little shiny square boxes with knobs and dials will be coming off that platform. Trucks will be picking up stuff, not dropping it off."

Striding toward them, his lean body hunched against the brisk autumn wind, came Bill Laws, a bent, unlit cigarette stuck between his thin lips, hands shoved deep in his pockets. "Well," he began wryly, "it isn't much, but it's going to be a lot of fun. We may go down, but we'll go down having one hell of a good time."

"Jack just said we were going to be rich," Marsha said disappointed, lips drawn together in a mocking pout.

"That comes later," Laws explained. "That's when we're too old and broken-down to have any fun."

"Has Edith Pritchet showed up?" Hamilton inquired

"She's hanging around somewhere." Laws gestured vaguely. "I saw her Cadillac parked up the road apiece."

"Does it run?"

"Oh, yes," Laws asserted. "It runs very well. We're definitely not in *that* world, any more."

A small boy, not over eleven, came scampering excitedly up. "Whatcha gonna build?" he demanded "Rockets?"

"No," Hamilton answered. "Phonographs. So people can listen to music. It's the coming thing."

"Gee," the boy said, impressed. "Hey, last year I built a one-tube, battery-operated, headphone-type receiver.

"That's a good start."

"And now I'm building a TRF tuner."

"Fine," Hamilton told him. "Maybe we'll give you a job. Assuming, of course, that we don't have to print our own money."

Picking her way gingerly over the not-yet-landscaped ground, came Mrs. Edith Pritchet. She was wrapped in a heavy fur coat, and an elaborate hat sat on her henna rinsed curls. "Now, don't bother Mr. Laws and Mr. Hamilton," she instructed her son. "They've got a great deal to worry about."

Sulkily, David Pritchet retired. "We were discussing electronics."

"That's a large amount of equipment you've put

chased," Mrs. Pritchet said doubtfully to the two men. "It certainly must have cost a lot of money."

"We're going to need it," Hamilton said. "We're not assembling amplifiers from standard parts; we're designing and building our own components, from condensers up to transformers. Bill has schemata on a new kind of frictionless cartridge. It should make quite a hit on the hi-fi market—guaranteed absolutely no record wear."

"You degenerates," Marsha said, amused. "Catering to the whims of the leisure class."

"I think," Hamilton said, "that music is here to stay. The question is: how do we handle it? Operating a hi-fi rig is getting to be an art in itself. These sets we'll be turning out will take as much skill to run as to build."

"I can see it now," Laws said, grinning. "Slender young men sitting on the floors of their North Beach apartments, rapturously tuning knobs and switches, as the incredibly authentic roar of freight engines, snow storms, trucks unloading scrap iron, and other recorded oddities thunder out."

"I'm not so sure about this," Mrs. Pritchet said dubiously. "You two seem so—eccentric."

"This is an eccentric field," Hamilton informed her. "Worse than fashions. Worse than catering for stag parties. But immensely rewarding."

"But can you be certain," Mrs. Pritchet persisted, "that your venture will be a financial success? I don't like to invest unless I'm assured of a reasonable return."

"Mrs. Pritchet," Hamilton said severely, "it seems to me I once heard you say you wanted to be a patroness of the arts."

"Oh heavens," Mrs. Pritchet assured him, "there's nothing more vital to society than a firm sponsorship of cultural activities. Life without the great artistic heritage created by generations of inspired geniuses—"

"Then you're doing the right thing," Hamilton told her. "You've brought your loot to the right place."

"My—"

"Your lute," Bill Laws said. "You've brought your lute to the right place. We're in the music business; with our rigs, the masses are going to hear music like they've never heard before. At hundreds of undistorted watts. At tens of thousands of cycles flat. It's a cultural revolution."

Putting his arm around his wife, Hamilton hugged her enthusiastically against him. "How does it look to you, honey?"

"Fine," Marsha gasped. "But be careful of me—my burns, remember."

"You think it'll be a success?"

"I certainly do."

"That should satisfy anybody," Hamilton said to Mrs. Pritchet, as he released his wife. "Right?"

Still doubtful, Edith Pritchet fumbled in her voluminous purse for her checkbook. "Well, it seems to be a good cause."

"It's a good cause, all right," Hamilton agreed. " 'Cause if we don't get the money, we won't be able to operate."

With a sharp snap, Mrs. Pritchet closed her purse. "Perhaps I had better not get myself involved."

"Don't pay any attention to him," Marsha urged quickly. "Neither of them knows what he's saying."

"All right," Mrs. Pritchet agreed, finally convinced. With great care and precision, she made out a check underwriting their initial expenses. "I expect to get this back," she said sternly, as she handed the check to Laws. "As per the terms of our agreement."

"You will," Laws said. And immediately leaped back n pain. Clutching his ankle, he bent angrily down and crushed something small and wriggling with his thumb.

"What is it?" Hamilton demanded.

"An earwig. Crawled up my sock and bit me." Grinning uneasily, Laws added, "Just a coincidence."

"We *hope* you'll get your money back," Hamilton explained to Mrs. Pritchet, just to be on the safe side. "We can't promise, naturally. But we'll do our best."

He waited, but nothing bit or stung him.

"Thank God," Marsha breathed, with a glance at the check.

Heading eagerly toward the corrugated-iron shed, Bill Laws yelled, "What are we waiting for? Let's get to work!"